Reel Murder

"A breezy, quick read, with oddball characters and a warm, tropical setting."   —The Mystery Reader

"A well-paced story."   —I Love a Mystery

"[R]ich characters and a moving plot that will keep you guessing until the last wonderful page."
                    —TwoLips Reviews

"With a lively cast of characters, including Maggie's hilarious mother, and a spellbinding mystery to solve, Kennedy continues to delight and surprise her readers with this winning addition to the cozy mystery genre."   —Fresh Fiction

"There is no doubt . . . *Reel Murder* is nothing but a win-win for the reader."   —Once Upon a Romance Reviews

Dead Air

"If you're thinking of committing murder in South Florida, beware of Mary Kennedy's delightful radio psychologist, Maggie Walsh, one of the most appealing amateur sleuths to come along in years. Hook her up with Jessica Fletcher and no murderer shall ever go unpunished."
          —Donald Bain, author of the *Murder, She Wrote* series

continued . . .

Other Talk Radio Mysteries
by Mary Kennedy

Dead Air
Reel Murder

STAY TUNED
FOR MURDER

A Talk Radio Mystery

Mary Kennedy

AN OBSIDIAN MYSTERY

OBSIDIAN
Published by New American Library, a division of
Penguin Group (USA) Inc., 375 Hudson Street,
New York, New York 10014, USA
Penguin Group (Canada), 90 Eglinton Avenue East, Suite 700, Toronto,
Ontario M4P 2Y3, Canada (a division of Pearson Penguin Canada Inc.)
Penguin Books Ltd., 80 Strand, London WC2R 0RL, England
Penguin Ireland, 25 St. Stephen's Green, Dublin 2,
Ireland (a division of Penguin Books Ltd.)
Penguin Group (Australia), 250 Camberwell Road, Camberwell, Victoria 3124,
Australia (a division of Pearson Australia Group Pty. Ltd.)
Penguin Books India Pvt. Ltd., 11 Community Centre, Panchsheel Park,
New Delhi - 110 017, India
Penguin Group (NZ), 67 Apollo Drive, Rosedale, North Shore 0632,
New Zealand (a division of Pearson New Zealand Ltd.)
Penguin Books (South Africa) (Pty.) Ltd., 24 Sturdee Avenue,
Rosebank, Johannesburg 2196, South Africa

Penguin Books Ltd., Registered Offices:
80 Strand, London WC2R 0RL, England

First published by Obsidian, an imprint of New American Library,
a division of Penguin Group (USA) Inc.

First Printing, January 2011
10 9 8 7 6 5 4 3 2 1

For Sandy Harding

ACKNOWLEDGMENTS

Thank you to my wonderful agent, Holly Root. She accomplishes miracles and makes it all seem effortless.

Thank you to the excellent team at Penguin Obsidian for their enthusiasm, their creativity, and their marketing savvy. You're the best.

I'm very grateful to my husband, Alan, my computer guru.

A big thank-you to Gail Link, author, friend, and RWA Bookseller of the Year.

A shout-out to the fabulous Becke Davis, talented author, dear friend, who does such a great job with the Barnes & Noble Mystery Book Club.

Hugs and thanks to Bob and Jill TenEyck, who continue to be my number one fans.

To Lieutenant Colonel Lisa Schieferstein and the brave men and women of the 389th Renegades. Thank you for your service. You are my heroes.

As always, thanks to Mark Bouton, fellow mystery author and friend, for all his expertise on crime solving, forensics, and the FBI.

Chapter 1

You would assume that people who talk to the dead would be as pale as vampires, their luminous eyes filled with unspoken secrets and timeless wisdom. You would expect them to speak in hushed tones, their voices floating like whispers on a tropical breeze as they invoke spirits from the beyond. You'd probably picture them as quiet and introspective, pondering the mysteries of life and what lies beyond the grave.

You would be wrong. Dead wrong.

Chantel Carrington, the new "psychic sensation" in Cypress Grove, is none of the above. Everything about Chantel is larger than life, strictly va-va-voom. Think of one of those giant Macy's Thanksgiving Day Parade balloons bobbing over Manhattan.

Big. Brash. Garish. Inescapable.

Oh, yes. And full of hot air.

From her booming "Hello, dahlings!" as she rolls down the WYME corridors to her eye-popping Hawaiian muumuus, Chantel steals the spotlight every time.

Today she was the featured guest on my afternoon radio talk show, *On the Couch with Maggie Walsh.* She's been on the show four times in the past two weeks, and I hate to admit it, but each time the ratings have skyrocketed.

It seems that my entire listening audience is jonesing to communicate with the dearly departed, and Chantel does her best to accommodate them. Cyrus, the station manager, is so thrilled with her otherworldly chats that I'm sure he salivates, just thinking about all that extra advertising revenue pouring into WYME.

Vera Mae, my producer, and I are less happy with the arrangement.

When I first arrived in Cypress Grove to host my own radio show, I'd been pretty naive about the topics I'd be covering. A former clinical psychologist with a cushy Manhattan practice, I'd gained quite a following for my work in what the shrinks call "behavioral medicine."

Behavioral medicine is based on the idea that if you change your thinking, you can change your behavior, leading to a more positive mental outlook. No Freudian claptrap, no endless discussions of your dreams or Jungian archetypes.

But after a few brutal winters in the Big Apple, I'd become sick of the city, frustrated by the skyrocketing real estate prices, and worst of all, I discovered I was tired of listening to people's problems all day long. Yes, tired of listening to people's problems.

Some days I felt like I was trapped in a *Jerry Springer* marathon.

A shocking revelation, right? Practically career suicide to say it publicly, but there you have it. I was whipped, emotionally drained, with nothing left to give.

I had total burnout.

So what did I do? I diagnosed the problem and wrote my own prescription. I made an executive decision, as The Donald would say. I knew I needed a complete change of pace, and I made it happen. I closed up shop, transferred my patients to a trusted colleague, sold my IKEA furniture, and moved to a sleepy Florida town.

Dr. Maggie, heal thyself.

At least, that was what I thought I was doing. I picked a town that was more like Mayberry than Manhattan, a place that was north of Boca, not too far from Palm Beach, and a pleasant ride to Fort Lauderdale. As the chamber of commerce says, "Cypress Grove: we're near everyplace else you'd rather be!"

I figured I'd use my clinical expertise and introduce my listening audience to the hottest topics in behavioral medicine, featuring the latest news in mental health issues. I'd select a topic and invite a fascinating guest expert to join me on the airwaves.

Except for one tiny problem. Where was I going to find a bunch of fascinating guests? It had never occurred to me that we'd have trouble persuading A-list experts to make the trek to Cypress Grove to appear on my show. We don't pay our guests, so unless they're hawking a book or a tape, there's really not much in it for them, except for the proverbial fifteen minutes of fame. And all the stale glazed doughnuts they can scarf down in the break room.

When Chantel Carrington blew into town last month to promote her latest book, *I Talk to Dead People—and You Can, Too!* I invited her to do a guest spot on my show. It was against my better judgment, but I knew Cyrus would be pleased, and frankly, my ratings could use a bit of a boost.

During the last Nielsen ratings, *On the Couch with Maggie Walsh* tied for last place, right down there with *Bob Figgs and the Swine Report*. I was running neck and neck with a show that features pigs!

I had no idea Chantel would be such a huge success and,

worst of all, that she would pick Cypress Grove as the perfect place to work on her next book. Before you could say woo-woo, she'd rented an apartment near Branscom Pond and was hosting séances in town.

So here I was, entertaining her as a guest on my show and making the best of a bad situation. I was making lemonade out of lemons.

Ironic, really, because this is the same annoying bit of advice I used to give my patients. Funny how our bromides come back to haunt us.

Chantel was carrying a cup of Starbucks coffee as she breezed into the studio and collapsed into a chair next to me at the control board. Chantel is a large woman in her late forties, with violet eyes (colored contacts?) and a mane of black curls trailing gypsy-style down her back.

She favors bright red lipstick and odd-looking Z-CoiL shoes that make her look like she might levitate up to the ceiling or spring into the netherworld without warning. Today she was wearing a peekaboo lacy white shawl over a yellow muumuu festooned with bright blue parrots.

"Two minutes till airtime," Vera Mae yelled from the control room. She glanced at me and made a two-fingered peace sign. I nodded back. Then Vera Mae spotted Chantel's coffee, shook her head, and thinned her lips in disapproval. Uh-oh. No one is allowed to have food or drinks in the studio, but Chantel seems to be a law unto herself. I knew Vera Mae would dart in at the first commercial break and whisk the coffee away.

Chantel fanned herself with a copy of the daily traffic log. She had a thin layer of perspiration on her upper lip, and her face was flushed a sickly shade of Pepto-Bismol pink.

"I should have worn something cooler today," she confided. "You'd think the weather guys would get it right for once."

She tugged at the shawl, which she wore Martha Washington–style, fastened in front with a tortoiseshell brooch.

I bit back a smile. Why would a psychic need the Weather Channel?

"Live in thirty seconds." Vera Mae slapped her headphones on and pointed to the board. It was already lit up with callers. We'd been running talk-to-the-dead promos for the last three days. We usually don't get this many callers unless we're giving away tickets to a Reba McEntire show or offering a free cut and style at Wanda's House of Beauty.

"Showtime," I said to Chantel, who licked her lips and squiggled her hips a little in her chair, gearing herself up for her big performance. I grabbed my headphones just as Vera Mae pointed at me and mouthed the word "Go."

Vera Mae's towering beehive quivered with excitement as she leaned over the board. I've tried to get Vera Mae to ditch her Marge Simpson volcano of carrot-colored hair, but she believes "the higher the hairdo, the closer to God."

There's always that electric moment when the phone lines open and I feel a little rush of adrenaline thumping in my chest. Okay, this was it. We were live on the air in south Florida.

"You're on the couch with Maggie Walsh," I said, sliding into my trademark introduction. "Today we have the renowned psychic and bestselling author Chantel Carrington with us. Welcome to the show, Chantel. It looks like the lines are flooded with calls. Are you ready to get started?" This question, of course, was strictly a formality. I could see that Chantel was more than ready; she was practically quivering with anticipation, like Sea Biscuit at the starting gate.

"Ready!" Chantel sang out, looking giddy with excitement.

"So, Vera Mae, who do we have first?"

"We have Sylvia on line one, Maggie. She's calling from Boca, and she wants to communicate with Barney, who passed recently. It was just last week, in fact—"

"So sorry for your loss, Sylvia," Chantel cut in smoothly, talking over the tail end of Vera Mae's comment. "Can you tell me a little bit about Barney? I'm getting some strong vibes that you were lifelong partners." She pursed her lips, staring up at the ceiling for a moment, as if seeking inspiration.

I followed her gaze. All I saw were some loose sound-proofing tiles, so I turned my attention back to the control board.

"We were together for eight years." Sylvia sniffled. It sounded like she was biting back a sob. Interesting she used the word "together," and she didn't say "husband." I imme-diately wondered, was Barney a boyfriend? Fiancé? Friend with benefits?

"Eight wonderful years," she went on. "After Barney died, my bed was so lonely at night, I cried myself to sleep. I just couldn't believe he was gone." I watched as Chantel whipped out a notepad and scribbled, *Eight years. Cries herself to sleep. Guilt? Unresolved issues?* Then she scrunched up her face in a fake-sympathetic look, her forehead creased in con-cern.

"But he's not really gone," she interjected. "You know that, don't you, Sylvia? He's watching over you this very minute. I can feel his love. Can't you?" Chantel was making notes as she talked, spouting the familiar lines by rote.

The idea of the dead watching over us is one of her favor-ite themes. The dead aren't really gone on Planet Chantel. They are just out of sight, like the sun when a cloud passes in front of it. They're still with us; we just can't see them.

Sylvia tried to rally. "Well, I know you say that in your

book, Chantel, and I really do try to believe it, but sometimes I wonder—"

"There's nothing to wonder about." There was a steely edge to Chantel's voice. "You *must* stay positive and believe that you'll see Barney again. Remember, our lives here on earth are short, ephemeral," she said, warming to her subject.

She lifted her right hand for emphasis, and a half dozen little gold bracelets clanked together. Vera Mae winced as the mike amplified the sound and the arrow on the volume meter flipped into the red. I pointed to the bracelets, and Chantel—ever the media pro—slapped her left hand over her wrist to stop the jangling sound.

"If you've read my book *I Talk to Dead People*, you should have a good understanding of my views on mortality, Sylvia. There is no room in your heart for doubt. You must choose love and optimism over doubt and despair."

I glanced into the control room and saw Vera Mae give me a little eye roll. We'd been forced to listen to Chantel's spiel over and over, and it was getting old. Plus, Chantel never missed a chance to mention the title of her book. Once or twice was okay, but her shameless self-promotion was beginning to grate on my nerves.

Yesterday Vera Mae threatened to hang a Chinese gong in the control room and give it a good whack every time Chantel plugged *I Talk to Dead People*. I caught myself drumming my fingertips on the console and made a conscious effort to stop. I glanced over at Chantel as she mouthed her all too familiar clichés. They were so cloying, they made my teeth ache.

I stared hard, narrowed my eyes, and tried to send her a psychic message. *Chantel, please don't say our time here is like a drop of water in the ocean. Please, I'm begging you.*

"Our time on earth is like a drop of water in the ocean," she said.

So much for thought transference. Or maybe she'd heard me and had decided to tune me out. I watched as she leaned forward, her bloodred lips aiming for the mike like a heat-seeking missile.

Not the grain of sand analogy again . . .

"We're like a grain of sand on the beach."

Ouch. I knew what was coming next. Think eye. Blink. Millisecond. Here it comes.

"Believe me, Sylvia. Our life on earth is over in the blink of an eye."

Hmm. I glanced at the clock. Life might be over in the blink of an eye, but this show felt like it was stretching into tomorrow. We were two minutes into the first hour, so that meant it was time for Chantel to plug one of her books. Again.

"In chapter three of my sequel, *Dead People Talk to Me*, I'll be covering this topic in some detail."

Aha, right on schedule. And now she was hawking the sequel to *I Talk to Dead People*, a book that wasn't even in print yet! Genius, right? Chantel glanced up just in time to catch Vera Mae making a throat-slitting gesture. She glared at Vera Mae for a long moment, while I ducked my head and pretended to be studying my notes.

"Yes, but to answer Sylvia's question," I prodded. I looked up and plastered an innocent-looking smile on my face.

"I was *getting* to that," Chantel said testily. "I want you to know I'm feeling very strong vibes from Barney right this minute, Sylvia. In fact, he's here in the studio." She looked past me and gave a faint smile. "I can practically reach out and touch him. Do you see him, Maggie? He's right behind you."

Wh-a-a-a-t? He's here in the studio? Standing behind me? Yowsers!

Vera Mae gave a startled yelp and dropped all her show notes on the floor. As she scrambled to pick them up, my heart thumped in my chest and my pulse zoomed into overdrive. A little rash of goose bumps sprang up on my arm, and I willed them away. I thought I felt a cool breeze fluttering somewhere behind my left shoulder, or was I imagining it? I refused to turn around; I wasn't going to play into her silly game.

I forced myself to maintain eye contact with Chantel. She was obviously a master manipulator and was playing tricks with my head, making me doubt my own perceptions. I hated to admit it, but she was good, very good.

I don't believe in ghosts. Again, there was another little puff of cool air behind me, and the papers ruffled slightly on the console. It was my imagination. *It had to be.* Or maybe the always-temperamental air-conditioning unit was pumping out erratic blasts of icy air. That was why the papers were moving ever so slightly on the counter top.

No way was it a sign from the dearly departed Barney!

Was it?

I don't believe in ghosts.

Do I?

"Yes, he's here," Chantel continued, her voice low and silky. "I feel his presence. Don't you feel it, Maggie?"

"Well, um, actually—"

"You *would* feel it if you were more open to it."

You mean I'd feel it if I were open to mass hysteria like your crazy followers. Call me Galileo, but I believe in science, not superstition. There is no way I'm going to fall for this. As a psychologist, I know all about the power of suggestion, and—

"Barney is standing right next to you, practically scream-ing to be heard."

He is?

I was sure pure shock registered on my face, because she added, "I'm speaking metaphorically, of course. His spirit, his aura, is in the room, not his corporeal form. I'll send you an advance copy of my next book, Maggie, and you'll learn how to tune in to the spirit world."

See what I mean? Chantel has an uncanny ability to steal the show, put me down with a snide remark, and draw the conversation back to herself. Who could compete with her "I see a dead guy in the studio" shtick? Ghosts trump psy-chological insights with the audience every time. Trust me.

"Ohmigod, Barney's in the studio? Is he all right?" Syl-via shrieked through the headphones. I jumped in surprise, my right elbow slipping off the console. I'd been so caught up in the saga of Barney the Friendly Ghost, I'd completely forgotten about poor grieving Sylvia, waiting patiently on the other end of the line.

"Ask him if he needs anything! Does he look good? Is he happy?" Sylvia was so excited, she was almost hyperventi-lating.

"He's very happy, Sylvia," Chantel said warmly. "He has everything he needs. And he looks fine to me." Chantel gave me a sly smile. "How does he look to you, Maggie?"

Ah, a trick question. How would a dead person look? I thought for a minute and drew a blank.

"Well, I guess he looks . . ." *Dead?* I wanted to say. I started to sweat a little, even though the AC was cranked up to the max. I thought I heard a faint cough sound behind me. *Do ghosts cough?*

This time I really had to force myself not to look around. I was developing a nervous tic in my left shoulder, and I was stammering a little, which is also something I do when I get nervous. "I mean, I think he looks—"

"Maggie thinks he looks fine, too, Sylvia," Chantel interjected. Then she waited a beat, lowering her voice to a funereal tone. "But he's worried about you, dear. He doesn't want you to be sad or unhappy at his passing."

"But I miss him!" Sylvia wailed. "Of course I'm sad and unhappy."

"Barney wants you to know that you didn't do anything wrong," Chantel said firmly, her forehead wrinkling in thought. "There's nothing you could have done differently. He knows you feel troubled about something. It seems like he left this earth very quickly. That is correct, is it not?"

Chantel always tries to get "those left behind" to agree with her as part of her shtick. Then she builds on what they say, or changes tack if she thinks she's veering off course.

Dead air for a beat. "No, not really." Sylvia sounded confused.

Chantel frowned. "He passed unexpectedly, did he not?" Her tone was wheedling, argumentative, like Sam Waterston's when he's grilling a witness on *Law & Order*.

"Well, no—"

"One minute he was here, and the next he was not. That is correct, is it not?" Chantel was in rare form. She could give James Van Praagh a run for his money any day.

"I suppose so—"

"Then that's *unexpected*, right?" She gave a derisive little snort, very unladylike. "Here one moment and gone the next. You can't *get* much more unexpected than that, sweetie." She snapped her fingers for emphasis, and all the bracelets jangled together again.

"Yes, if you put it that way."

Chantel closed her eyes for a moment and put her fingertips to the bridge of her nose, as if lost in thought. "I'm sensing there was a problem with his heart, or it might have been cancer."

Heart disease or cancer. A safe choice. Don't most people die of those things?

I mean, she could have gone out on a limb and said "leprosy" or "malaria," but why should she? Nothing like hedging your bets. I found myself hoping that Barney had died in a bizarre way.

Maybe an avalanche? Admittedly, an avalanche would be a rarity in southern Florida, but I would have loved to see Chantel try to talk her way out of that one.

Or maybe a hang-gliding accident. That would certainly throw Chantel for a loop. Or maybe he was eaten by a shark or—

"But he didn't have heart trouble, and his cardiac function was fine." *Uh-oh.* A doubtful note was creeping into Sylvia's voice. Grief stricken or not, she wasn't falling for what Vera Mae calls Chantel's phony-baloney.

So now what? It looked like Chantel was way off target, and that meant it was time for a quick backpedal.

"Of course he had heart trouble! When he died, his heart *stopped*, didn't it?"

"Yes, that's true, but—"

"There are no buts about it. He died because his heart stopped. That means he had heart trouble. Period." Chantel sat back in her chair and folded her arms over her chest, looking smug and vindicated. Chantel Carrington, the psychic cardiologist.

Dr. Oz, eat your heart out.

Vera Mae and I locked eyes as she gave a little shrug. *But doesn't everyone die because their heart stops? Isn't that the definition of dying?* I bet our thoughts were chugging along the same track, because she gave me a tiny eye roll.

Chantel took a quick peek at her notes. Better get off the details of Barney's passing and jump into something else fast.

"Is he still there in the studio?" Sylvia asked.

"Yes, he is. In fact, Barney is telling me right this minute that you were his soul mate, the love of his life," she said slowly into the mike. "But you already know that, right?" Her tone was as treacly as molasses.

Sylvia gave a tremulous laugh. Chantel was winning her back. "Oh, yes, I do know that." A pause. "I hope he realizes it was his time. At least that's what Dr. Harper said."

Dr. Harper? Chantel hesitated, looking blank for a moment. She opened her mouth like a guppy, snapped it shut, and then took a deep breath through her nose. "Barney knows that Dr. Harper made the right decision." She spoke slowly, the way people do when they're not quite sure of what they're saying.

Had Barney been on life support? I wondered. Maybe Sylvia felt guilty about pulling the plug. I couldn't think of any tactful way to ask, so I remained silent.

Luckily Chantel talks enough for both of us.

"Barney tells me his loved ones were all with him when he passed," Chantel continued. "That must be a comfort to you."

"But that's impossible. Barney didn't have any relatives. They all died years ago."

Chantel blinked. She was off her game today. "Well, when I said they were *with* him, I meant they were *waiting* for him on the other side. You know, after he went into the white light and crossed the Rainbow Bridge."

Nice save, Chantel.

"Oh, I see what you mean."

Out of the corner of my eye, I saw Vera Mae making a quack-quack motion with her hands, a sign that a commercial was coming up. Time to wrap this up till the next segment.

"I'm afraid we have to take a break now—," I ventured.

"Wait!" Sylvia pleaded. "I have to ask one more question. Does Barney know about Harold?"

Harold? It's awful when a caller says something out of left field, and I saw a flash of panic in Chantel's eyes. She bit her lip uncertainly, and some of her flame red lipstick smeared onto her front teeth.

Who was Harold? An illegitimate son? A business partner? A new romantic interest?

"I think he does," Chantel told her. "Yes, he's nodding his head." I resisted a ridiculous impulse to look around and see whether the ghostly Barney really was nodding in approval.

"And he's okay with that?" Sylvia asked breathlessly. "Because Harold's sleeping with me now. I know it seems a little soon, but it was just one of those things."

Harold is sleeping with her, and Barney just passed last week? I felt like I was caught up in an episode of *The Young and the Restless*. Or maybe *One Tree Hill*.

"I . . . Yes, I believe Barney is okay with that," Chantel said. She swallowed, clearly flustered. "Barney seems to be drifting away now, so I'm afraid I can't be more specific. . . ."

"I never thought I'd get another Pomeranian, but I bought Harold from the same breeder that Barney came from." Sylvia was talking in a rush. Pressured speech, the shrinks call it. "He's got papers and everything. I may show him at Westminster next year."

Same breeder? Westminster? Suddenly it all made sense.

"Barney's a *dog*?" I blurted out.

"Of course he's a dog," Sylvia huffed. "A prizewinning Pomeranian. What did you think he was? I had to have him euthanized last week. His kidneys went. Dr. Harper said it was time. I just wanted to see if he was doing okay and to tell him about Harold."

I was speechless, but Vera Mae took up the slack. "And so the circle of life continues," she muttered into her mike. "We're coming up on a break, and we just have time for a quick word from our sponsor, Wanda's House of Beauty."

The moment we went to break, Chantel and I whipped our headphones off and stared at each other in stunned silence.

Chapter 2

"And we're out. For two minutes!" Vera Mae yelled from the control room.

Her cone of lacquered hair tottered a little as she leaned down to jam a cassette into the deck. An annoying jingle from Wanda's House of Beauty flooded the studio, and Vera Mae motioned for me to read the live copy that was sitting in front of me.

The thirty-second spot is called a "doughnut" because it opens and closes with music; there's a "hole" in the middle for me to say my lines. This means there are ten seconds of music and ten seconds for me to read the ad copy, and then the music returns before fading out in the last ten seconds. It's a good deal for the sponsor. It saves on production costs, and it's very flexible; we can change the ad copy without recording a whole new commercial.

"Don't miss our midweek special," I said into my mike. The music was jacked up too high, and I practically had to shout to make myself heard. I felt myself wincing as I read the lines. Vera Mae is supposed to lower the volume for the voice-over part of the commercial, but I figured she was still rattled from Sylvia's call. I know I was.

"Thirty percent off on highlights, this week only." I was racing through the lines. It looked like too much copy for ten seconds, and the words were tumbling over each other. "Single-process color is only forty dollars, and that includes being blown out of this world."

Blown out of this world? Where had that come from? I felt like my brain had slammed into a wall. Chantel snickered, sitting back in her chair.

"I mean, that includes a *blow-dry*," I said hastily.

Music up and out. I saw Vera Mae bent over the control board, flipping dials, booting up the music for the end of the spot.

"Nice commercial," Chantel said in her Queen of Snark voice. "Did you write it?"

"No, we have a copywriter." I paused. "Well, she's sort of a copywriter. It's Irina, the girl at the front desk."

Chantel laughed. "Sort of?" she mocked. "I'll say."

Irina strikes again! I bit back a sigh. Irina is our beautiful blond receptionist from Sweden. She manages pretty well in English, but jokes and double entendres go whizzing right by her. Cyrus, in one of his typical cost-cutting moves, decided that Irina could double as a copywriter, churning out radio copy in addition to handling the reception desk.

I knew it was time to talk to Cyrus again about hiring a real copywriter. Someone who understands the English language. This was getting ridiculous. A few more bloopers like this, and the FCC would pull me off the air.

Vera Mae ran a promo for a Cypress Grove celebration for the next sixty seconds and muted the sound. She opened her mike, and her voice floated into the studio.

"I can't believe it. Barney was a dog! A show dog!" She grabbed her midsection and chortled. "I have to tell you, Maggie, I never saw that one coming."

"Barney was a dog," I mused. "I was sure he was her boyfriend. I was really blindsided by that one." I turned to my guest. "How about you, Chantel? I guess Sylvia caught all of us off guard."

"She didn't catch me off guard, not for a second." My guest was playing it cool, inspecting her bloodred nails. They looked phony, like acrylics. Her fake-violet eyes glittered with amusement, and she ran her hand through her gypsy curls. I wondered whether they were fakes, too, maybe extensions?

"You mean you *knew*? How did you figure it out?"

"I didn't have to figure it out. I knew it from the first word out of Sylvia's mouth." She gave me a nasty smirk. "And don't forget—I *saw* Barney in the studio. Apparently you didn't." She threw a meaningful glance over my left shoulder, but I refused to take the bait.

I smiled at her, but I didn't turn around. *No more head trips, Chantel!*

She wrinkled her nose like Samantha does on those *Bewitched* reruns. "Poor Barney, I think he needs a bath because he's got a major case of doggie odor." She waited a beat to see whether I would react. I didn't. "You know he's still with us in the studio, right? He's standing right behind your right shoulder, Maggie. He's moved a little closer."

Liar, liar, pants on fire.

I swear I caught a puff of hot doggie breath on my shoulder just then. And a faint whiff of liver treats.

"Well, that was a doozie of a show," Vera Mae said later. "Holy moley, that call about Barney was the worst."

"I thought the caller who wanted to talk to her dead cat was the worst."

"Damn straight. I halfway expected Chantel to channel Mr. Whiskers for her, but you notice how she sidestepped that one by saying we'd be doing a whole segment on departed pets next week. Pretty clever, the way she gets some promo for herself."

The show was finally over. Chantel had left the studio, blowing air kisses to the staff, and I was going over programming notes with Vera Mae in my tiny office. It's really more of a cubicle than an office, with piles of books and papers scattered everywhere, along with newspaper clippings for show ideas, and stacks of correspondence.

You'd be surprised how many publicists send me press packets, jammed with tricolor foldouts and head shots. Either they think we have a bigger market share than we really do, or they just send out mass mailings to convince their clients that they're covering all the bases for them.

As the show's producer, Vera Mae is the one who's really responsible for booking the guests, and she combs through all the big south Florida papers, the *Miami Herald*, the *Sun Sentinel*, and the *Palm Beach Post*, for story ideas. But a lot of locals feel they know me because they tune in to my show every day, so they send the material directly to me. It's always hard to say no to someone who's a faithful listener of *On the Couch*, but the truth is, I have to refuse most of them. The trick is to do it without ruffling their feelings.

"I have a splitting headache," I said, reaching into my bag for a couple of aspirin. "Chantel was off her game today, wasn't she?"

"Completely. That girl wasn't getting anything right, bless her heart."

Whenever Vera Mae says "bless her heart," it means, "I'd like to wring her gosh-darn neck."

"I don't suppose Cyrus will care, though. We'll still have to invite her back next week."

"Oh, she'll be back like clockwork," Vera Mae said glumly.

"All Cyrus cares about are the ratings, sugar." She was nibbling on a Twizzler, the latest in her string of stop-smoking strategies. Before Twizzlers, she worked her way through a candy mountain of malted milk balls and Reese's Pieces. "For some reason, your listeners are connecting with her, and that's a fact. You know, we're running those séance spots every hour on the hour. Who knew that dead folks would have so much to say?"

"That reminds me," I said, my spirits sinking. "I'm supposed to go to one of Chantel's séances tonight. For some reason she wants me to see her in action. Maybe she thinks it'll give me some new insight into her spirit work, as she calls it."

Vera Mae pulled a face. "I promised her I'd go, too. Do you want to go together? It's down at the historical society on Water Street. We could order in a pizza and go straight from here." She gave a wry smile. "My car's still in the shop. I don't know what in the world Jeb Peterson is doing to it, so if I could hitch a ride with you, that would be great."

"Sounds good. Lark and Lola want to come, too. So we'll swing by my place and get them on the way, if that's okay."

"Of course it is. The more, the merrier. You know what they say—misery loves company," Vera Mae added wryly.

Lark, my twenty-three-year-old roommate, is into all things New Age and would never forgive me if I denied her the chance to go to a ghostly encounter. And Lola, my glamorous fiftysomething mother, is game for anything that will improve her "art."

Lola is an aspiring actress who's appeared in a string of B movies, and she's always up for a new experience. It's doubtful she'll ever be called on to play a medium or psychic on-screen, but she's a confirmed people watcher, and a séance was the perfect place to do it.

I opened a press packet that included a self-published book

on Cypress Grove history, written by Professor Bernard Grossman, a local author. It had a cheesy cover and a gluey binding, but it was obviously a three-hundred-page labor of love. I held it up for Vera Mae. "Save or toss?"

"I'll take it, sugar." Vera Mae peered at the cover. "You know, I can probably get some good material out of here for those time capsule promos." For the past month, we'd been running a major promotion called "Take Me Back in Time," in honor of an upcoming Cypress Grove event.

Several decades ago, the town council buried a time capsule under the courthouse, with the stipulation that it would be dug up in a hundred years. But a few months ago, a developer named Mark Sanderson started negotiating to buy the courthouse. He doesn't care about the ugly mock-Gothic building; all he's interested in is the prime real estate it stands on. Sanderson plans on razing the courthouse and building a towering condo project on the valuable two-acre lot in the center of town. So that means the time capsule is going to be unearthed in less than two weeks, way ahead of schedule.

Cyrus, who always has an eye out for ratings, decided we could get some mileage out of the time capsule story by running contests, offering prizes to listeners, and interviewing local historians.

Vera Mae had assigned the project to Kevin Whitley, our college intern, mostly to give him something to do. Kevin is barely twenty, but he dresses like someone forty years older. Today he was sporting Larry King suspenders, a Matlock seersucker suit, and wire-rimmed glasses. He's annoyingly cheerful, as effervescent as a club soda.

"Great show, Dr. Maggie, Miss Vera Mae." He's also unfailingly polite. He was on his way to the production office with a pile of tapes, but he stuck his head in my cubicle to say hello.

"Do you really think so, Kevin?" I asked. He seemed blind to the fact that the show had been a train wreck from start to finish. I wondered what it would take to burst that sunny bubble of optimism he carried around with him.

"Oh, yes, ma'am, I did. I always do enjoy hearing Miss Chantel. I learn something new every day from her." He gave a toothy grin, which along with his weak chin, gives him an unfortunate resemblance to Eeyore.

"You don't think we've done this topic to death, Kevin?" Vera Mae asked. "No pun intended," she added with a grin.

"No, ma'am! I don't think your listeners will ever get tired of talking to dead people. In my own family, we have loads of people who talk to the departed on a daily basis."

And they're not hospitalized? Or on medication?

His tone was solemn and so reverential that I resisted making a cheap joke. "It seems to be the women in the family, mostly." He wrinkled his forehead in thought. "Come to think of it, the women are the ones who have all the psychic powers in the Whitley clan. They just love to keep up with relatives who've passed."

I exchanged a look with Vera Mae. "And why do you suppose that is, Kevin? Why would women be more in touch with the spirit world than men?"

"I'm not really sure. I think that maybe women have more to say. They're just better at connecting with people, you know?"

"Damn straight we are," Vera Mae said. "You got that one right." She turned to me. "Maggie, didn't one of your guests say that women talk six times as much as men?"

I nodded, not sure where the conversation was heading. "There's a famous study on male-female communication," I said. "The researchers discovered that in a one-on-one conversation between a man and a woman, a woman uses six times as many words as a man does. Maybe that's what you're thinking of."

"It doesn't surprise me. Men don't listen to us, so we have to repeat everything half a dozen times," Vera Mae said darkly.

As soon as Kevin made his way to the production room, I decided it was time to broach the subject of Irina.

"You're going to talk to Cyrus about hiring a real copy-writer, right? That House of Beauty commercial was awful. I nearly said 'blow job' on the air."

Vera Mae laughed. "I know you did, sugar, and I'm real glad that you didn't. The phones would be ringing off the hook with furious callers." She sighed. "I really meant to read over that copy before I put it on the schedule, but you know, things get crazy around here. I don't always get the time to do the things I should be doing."

"It's not your fault, Vera Mae. It's Irina. She's just not cut out to be a copywriter. English is a second language for her. Why can't Cyrus see that?"

"He can't see past saving a few bucks, honey, and that's a fact." She scooped up a pile of press packets. "But don't worry. I'll talk to him. I'll just fib and tell him Wanda com-plained," she added with a wink. "A word from the sponsor always gets his attention. You better believe it."

Chapter 3

The last moments of sunset were streaking across the western sky when Vera Mae and I left WYME for the séance at the historical society. But first we had to swing by my mock-hacienda-style town house to pick up Lark and Lola. As we turned onto the leafy street lined with banyan trees, I thought how lucky I was to have found this place. It's a three-bedroom unit in a quiet residential neighborhood just ten minutes from WYME.

A row of fragrant gardenia bushes separates my building from the Seabreeze Inn, a bright yellow and white Victorian B and B right next door. Ted Rollins, the manager and owner of the Seabreeze, was hosting one of his nightly wine-and-cheese receptions, and I spotted a dozen or so guests mingling on the wide front porch.

It was a lovely evening, the air soft and balmy, the cicadas humming in the trees. Lark and Lola were sitting outside on the front step, deep in conversation.

I was relieved to see that my mom was decked out appropriately for the occasion. She was wearing a pair of white capri pants, a striped navy-and-white boater's sweater, and four-inch stiletto heels. This is a pretty tame outfit for a woman who's fond of shopping at Wet Seal. The term "age appropriate" never crosses her lips; as she says, she'd "rather dress like Nicole Richie than Helen Mirren."

She figures the "classic look" is a slippery slope for a woman of a certain age. You'll never find her in a pastel pantsuit and sensible pumps. She finds the whole idea of "dressing her age" terrifying. As Lola says, "Why, the next you know, I might be ordering the early-bird special at Applebee's and dating a man named Sid who wears a rug."

At fifty-eight, Mom has the style and panache of one of those long-dead actresses of the silver screen, Dorothy Lamour, Ava Gardner, Marilyn Monroe. She dresses a little young, but since she never tells anyone her real age, it probably doesn't matter. Mom has been known to fudge the truth. The résumé stapled to the back of her head shot still lists her as "thirty-eight," but a more accurate listing would be "thirty-eight and holding."

Think about it. I'm thirty-two. At the rate she's going, she'll soon be younger than I am, and she's been known to introduce herself as my sister. According to Lola, she's younger than every actress in Hollywood, with the possible exception of Dakota Fanning.

Lola and Lark sprang to their feet when I pulled up in front of the town house.

"This is going to be an amazing evening," Lark said, climbing into the backseat after Mom. "I've never been to a séance, although I have seen auras around people."

"Is that so?" Vera Mae asked diplomatically. "Too bad you're weren't in the studio today. You might have seen Fido's aura." Vera Mae winked at me.

"You mean Barney," I corrected her.

"Who's Barney?" Lark asked.

"He's a dog." I checked my watch and pulled away from

the curb. We'd be a little early for the séance, but I wanted to get a good seat.

"A dead dog," Vera Mae offered.

"Well, you can't leave us hanging," Lola said. "I missed the show today. What happened?"

"It's a long story. I'll tell you all about it later," I promised.

"Do you suppose the press will be there tonight?" Mom asked breathlessly.

I glanced in the rearview mirror, and I could see her touching up her lip gloss. I wouldn't be surprised if she'd tucked a few extra head shots in her tote bag. Mom likes to be prepared. She once chased a guy with a beard who was wearing a baseball cap five blocks down Rodeo Drive. When she finally caught up with him, she realized it wasn't Steven Spielberg.

"The press? I don't think so," Vera Mae said. "Not unless the *Cypress Grove Gazette* sends someone. What about that reporter friend of yours, Nick Harrison? Do you suppose he'll be at the séance, Maggie?"

"No, I remember distinctly that Chantel said she didn't want any media present. The event is open to the public, so she can't keep them out, but she certainly isn't encouraging it. The presence of reporters disturbs the spirits, she told me."

"Ha! I bet Chantel said that because she's afraid they'll run an exposé on her. The reporters must know this is all a load of malarkey. You know, someone should do a little investigating on that girl, Maggie. She gave us that press packet, and we've been accepting it as gospel truth." Vera Mae raised her eyebrows. "Maybe there are some dark secrets in her past."

An interesting idea. I made a mental note to ask Nick to do a quick background check on Chantel Carrington for me.

Nick is a first-rate investigative reporter who's covering arts and entertainment features for the tiny *Cypress Grove Gazette* while he waits for his big break. He'd love to move to the *Miami Herald* or the *Palm Beach Post*, but things are tough in the newspaper business right now, so he has to stay put in our little town.

"Are you saying Chantel is a fraud, a charlatan?" Lark piped up. "That's disappointing, because a lot of people believe in her."

She gave a tiny shake of her head, and her blue eyes looked troubled. Lark is determined to think the best of everyone and doesn't share my cynical view of humanity. In many ways, she and I are polar opposites. Lark is an incurable optimist and believes in cosmic harmony, yin and yang, and the idea that the universe sometimes bestows blessings in the form of apparent disasters.

"Well, you just have to take it for what it is," Vera Mae said kindly. "Think of what Chantel does as entertainment. You know, a performance, a stage act."

"But it can't just be entertainment. I've had a strong feeling all day that I was meant to come to her séance tonight. I feel a cosmic connection to her."

"Then you're setting yourself up for disappointment, sugar."

Lark believes that we're destined to meet every single person we encounter in life, either to learn something from them or to teach them something. She's into all things New Age: chakras, karma, auras, and the *I ching*.

Her favorite movie is *Forrest Gump*, and I love anything by Woody Allen.

I think that says it all.

"I'd sure like to get a rundown on her background," Vera Mae said. "What do we really know about her anyway? Have you ever seen her business card? It says she's a professional psychic, a medium, a seer, and an oracle. She calls herself an oracle! She's not lacking nerve. That's for sure."

"It actually says oracle on her card?" *Oracle.* That seemed a little over-the-top, even for Chantel. "I wish I'd known that. I could have used that on the show today."

"I don't think I've ever met an oracle," Lark said, awed. "Or a seer, for that matter."

"Oh, seer, schmeer," Mom interjected. "People can say whatever they like. I could say I'm Suzanne Somers, but who'd believe me?" She twisted a long, loopy strand of golden hair around her index finger. Mom had extensions hot-glued onto her own locks last week and she couldn't resist playing with them.

"Well, you do look a little like her," Lark said, ever tactful. "Around the eyes."

"Do you think so?" Mom brightened and whipped out her compact. "Really?" Mom smiled at her reflection, flipped her extensions back over her shoulder, and pursed her lips. "I don't know. Maybe if they photographed me from a certain angle, in the right light. Of course, they'd have to use those soft pink lightbulbs. They're very flattering, you know."

Vera Mae and I exchanged a look. *Soft pink lightbulbs? Who's she kidding?*

It would take more than pink lightbulbs to make Mom look like Suzanne Somers.

It would take a pair of rose-colored glasses.

Or maybe a bad case of cataracts.

Chapter 4

It was nearly seven when we arrived at the Cypress Grove Historical Society on the south end of Water Street. I nosed my Honda Accord into the parking lot behind the imposing pale gray Victorian mansion that sat squarely on a corner lot.

Althea Somerset was hosting Chantel Carrington's appearance tonight. Althea, one of Cypress Grove's most prominent citizens, sits on the board of several local charities and is an enthusiastic town booster. The historical society is her passion in life, and she's been the director for more than three decades, working for a minuscule salary and living in a small apartment on the top floor.

Althea is an imposing woman, tall and slender. Pushing eighty, she's always stylishly dressed in her trademark pearls and designer pumps. Tonight she was wearing a pale blue Marc Jacobs dress with a high neckline; her silver hair was swept up into an elegant French twist and secured with a silver comb.

I find it hard to believe that Althea really believes in Chantel's ghostly chats, but she certainly understands the power of publicity. She'd told me the other day that membership in the historical society was down and donations were at an all-time low. I noticed she'd discreetly placed a pile of membership brochures in a silver dish sitting on an antique armoire.

"So glad you could make it, Maggie," she said, giving me a hug. "And you brought Vera Mae and Lark. And oh, Lola, I was hoping you'd be able to join us."

Lola loves being anyplace where there's an audience. She took a moment to check herself out in the elaborate rococo mirror hanging in the entryway before greeting Althea.

"This came from one of the Flagler mansions," Althea said proudly. "A very valuable piece I just added to the collection." I bit back a smile. She didn't realize Lola was admiring herself, not the gilded mirror, festooned with pudgy cherubs and water nymphs. "As you know, the Flaglers came here in the nineteenth century and made significant contributions to the area." She looked hopeful, as if she was trying to spark some interest in the philanthropies of the famous family.

"Oh, yes, lovely," Mom said politely. She gave a quick tug to her sweater. It was riding up just a tad in the back, and I knew she didn't want anyone to catch a glimpse of the Spanx she wore under her form-fitting white capris.

Althea pointed out a few more new acquisitions before ushering us into the dimly lit parlor to the left of the front hall. It was the size of a small ballroom, with high ceilings and elaborate millwork, but there was nothing airy or festive about it. It was oppressive, with faded Orientals, somber paintings in muddy tones, and heavy Victorian furniture. Burgundy velvet drapes covered the Palladian windows, and I noticed that someone had pulled them tightly shut for the evening's event.

To keep the spirits in? Or the gawkers out?

"Where would you like us to sit?" I asked, motioning to

the rows of folding chairs that were arranged in front of a small stage at the far end of the room. Probably thirty people were already seated, fanning themselves with programs, talking quietly. The air-conditioning was either on the fritz or too old to be effective, because the room was sweltering.

Althea hesitated. "Chantel is going to choose a few people to join her onstage tonight. Would any of you be interested?" She kept her voice low and glanced over her shoulder, probably worried that she'd spark a stampede of volunteers. "She wants people who are attuned to the spirit world and will bring positive energy to the group." She gave a very slight emphasis to the words "spirit world," and I felt she wanted to give me a tiny eye roll but was too ladylike to really do it.

"Well, holy moley, count me in, Althea," Vera Mae said. "I have a passel of dead relatives I'd like to contact. I'd like to give a piece of my mind to a few of them, and one or two owe me money." Vera Mae grinned at Lark. "You want to be part of the séance, too, don't you, sweetie? I heard you're into all that heebie-jeebie stuff."

"I'd be honored, if Chantel will allow me," Lark said a little breathlessly. Out of the corner of my eye, I saw Althea wince at Vera Mae's use of the term "heebie-jeebie."

"Just make yourselves comfortable, and I'll let Chantel know that you'd like to participate," Althea said, hurrying away to meet some latecomers.

We settled into seats in the back row just as Chantel approached a podium at the far end of the parlor. A single spotlight was focused on her from below, giving her face an odd, otherworldly cast, like someone out of *The Blair Witch Project*.

"Good evening, everyone," Chantel began. "Miss Althea wanted to give me a lovely introduction, but I told her I'm not the focus of the attention tonight." She gave a long, stagey pause. "The spirits are the real stars tonight. It's not about *me*. It's about *them*."

She gave a mock-humble smile, folded her palms over her chest, and looked skyward for a moment. "I am but a channel, a vessel to hold their psychic energy as it rains down upon us." She made a fluttery motion with her fingers as if suggesting a spiritual downpour from the heavens.

I nearly looked up at the ceiling but stopped myself just in time.

"The spirits will be lucky if they manage to get a word in edgewise with Chantel running her mouth like this." Vera Mae nudged me with her elbow. "She's not fooling anyone with this humble act. Look at that pile of books she's got stashed on the table up there. You know darn well she expects people will buy them. I doubt she's handing them out for free."

Chantel glanced our way, raised one of her plucked-to-death eyebrows, and frowned.

"Shhh," I cautioned Vera Mae.

"And she's got more copies scattered on end tables all around the room," Lola whispered. "You can't walk two feet without bumping into a copy of her book. She knows how to promote herself, doesn't she?" she added, an envious note creeping into her voice.

Chantel moved toward a round wooden table, and Althea took her place at the podium. "While Chantel readies herself to receive the spirits, I would like the following people to approach the front of the room." She called out six names, including Vera Mae's and Lark's.

"Wish me luck," Vera Mae whispered as she made her way up the aisle with Lark.

"Knock 'em dead," Lola said warmly to Lark.

"I'd like you to join us at the table as well, Althea." Chantel smiled, motioning for the others to take a seat. "Please sit to the right of me."

I noticed that Chantel had taken the choice seat, smack-dab in the center, so everyone in the audience would have a good view of her. Mom was right. She was a genius at hogging the limelight.

"Oh, no, I couldn't—," Althea protested.

"You must." Chantel spoke in a flat robotic voice, like an android in a bad sci-fi flick, and I wondered whether she was going into some sort of trance. "The spirits are asking that you join us." She paused, tilting her head on one side, as if listening to a ghostly command. "In fact, they are *insisting* on it." Althea nodded and quickly took a seat next to Chantel.

"Wow, it's sort of like a command performance," Mom felt compelled to explain to me. "I remember the time Princess Diana asked that John Travolta be included in a White House dinner she was attending. She said she'd always wanted to dance with him, and—"

"Mom, please. People are staring at us."

"Well, I'm just saying that if a spirit asks you to be present, you have to oblige. You can hardly say no to a ghost."

"Fine," I said with a resigned sigh. I wondered whether Mom was going to talk throughout the entire séance. She'd jabbered nonstop through the entire three hours of *The Lord of the Rings*, so it wouldn't surprise me.

"Oh, for heaven's sake, you're no fun at all," she whispered as the lights suddenly lowered.

"Either the lights are getting dimmer, or I've got a brain tumor," Vera Mae called from the front of the room, drawing a big laugh from the crowd and a frosty look from Chantel.

"I will require almost complete darkness and total silence"—she shot a hostile look at Vera Mae—"for my work to be successful tonight." Vera Mae grinned out at the audience, not the least bit embarrassed by Chantel's reproach.

The lights dimmed a little more until the room was almost completely in shadows. I realized the only lighting was coming from a collection of ornate wall sconces strategically placed throughout the room.

Chantel lit a fat white candle in the center of the round table. She stared at it fixedly for a few moments and then leaned her head back, letting her eyelids flutter shut. There was something hypnotic about the setting, and I wondered whether it was deliberately planned that way. The shadows, the flickering candle light, the airless room—were they all part of an elaborate ruse, designed to make the audience more susceptible to a visit from the beyond?

Then she ordered everyone at the table to join hands. Vera Mae, Lark, and Althea, along with the four women selected from the audience, smiled shyly at one another and complied.

"I'm feeling a familiar presence," Chantel said softly. "Michael, is that you?"

I knew from Chantel's appearances on my show that Michael seems to know everyone in the spirit world and Chantel uses him to channel appearances from the dearly departed.

I picture him as a good-natured bouncer, guarding the rope line of Club Underworld. If you want to mingle with the dead, it's a good idea to be one of Michael's BFFs.

Suddenly a wisp of white smoke appeared in the air above the table and hovered there, dancing. A gasp went up from the audience. The smoky thread was baffling to me. It was stifling hot in the room, utterly still. So how to explain the smoke? And why was it dancing around above Chantel's head? I squinted into the darkness, but the smoke was already dissolving into gossamer threads, melting as fast as a snowflake on a windowpane.

"Ah, he's here," Chantel said with a deep sigh. "Now our journey can begin."

I glanced at Mom, who was staring raptly at the stage. It was impossible not to admire Chantel's stage presence. Charlatan or not, Chantel had the audience in the palm of her hand. She knew how to keep them on the edge of their seats, hanging on her every word.

"Michael is telling me that he has a very important message for someone sitting at this table."

I couldn't read Vera Mae's expression in the dimly lit room, but I noticed the change in her body language. Vera Mae, along with everyone else at the table, suddenly leaned forward, bodies tense, probably wondering whether Michael was speaking directly to them.

"Do you suppose it's a stock tip?" Mom whispered. "My investments have really tanked, and I could use some insider advice—"

I silenced her with a look.

"Michael says that someone here is in great danger," Chantel said solemnly, still with her eyes closed. *Great danger?* I could dimly make out Vera Mae's head whipping around behind her.

I sincerely hoped Barney wasn't making a return appearance. I'd had enough of that dog to last several lifetimes.

"The danger comes from an unexpected source." Mom opened her mouth to say something, but I squeezed her wrist. Hard. "There is an unbeliever threatening Cypress Grove. An evil presence is in our midst."

Another small murmur went up from the audience. Now everyone was getting into the act. Mentioning an "evil presence" was a smart move on Chantel's part. That's the kind of thing that gets everyone's attention.

"And all of us here tonight are in grave danger. There are lies and secrets lying deep beneath the surface. A smiling face holds a dagger." *Yowsers.* I felt a little tingle go down my spine and willed it away. I knew it was all part of Chantel's shtick, but I thought I felt the presence of something sinister, an evil spirit lurking in the stuffy parlor.

"Michael," Chantel said in her rich contralto, "can you tell us anything more about this danger? What can we do to avert a tragedy in our little town?"

At least ten seconds of complete silence. Either Michael didn't have an answer or he was slow on the uptake. If Michael were an 8-Ball, he could just say, *Ask again later,* but apparently this isn't an option for spirit guides.

"Michael says that some things should be left alone. Some stones should be left unturned. Some plans must be abandoned."

Michael, the master of the cryptic remark. He could have been channeling Yoda.

"Huh? Stones left unturned?" Mom said under her breath. "What does that mean? He's not being very helpful, is he?"

"If we don't heed his warning, the consequences"—Chantel waited a beat—"will be dire. Michael says that greed and avarice will lead to total annihilation."

Annihilation? What she was saying was absolute hocus-pocus, but I have to admit it was effective. It certainly made me sit up and take notice. Annihilation is serious stuff, after all. It's bound to be a much bigger deal than simply paying a library fine or getting a ticket for jaywalking.

I was still pondering what had just happened when the lights suddenly started coming back up. It was so steady and gradual, I realized they must have been on a dimmer switch all along. Maybe the wall sconces were wired that way, but how did Althea turn them up and down? She'd spent the whole time sitting next to Chantel, so someone else from the society must have dimmed them. I felt myself blinking in the yellowish light, still watching the stage for signs of movement.

So this was it. The séance was over.

Chapter 5

Chantel had been slumped back in her chair throughout the séance, but now she suddenly sat bolt upright and stared out at the audience. Her voice was thin and reedy, as if the séance had sucked every ounce of energy out of her. Her skin looked sallow, and even her trademark gypsy curls seemed lifeless, trailing limply down her back.

"Michael has spoken," she said solemnly. "His message was intended for someone at this table, or maybe for all of you. Look deeply into your heart, and you will know if Michael was speaking directly to you."

She turned her magnetic gaze on each person at the table, one by one. I noticed that Althea looked uncomfortable and touched her hand to her throat, while Lark appeared fascinated and stared right back at Chantel. Vera Mae, impish as always, flashed a wide grin. I held my breath, hoping Vera Mae wasn't going to crack a joke.

"We have learned something valuable tonight," Chantel continued. "The danger Michael spoke of is real. It might affect everyone in our little town." She made a broad gesture that included the whole audience. "All of us need to be very care-

ful about the choices we make and the people we trust. Evil
is afoot in Cypress Grove."

There was a long moment of silence. It was as if the audience was collectively taking a deep breath, trying to absorb
the somber warning.

"If you'd like to hear more of my chats from beyond, be
sure to tune in to my visit on WYME later this week," Chantel said briskly. *Aha.* The old Chantel was back, full of brassy
confidence, flaunting her megawatt personality and high-
voltage smile.

She was on full power now. "I'll be taking calls on Maggie Walsh's show, and if we're very lucky, Michael might
drop by to join us." She gave a coy smile. "Or who knows?
Maybe a few other spirits will show up."

"Can Michael just chat with Chantel whenever he feels
like it? And how does she know he's going to be available
for your show?" A hint of mischief flashed in Lola's eyes.

"A good point. I'll be sure to ask her."

Chantel whipped out a Sharpie and started autographing
books for people who'd lined up to buy a copy of *I Talk to
Dead People* in the front of the room. Vera Mae and Lark
made their way along the edge of the room just then, and
Althea joined us a few minutes later as we prepared to
leave.

As we were saying good-bye, I spotted a landscape painting hanging in the front hall. It was a rather uninspiring pas-
toral scene, done in shades of muddy browns and tans, but
something about it caught my eye.

Who's the artist? I peered to look at the lower right-hand
corner more closely. The lighting was dim in the front hall,
but I could see that it wasn't signed.

"I found this in the stockroom downstairs a few years

ago," Althea said, coming up next to me. "Pity it's not signed. I just hung it here in the hall and forgot about it."

"There's something about this painting," I said. "Something I can't quite put my finger on. You don't know anything about it?"

"Well, this is probably wishful thinking, but I wondered if it might be a Joshua Riggs," Althea said, a little note of hope creeping into her voice. "Wouldn't that be something?"

I frowned. "Joshua Riggs? I have to confess I haven't heard of him."

"He's a British landscape artist, and he often didn't sign his paintings. It's practically a trademark."

"That seems very odd to me. Why in heaven's name wouldn't he sign his work?" Mildred Smoot had joined us. Mildred, the town librarian, is in her late seventies and an amateur artist. She reached for a pair of bifocals that hung on a beaded chain around her neck and peered at the painting. "It's not very good technically, is it?" She shook her head in disapproval. "I wouldn't get away with this in my watercolor class. And the draftsmanship is horrendous. It looks as though he dashed it off in an hour or two. Not my cup of tea, I'm afraid."

"It does have a sort of unfinished, amateurish look to it," Althea agreed. "But that's how Joshua Riggs painted in his later years. His early paintings are the valuable ones, the ones he did before the middle of the nineteenth century. In his later years, he fell onto hard times and ended up destitute, living in a friend's attic."

"Really? I hadn't heard that," Mildred murmured.

"According to his biographer, poor Joshua became quite paranoid and eccentric. He always thought people were out to steal his paintings, so he decided to hide the really good ones. He'd paint a second picture right over the first one. The top one is a decoy."

"A decoy? What an interesting idea," Mildred exclaimed. "Do you suppose there's something wonderful hidden behind this one?"

I moved closer for a better view and discovered something odd. The painting was in a massive gold frame, and there was a tiny trace of blue paint in the bottom right corner. But there was no blue in the painting. Could there be another painting underneath? And somehow a streak from the hidden painting ended up on the frame? It seemed farfetched, but not impossible. "Maybe someone could X-ray it to see if there's another painting underneath," I suggested. "Someone who specializes in restoring paintings, an art expert, could do that for you. I know they do that at the museums in New York."

Althea considered this for a moment. "I doubt we have anyone like that in Cypress Grove, but I did make arrangements to have it reframed first thing tomorrow morning." She paused. "Maybe the framer will have some ideas, or know someone I can contact."

"I hope so," I said warmly. "I think you may be sitting on a gold mine, Althea."

"Do you really think so? I hope you're right," she said wistfully. "The historical society could certainly use the money." She pointed to a pile of paintings stacked up against the wall. "There are some of the other ones I found in the basement. Maybe I should go through all of them. Perhaps there are some treasures lurking there."

"If you find out that the painting really is valuable, make sure you tell Vera Mae. It will fit right in with some time capsule promos we're running this week, and it will be a good chance to mention the work you do here."

"Thank you, Maggie. I'll do that," she said warmly. "Every bit of publicity helps the society."

It was nearly nine o'clock when we got back to the town house, after swinging by Banyan Way to drop Vera Mae off at her condo.

"That was quite an evening," Lola said, kicking off her too-high heels and heading for the refrigerator. "I didn't believe that whole bit about Michael and his tales of doom and gloom—that was a bunch of hooey—but you have to admit, Chantel has an amazing stage presence. She really had the audience eating out of the palm of her hand." Mom let out a tiny sigh.

Was she a little envious? Well, if she was, who could blame her?

People were showering Chantel with lucrative book contracts and movie deals plus a chance to hit the lecture circuit and play at major venues. Chantel had created a great platform—talking to the dead—and was getting loads of media attention. When you thought of it, it was brilliant. Who could say she *wasn't* talking to the dead? As one of my professors once said, it's tough to prove a negative.

"Yes, she knows how to connect with the audience. She's that way on my show, too. She ropes in the listeners right away, and the lines are always jammed with callers."

I was feeling a little twinge of jealousy myself. If Chantel ever wangles her own show on WYME, I bet she'll outpace *On the Couch with Maggie Walsh* in a heartbeat. It's all about ratings, and Chantel knows how to work her magic, not just with the listeners, but with Cyrus Still, the station manager.

She's savvy about promoting herself, and I don't quite trust her. I have the feeling she'd step right over me to get to the top and would be willing to do whatever it takes. I still didn't understand her motivation, though.

Why would she be interested in a small market like Cypress Grove? Or was it a stepping-stone to something bigger? I'd never really believed her line that she came here for some much-needed peace and quiet in order to write. From what I've seen of Chantel, peace and quiet—and isolation—are the last things she needs.

"I wonder if she's had any theatrical training," Mom said. "Or maybe she's just a natural. Either way, I'd love to find out more about her. I have the feeling she's a fellow thespian."

A fellow thespian? A charlatan is more like it, I thought.

But it was interesting that Lola believed she recognized a fellow actress, a kindred spirit, in Chantel. Lola has been pursuing an acting career most of her life. At fifty-eight, she's still hoping to grab the brass ring, although the years may have dampened her over-the-top aspirations. In a youth-oriented culture, how far can Lola really go with her acting career, and what sorts of parts can she hope to play?

Lola has managed to snare some parts in B movies—the kind that go straight to video—and recently, she appeared in a Hollywood movie that was being shot right here in Cypress Grove. She got the part because of her friendship with Hank Watson, the director, but it still was an exciting time for her, and she loved being part of the production.

I was involved with the movie company as well, first as a script consultant, and then I found myself investigating a murder that happened on the set.

There's a bustling film business in Miami, and Mom still trots off to auditions every time she gets the chance. She's acquired a new agent, Edgar Dumont, who has an office in South Beach. He looks like he's been around since the golden age of Hollywood, but he does send her on "go-sees" and auditions for the occasional low-budget flick or television commercial. It's enough to keep her hopes up, I guess, because she never gives up on the business entirely.

"Intermittent reinforcement," the shrinks call it. Give a pigeon a few crumbs as a reward from time to time (but don't do it all the time) and it's more effective than a regular payoff. In other words, keep them guessing. Giving someone a few strokes occasionally and randomly will keep them coming back for more. Reward them every time and they lose interest in a hurry.

"Just call in the next time Chantel's on the show and ask her whatever you want," I suggested. "Vera Mae will make sure you get through. You can call Vera Mae on her private line. I'll give you the number."

"Well, I'd hate jumping ahead of the other listeners," Mom said. "After all, you're the host of the show. I don't want anyone to think I'm being pushy or asking for special treatment."

I laughed. "Are you kidding? Mom, I think I'm entitled to a few perks as a WYME talk show host."

I wondered whether she realized I'd taken a huge pay cut to move to Florida and work at WYME. Even though it was expensive to live in Manhattan, I'd made a good living from psychology, especially since I specialized in forensic work.

I also had a small "concierge practice" on the side and saw only a dozen or so patients every week. I always thought of them as the "worried well" because they were high-functioning types, mostly high-powered executives and a few show business personalities. They didn't use their health insurance cards because they didn't want to leave a paper trail of their sessions with me, and they always paid out of pocket. Some of them even paid me a monthly retainer to make sure that I'd always be available to them.

Being a radio talk show host in a small market has a lot

of positive things associated with it, but money isn't one of them. It's fun, it's entertaining, you meet some terrific people, you become an instant celebrity, and you have your own parking spot.

But you don't get rich. Trust me.

Chapter 6

I bent down to hug Pugsley, who, even thirty minutes after our return, was still circling my ankles, yipping with excitement, delirious with joy at our return. Pugsley is the furry love of my life, a three-year-old rescue dog who understands my most intimate thoughts and feelings. He's the next best thing to a soul mate and gives me what every woman craves.

Unconditional love and a ton of sloppy kisses.

Pugsley never has a bad day. I feel happier just being around him.

I scooped him up and settled down with him at the kitchen table. The kitchen is a cozy place, with oak floors, exposed beams, and cream walls dotted with abstract canvases ainted by local artists. Lark has an excellent eye for color, and she's picked them up for a song at neighborhood yard sales.

Pugsley squirmed in my lap, watching Mom at the refrigerator, probably angling for a treat. We try to keep him on what Lark calls a heart-healthy diet, but we allow for the occasional snack. After all, what's life without a few Liv-a Snaps now and then?

Mom pulled out a plate of blueberry-walnut scones and set it down in front of me while Lark filled the electric teakettle. Exotic teas and homemade goodies have become an evening ritual for us, and I'm very fortunate that Lark loves to cook. She's into organic food and makes everything from scratch, using whole grains, flaxseed, soy powder, and other heart-healthy nutrients that she stashes in glass canisters. If she wasn't so dedicated to her paralegal studies, I think she would make an excellent personal chef.

"I'm curious about your reaction to the séance, Lark," Mom said to her. "Did you feel anything special when you were sitting there at the table tonight with Chantel?"

Lark looked pensive for a moment and then ran her hand through her choppy blond hair. Lark has a winsome look about her, and with her delicate bones and slim stature, people often mistake her for a teenager.

"I can't really say," she said finally, carefully measuring out some fragrant peach-vanilla tea into the pot. "I felt *something*, but maybe it was just the power of suggestion. Chantel has a very strong aura around her, you know. She comes across much more forcefully in person than she does on the radio."

"It was hard for us to tell anything, sitting way back in the audience," Mom said.

I suddenly remembered the puff of white smoke that danced for a few minutes in the air and then disappeared. I asked Lark about it.

"Yes, I saw it, too," she said quickly. "It seemed to come out of nowhere." She wrinkled her nose. "The funny thing is, it had a strange odor to it. Like a chemical smell."

"Really? That's interesting." Maybe Chantel had released a vial that contained some sort of vapor that hung over the table for a few minutes before vanishing. It was a little odd, but I suppose it added to the air of mystery. I made a mental note to ask Nick Harrison, my friend at the *Gazette*, to check it out. I was sure Nick would have some ideas on magic tricks, or he'd at least know whom to ask. He has terrific connections on both coasts along with the tenacity of a pit bull when he's hot on the trail of a story. I wrote *Call Nick* at the top of my to-do list before turning in to bed at eleven o'clock, with Pugsley nestled happily at my side. He fell asleep within minutes, caught up in a doggie dream, his tiny feet making galloping motions as if he was chasing a rabbit.

I reached over to pet him, my own thoughts going back to Chantel's séance. Her silly conversation with Michael the spirit guide. Her blind ambition. Was she trying to take over my show? And what about her somber prediction that there was danger afoot in Cypress Grove? She warned that disaster would strike us, all because of greed, avarice, and some very dark secrets.

You notice how she kept the warning completely general, never specific. It would fit any situation, any set of circumstances, just like the horoscope column in the local paper. Who'd believe such nonsense?

I rolled over and gathered Pugsley in my arms like a teddy bear, but I couldn't turn off my thoughts. Then I answered my own question. *Who'd believe in Chantel?* The same people who believed in crop circles, Area 51, and the idea that the Nazis had a base on the moon. Oh, yeah, and the wacky notion that supermarket bar codes were actually part of a secret government plot to control our thoughts and behavior.

Conspiracy theories. They might make for an interesting show, and I decided to run the idea past Vera Mae when I got to the studio the next day.

And that's the last thing I remember before I fell into a deep, dreamless sleep.

The next morning was a perfect south Florida day, bright and sunny, with just a few puffy clouds drifting across a paint-box blue sky. I opened the sliding glass door to our tiny balcony, and Pugsley went flying outside while I plugged in the coffeepot.

I like to linger on the balcony with a cup of high-octane Hazelnut Delight before starting my day, and if Mom's staying at the town house with us, she always joins me. Mom has her own place in Miami, but she visits frequently, and I'm glad I paid a little extra to have a three-bedroom unit.

The balcony is tiny, probably only fifty square feet, and simply furnished with a couple of navy canvas deck chairs I picked up at Tar-zhay plus a small wicker table. But it overlooks a pretty little fountain that spills into a pond and a nice little garden bordered by some magnolia bushes at the end of the property.

I got the coffeepot going and then sat out on a deck chair, watching the copper green metal dolphins twirling in the spray, the droplets looking like tiny crystals as they landed on the terra-cotta tiles edging the pond. It was one of those mornings that makes me grateful to be living in south Florida, a day when all is right with the world.

Mom came out on the balcony to join me, wearing a silk Japanese dressing gown, reading a copy of *Variety*. Even though we're three thousand miles from Hollywood, she likes to stay "plugged in," as she calls it, and follows all the latest casting news in Los Angeles.

"They're holding auditions for a Lifetime movie," she said. "And listen to this: they're looking for a *young* Mia Farrow." She paused dramatically. "A *young* Mia Farrow! Can you believe it?" She sounded shaken. "I remember her in *Rosemary's Baby*," she said quietly. "She was wonderful in that movie. And she looked so young, hardly more than a girl." Mom looked wistful, her blue eyes thoughtful.

"Well, yes, Mom, of course she looked young. She *was*

young. You have to remember, *Rosemary's Baby* was filmed more than forty years ago. She's a beautiful woman, but it's been quite a while since she could play an ingenue."

I wondered whether Mom realized that Mia Farrow is playing grandmother roles at this stage of her career. Lola probably did know this on an intellectual level, but maybe she blocked the information out of her mind. I think she would find it depressing beyond belief if she let herself dwell on it.

"Time flies," Mom said with a heavy sigh. "I haven't seen her on the screen very much recently." I knew what she was thinking. If Mia Farrow was getting older, that meant she was getting older as well.

She flipped through the paper for a few moments and then tossed it aside. "All the casting notices seem to be for girls in their twenties and thirties," she said, giving a little frown. "Well, no surprises there. That seems to be par for the course." She pursed her lips and stared out into the sunny garden, apparently lost in thought.

"Do you have an audition today?" I spotted a script in her lap.

"Yes, it's just a small part, but I better get cracking on it. My memory isn't what it used to be." She paused. "Lately, I seem to have trouble concentrating. That's why I turned off the TV and the phone this morning."

"I noticed." Mom needs complete silence when she has to memorize lines. "I'm sure you'll do a great job."

"Don't be so sure." She made a face. "There will be tons of young girls auditioning. And then there's me. I bet I'll be the oldest person in the room." She heaved a little sigh.

Mom knows that Hollywood isn't kind to "women of a certain age," and as she says, the clock is always ticking. There's only a small window of opportunity for them to practice their chosen craft. For every Sally Field, Meryl Streep, and Helen Mirren, there are thousands of actresses who never work in their "mature" years. The parts just dry up, and no one sends them out on auditions. They simply become invisible.

Sometimes the same thing happens to male superstars.

"The Tab Hunter story comes to mind." Mom smiled. "You've heard it, right?"

I nodded. "The four stages of Hollywood stardom." I smiled, remembering the old joke. *Get me Tab Hunter. Get me a Tab Hunter type. Get me a young Tab Hunter. Who the hell is Tab Hunter?*

Lark called out that the coffee was ready, and I brought out two mugs on a tray with a couple of croissants. Mom and I sat side by side, enjoying the bright Florida sunlight, the dazzling bougainvillea, and the sweet smell of magnolia drifting across the soft breeze.

Nothing bad could happen on a day like this, I thought.

I couldn't have been more wrong.

Vera Mae called me on my cell around noon, just as I was getting ready to leave for the station. I had dressed casually in a pair of white capris and a sleeveless yellow blouse from Ann Taylor. I was just stuffing my cell phone in my tote bag when I realized it was vibrating. I quickly flipped the lid open, and before I could even say hello, Vera Mae's voice raced across the line.

"Holy moley, girl, haven't you heard the news? Are you watching channel six?"

"What's up?" I said idly. I was doing a mental rundown of what I needed to stash in my tote: show notes, briefcase, water bottle, day planner, granola bar. I had the vague feeling I was forgetting something. Maybe hair spray? My shoulder-length auburn hair turns into a fuzzball when it's humid, and I have to use industrial-strength products to tame it.

"What's up? Miss Althea is dead—that's what's up. I thought surely you'd have heard by now."

Althea dead? I tuned out everything except those two words. A muscle jumped in my cheek, and my head throbbed with the news. While I'd been sitting outside enjoying the sunny day with Lola, Althea Somerset had died. I shook my head in disbelief at the randomness of events.

If I shared Lark's view of the world, I'd have no trouble accepting this odd dichotomy. Lark believes that whenever the cosmos favors you with good fortune, it immediately sends a bolt of darkness and sadness. Every joyful moment is followed by tragedy. Yin and yang, Lark calls it. Sunny days are always balanced by rain. I'm glad this philosophy makes Lark happy, but I don't buy it.

"Althea Somerset? But what happened? She was fine last night," I said idiotically. My mind was doing loops at the impossibility of it all. It always amazes me what pops out of people's mouths when they're hit with the news of someone's death.

I wasn't a close friend of Althea's, but she'd been kind to me when I was new in town, feeling my way. I felt a wave of sadness at her passing, and I took a deep breath to steady myself.

"She was murdered in a home invasion." Vera Mae paused; her voice sagged. "Right there at the historical society. Bludgeoned to death with a fireplace poker." Vera Mae had known Althea for more than two decades, I remembered. No wonder she was upset. "It was all over the news a few minutes ago."

"We've had radio silence here this morning," I said. "Lola was studying her lines. She's going on an audition tomorrow. You know how she is when she's memorizing a part. No one can make a sound." I walked away from the kitchen, down the little hallway that leads to my bedroom.

Lark and Lola had headed out the front door for a shopping trip at Sawgrass Mills just a few minutes earlier. I felt a little pang when I realized they'd find out the news as soon as they turned on the car radio. I tried to gather my thoughts, which were scrambling like leaves in the wind.

Sudden death was shocking enough, but murder was unthinkable. And why Althea? It was impossible to think of her as a murder victim.

"I need to call Rafe," I said quickly. "And Nick Harrison."

I knew Nick, my reporter friend at the *Cypress Grove Gazette*, would be on top of the news and was probably already out interviewing sources. Even though he covers arts and entertainment, he never misses a chance to tackle the crime beat.

And Rafe, my on-again, off-again boyfriend, who happens to be a detective with the Cypress Grove PD, was probably working the case right this minute. I needed to get information from both of them, and I needed it fast.

"Well, Rafe's already called here for you. I told him we were both at that séance last night, along with Lola and Lark. It's weird to think that we were probably some of the last people to see her alive, isn't it?"

Along with about thirty other people, I thought. And of course Chantel. Could the murder be connected to the séance? But how? And who would benefit from Althea's death?

"How fast can you get in here?" Vera Mae asked, breaking into my thoughts. "I'm thinking of putting together a memorial show about Althea and her work with the historical society. We won't be able to get it ready in time for today, but we can certainly run it tomorrow." She paused. "And Cyrus wants me to step up those promos for the time capsule ceremony. That was one of Althea's pet projects." There was a little catch in her voice.

"I know, Vera Mae," I said softly. "That would be a wonderful tribute to her, a great way to honor her. We can work on the promos as soon as I get there. I'm on my way."

Chapter 7

I scrolled through my messages as I zipped out to my little red Honda parked on the street. Rafe had called my cell three times. Interesting. I thought of calling him back and decided against it. I knew he'd go ballistic if I tried to talk to him while I was driving, and I wanted to get to the station as quickly as possible.

I'd just pulled into the WYME parking lot and was scrambling out of my car when I heard a familiar voice behind me.

"I think you've done it again, Sherlock." A male voice, low and husky, with a sexy undercurrent that made my heart go flip-flop. I recognized the voice immediately, that sultry tone with a teasing edge could belong to only one person.

Rafe Martino.

"How's that?" My heart was thumping in my chest, but I tried to sound casual as I glanced over my shoulder. I grabbed my tote bag off the front seat, closed the car door, and took my time pushing my sunglasses on top of my head before I turned to face him.

We were standing just a few feet away from each other, and I felt a wave of emotion body slam me. Rafe was wearing a black T-shirt and dark denim jeans and looked like a million bucks. Life is unfair. It isn't standard cop attire, but he's a detective and often works undercover, so I guess he can wear whatever he wants.

Rafe and I have an on-again, off-again history, but my traitorous hormones always kick into high gear when I'm standing this close to him. It's like he's putting out pheromones that draw me back into his web. Is he even aware that he's doing it? I've often wondered about that. Something about the sexy little smile that plays over his lips tells me he knows exactly what he's doing.

"It looks like you've gotten yourself involved in another murder, Maggie," he said lightly. "You've heard about Althea Somerset, right?" I nodded and he went on. "Vera Mae tells me you were the last person to see her alive. I'd like to hear more about that." A smile, coaxing, played on his lips.

I decided it was time to set him straight. "What Vera Mae said isn't quite accurate, Rafe. I was *one* of the last people to see her alive." For a homicide detective, he was remarkably casual about his choice of words. Or maybe he was being deliberately obtuse, trying to throw me off guard, something he enjoys doing from time to time.

"There were at least thirty people at the historical society last night," I continued. "And a handful of them were chosen to actually get up onstage and participate in the séance. But you probably know all this, right?" I said, goading him a little.

"Of course. I have a copy of the guest list," he said in that maddening way. "Luckily Althea asked people to sign the register at the door. And Vera Mae filled me in on which guests Chantel chose to sit at the table with her. I know Althea was one of them. In any case, Duane and I plan on interviewing every single person who was at the historical society last night. And a few other people who might have knowledge of the case."

"Really? Other people?"

Rafe shrugged, not willing to give anything away. "Duane is checking out some collateral contacts for me."

"Have they established the time of death?"

"The coroner is still working on that. It could be late last night or early this morning. Duane is going to call the medical examiner's office for an update."

Officer Duane Brown is a freckle-faced rookie cop whom I secretly call Opie because he's a dead ringer for that kid from Mayberry. He barely looks old enough to get a library card, much less carry a gun.

Rafe rubbed his hand over his jaw, looking thoughtful. "But since you were right there last night, in the thick of things, I thought I'd start with you. And Chantel Carrington, of course. I figured I could talk to both of you at the same time. Vera Mae told me Chantel was coming into the station today."

"Really? That's news to me. She doesn't have a show scheduled." I thought for a moment. "Maybe she's hoping to cash in on some publicity for herself," I muttered. "That's exactly the kind of thing she would do. She probably thinks of Althea's death as a golden opportunity. It might even create some extra buzz for her new book." It would also boost my ratings the next time she appeared, but I decided not to point that out to him.

"Is that a fact?" His eyes narrowed a little at the corners, and I could see the wheels clicking in his mind. He reached into his back pocket and pulled out a tiny notebook.

"Oh, for heaven's sake, don't write that down," I said, only half seriously. Rafe makes copious notes about his cases, and I didn't want my snarky remark to be immortalized in a police report somewhere. "You know I didn't mean it. I'm just not a big fan of Chantel and her mumbo jumbo."

Officer Brown drove up just then in a black-and-white cruiser and slid into a parking place next to us. He jumped out, nodded to Rafe, and greeted me, looking uncomfortable in his scratchy serge uniform.

"Will you be doing a psychological profile on the perp, Dr. Maggie?" Opie asked me.

The perp?

I could see Rafe biting back a smile. Opie is a huge fan of detective shows—*CSI Miami*, *Law & Order*, and *The Mentalist*—and he sprinkles cop talk into every conversation. Opie is wildly impressed that I did forensic work back in Manhattan, and he has an idealized view of the field. And of me, for that matter. He says I remind him of Dr. Elizabeth Olivet, the classy police psychologist who used to be on *Law & Order*.

"Afraid not," I told him. "I just found out about the murder a few minutes ago. As far as I know, no *perp* has been identified. In fact, I don't think there are any suspects at the moment." I tossed a questioning look at Rafe, who was keeping a poker face. "And I really don't think the local police are too interested in anything I'd have to say," I continued. "They believe that good old-fashioned detective work trumps forensic psychology any day."

This is an old argument between Rafe and me. Rafe insists that forensic psychology is useless and refuses to believe it can reveal anything about personality and motive. I've helped solve two murders since moving to Cypress Grove. One victim was a New Age guru and the other a film star, but Rafe always acts as though he's two steps ahead of me.

Apparently Rafe decided to ignore my jibe. "Let's go inside. The heat's killing me today." The three of us crunched over the gravel to the glass double doors of WYME. Rafe was right. The temperature had ratcheted up a few notches. The noonday heat was scorching; it felt as if we were pushing against a solid wall of hot air, and it was hard to draw a breath.

Although I have to admit, it's easy to be breathless around Rafe. He has movie-star good looks going for him and an undeniable bad-boy charm. His finely chiseled features, smoky eyes, and black hair, worn on the longish side, add to his "renegade" look. His hair has a tendency to curl up in the back in a very sexy way, just like Simon Baker's on *The Mentalist*, and I found myself longing to reach out and touch it.

Today Rafe was wearing aviator sunglasses and channeling Horatio Caine, and there was a coiled readiness in his body. His eyes are watchful and his body language is always on high alert. I never can decide whether it's part of being a cop or just his personality style.

The word on the street is that Rafe never gets too involved with anyone—he's had a string of girlfriends, but he makes sure he can walk away at a moment's notice. Rafe always has an exit strategy; he's not the kind of guy who plays for keeps. I try to cool my jets when I'm around him, although sometimes it's a losing battle. But there's no sense in putting my heart on the chopping block and having Rafe do an Emeril Lagasse (*Bam!*) on it.

We'd barely entered the lobby when Big Jim Wilcox hurried over. "Look, it's Maggie Walsh and she's got the cops with her!" He was shouting, his big beefy face red with excitement. Big Jim is the fortysomething sports announcer at the station; he's been a thorn in my side since I joined what Cyrus calls "the WYME family." If we're a family, we're so dysfunctional, we should be headed for the *Jerry Springer* show.

To say that Big Jim is an idiot is giving him too much credit.

"So what really happened at that séance, Maggie? Did somebody snap and come back later and kill Althea? Or do you think a ghost was out for vengeance? Maybe it was some kind of divine retribution. I want an exclusive, you know." Jim was standing too close to me, as always, wearing too much Drakkar Noir, his eyes bulging with interest.

Even though Big Jim covers sports, he's trying to make the big leagues and keeps hoping for an investigative report to add to his demo reel. His biggest story to date is a human interest piece about Andy Layton, a high school sophomore who broke his ankle during football practice and had to sit out the rest of the season. That's not the kind of scoop that will propel Big Jim into a major market, I'm afraid.

When I first moved to Cypress Grove, Big Jim thought I'd gone insane and murdered my own talk show guest, a New Age guru. Even though the real killer was later brought to justice, Big Jim still harbors a nagging feeling that I must have been involved in some way. He believes "all shrinks are nuts," and he expects me to go berserk at any moment. Actually, he's hoping for it. I wondered whether he'd grab a tape recorder and try to get a comment from me. Or maybe he was wearing a wire and was hoping I'd say something incriminating. Nothing Big Jim might do would surprise me.

"Well, what is it, Maggie?" he nattered on. "A ghost did it, right?"

"I don't think Althea was murdered by a ghost," I said, keeping my voice level. I saw Opie whip out his notebook. I bet he was writing down every word.

"No? Well, you can't be sure, can you? You could do one of those psychological autopsies. I saw that on *CSI Miami*.

Now, that would bring in a lot of listeners." Big Jim paused to pop a breath mint and scratch his chin. "Although, come to think of it, how would you do an autopsy on a ghost? Bummer." He gave a cackling laugh. "I guess even an ace shrink like yourself can't figure that one out, can you, Maggie?"

I shook my head. Big Jim was an even bigger moron than I'd thought.

"Well, for one thing, a psychological autopsy is done on the *victim*, not the *murderer*. And it has nothing to do with a body. It's a way of reconstructing what the victim thought, felt, and did. You know what the cops always say: 'know the victim and you'll know the killer.' That's the theory behind the psychological autopsy."

"What was that again?" I turned around, and sure enough, Opie was frowning and scribbling in his notebook. "Know the victim and—"

"Know the victim and you'll know the killer," I repeated.

"Huh?" Big Jim looked perplexed. "Is that true? Because I'm sure I read in the *National Enquirer* that ninety percent of all murders are—"

"Look, we need to get started here," Rafe interrupted him. "Maggie, the first thing we need is a quiet place to talk to people. If you'll excuse us," he said pointedly to the sports announcer.

Naturally, Big Jim didn't get the hint. Rafe walked over to Irina, our beautiful blond receptionist, who was watching spellbound from her desk.

Whenever Irina sees Rafe, she blushes bright pink and her always-fragile hold on English slips away. She gave a girlish little giggle when she realized Rafe was headed her way.

"Miss Yaslov, could you please get Miss Vera Mae Atkins

for me? She's expecting us." Rafe stared at her for a long moment, while the synapses finally connected in her brain. Her face flushed an even deeper shade of salmon.

"Ya, I will be doing these things even now as I am speaking to you," Irina said, flashing him a gleaming supermodel smile. She had an impressive set of veneers, and I always wondered how she managed to afford them. I couldn't imagine cosmetic dentistry being a big item in Sweden so I assumed she had them done over here. "Ya, you will see. I am calling her now, at our present moment."

"Great, thank you." Rafe tossed her one of his heartbreaker smiles, and I thought she would swoon.

Irina reached for the intercom, never taking her eyes off Rafe. "Vera Mae Atkins, please to be coming into the lobby," she said. "Is urgent. Please to be coming now." She grinned at Rafe. "Ten-four!" she added in a burst of ingenuity. "Is correct, yes?"

"Yes, that's correct." His breath quickened beside me, and I knew he was fighting a laugh.

"Ten-four, ten-four," she chanted into the intercom. She was flushed and giggling, high on Rafe's approval.

Then, like a Chatty Cathy doll who never shuts up, she started to repeat the entire message. "Vera Mae Atkins, please to be coming to the lobby—"

"Oh, for heaven's sake, cut that thing off, girl!" Vera Mae said, bustling into the lobby. "Can't you see I'm standing right here? You don't need to get your panties in a twist."

Vera Mae was carrying a clipboard and looked frazzled. A few strands of carrot-colored hair had escaped from her towering beehive and were curling down the back of her neck.

"I've cleared out the break room. We can talk in there," she said to Rafe. "And if you need a second interview room"—

she glanced at Opie—"you can use my office." She turned to me. "Maggie, I've left a few messages on your desk. Nick Harrison called. He'd like you to call him back at the *Gazette* as soon as you can."

"Thanks. I'll do that." I was looking forward to hearing Nick's take on the murder investigation, especially since it was pretty obvious I wasn't going to get anywhere with Rafe Martino.

Vera Mae moved closer and lowered her voice. "And I think I should warn you, Chantel is here. She's in the ladies' room, getting all gussied up."

"Why did she come in here today?"

"Why do you think?" Vera Mae muttered. "She wants to channel poor Althea's spirit for today's show. She thinks her pal Michael can arrange it." The expression on Vera Mae's face told me what she thought of the wacky idea.

"What? That's outrageous!" I said, horrified. "Of all the cheap, tawdry, sensationalistic—"

"Don't worry, sugar. It's not gonna happen." Vera Mae had a steely look in her eyes as she touched me lightly on the arm. "Not in a million years. Ratings may be important, but we're talking about one of the town's favorite citizens. Cyrus knows better than to offend the ladies in the historical society. He knows a lot of them are married to some of our most valuable sponsors. He'd never hear the end of it." She gave me a shrewd look. "The ladies in the society wouldn't want to see Althea being used as part of Chantel's parlor game."

"I hope you're right about that." I had my doubts. I could see dollar signs dancing in front of Cyrus's eyes as he pictured Althea appearing live—or rather, dead—in the WYME studios today.

"I *know* I'm right on this one." She jutted her chin, tucked a few strands of loose hair back into her beehive, and used a bobby pin to hold them in place. "I've already talked to Cyrus, and he said he wouldn't allow it. Every once in a while, that boy surprises me," she said with a hint of a smile. "I think he's grown a backbone."

Vera Mae was much calmer than she'd been on the phone. I was sure she was still upset over Althea's death, but now that she was caught up in the details of her workday, she had to put sentiment aside. She had a show to produce.

"So what are we planning for *On the Couch* today?"

We all were squeezed together in the narrow hallway as we made our way down to the break room. Big Jim was trailing behind us, probably hoping to get an inside scoop on the investigation, but I knew Rafe would figure out a way to get rid of him.

Vera Mae glanced at her notebook. "I think we'll let the callers share some stories about how they knew Althea. The old-timers probably have some good memories to share. And I'm trying to get someone from the historical society over here for the second hour. I'm not sure if that's going to work out," she admitted. "Everyone who knew her is pretty devastated. I don't know if I can get anyone to agree to go on the air on such short notice."

I nodded. "We can go with two hours of calls, if we have to. Maybe get a history professor over here to talk about changes in the town over the years, and how the historical society documented all the milestones. That would honor Althea and it also would fit in with the time capsule promos. And you could try Professor Grossman. He wrote a book on south Florida history and he's been dying to get on the show. Remember? He's the one who's always sending over press releases."

"Good thinking! I've got his phone number in my files.

And Cyrus can probably get someone from the chamber of commerce to do a phone interview with us. Or maybe even sit in as a guest." Vera Mae took a pencil from behind her ear and started jotting down some notes. "I better skedaddle, hon." She glanced at her watch. "See you in a bit."

Chapter 8

"Lola and I really didn't see much from the back of the room," I told Rafe a few minutes later. "Chantel went into a sort of trance, and then Michael gave a little spiel about evildoings in town. He warned us that all of us were in danger. Or maybe just one person." I made a dismissive wave of my hand. "He was very cryptic. I'm not really sure what he meant."

"Michael?" Rafe had whipped out a notebook and stared at me, pen poised. "Do you have a last name on this guy? I need to talk to him."

"Good luck with that." I bit back a laugh "He's a spirit guide. Chantel channeled him, and he gave us this message from the great beyond."

"Oh." Rafe gave a rueful smile. "So he said everyone's in danger, but he didn't go into specifics?"

"That's right. There wouldn't have been time anyway. I don't know how long séances usually last, but this one was only a few minutes."

"Interesting," Rafe muttered, making a note.

"I think it was just a marketing opportunity for Chantel. People were lining up to buy her books after the séance." Rafe and I were sitting on cheap turquoise plastic chairs in the break room, while Opie was down the hall, interviewing Chantel in Vera Mae's office.

Rafe had asked Opie to get some background information about Chantel and the séance, but I think he just wanted to give the young officer something to do. I knew Rafe was planning his own interview with the flamboyant medium as soon as he finished talking to me.

"I have the feeling most of the people at the historical society had never met Chantel before last night," he said. He laid a small tape recorder on the table between us. "You don't mind if I tape the rest of this, do you?" he asked, catching my glance. He kept his tone deliberately casual, and he had his cop face on, closed and inscrutable.

"Of course not." Actually, I did mind a little, but I decided to play along. Seeing the tiny red light spring to life on the recorder made me uncomfortable, which was why I had never taped my sessions with my patients back in Manhattan. Switch on a recorder and people would freeze up, become guarded, reticent, and you'd have to dig a lot deeper to get information out of them. I relied on my memory and I made notes as soon as they left the room.

Of course, Rafe and I were having more than a conversation. I knew that everything I said would end up in police report someday.

"To answer your question, I'd guess that hardly anyone had met Chantel before last night. Vera Mae had met her here in the studio, of course." I paused. "And a lot of people in the audience knew her from her appearances on my show."

"How do people react to her?"

I smiled, remembering Vera Mae's nonstop commentary on the séance. "They think she's a little over-the-top, if you ask me. But still, it's all about ratings, isn't it? And after all, this is entertainment. I don't know how many people are true 'believers,' as Chantel calls them, but I think it's just a small percentage. Most people just find it intriguing."

"Tell me about Althea. It seems she was well liked."

"Very much so. I've never heard anyone say an unkind word about her. She did a lot for Cypress Grove, and the historical society was her passion in life."

"Doesn't it seem a little odd that she hosted a séance for Chantel? What could the two of them possibly have in common?"

"I think it was a shrewd marketing move on Althea's part. She needed to raise money and public awareness about the historical society, and she hoped Chantel would be able attract an audience."

"Althea was single?"

"Yes, widowed. I heard her husband died years ago. I really don't know much about her personal life. I'm pretty sure she was born in Cypress Grove, and I think she's lived here her whole life. I know she's had an apartment at the historical society for at least thirty years."

"I think I'm next," a sultry voice interrupted me.

Chantel. The woman had the stealth of a Florida panther. She was standing in the doorway to the break room (*posing* in the doorway would be more like it), and her flashing eyes were riveted on Rafe.

Rafe immediately switched off the recorder and got to his feet. "Ms. Carrington," he said politely.

"Are you ready for me?" she said expectantly. Without asking for an invitation, she plopped herself down at the table with us, her gold bracelets jangling on her wrist. "That handsome young man has finished with his part of the interview, and he told me to find you." She steadied her elbow on the table, cupped her chin in her hand, and gave Rafe a long, languorous look.

Rafe stared at her for a moment, stony-faced, and then turned back to me. "Was there anything you wanted to add to your statement, Maggie?"

"No, I think we're done here," I said lightly.

As I got up to leave, Chantel added, "Oh, I nearly forgot. Detective Martino, I was supposed to tell you that one of your crime scene techs called and left a message for you and Officer Brown. Something about a cat? He wants to know if he should call Animal Control."

"A cat?" Rafe looked blank.

"At the crime scene," Chantel said. "It seems they just discovered a cat hiding under the bed in a little apartment upstairs at the historical society. An orange tabby cat."

My brain finally kicked into gear. "An orange tabby. That's Mr. Big!"

Rafe's lips twitched. "Mr. Big?"

I wondered whether he was a fan of *Sex and the City*. It seemed improbable. I happened to know that Althea had come up with the name after her beloved female cat, Miss Tiny, passed away.

"Yes, that's Althea's cat. The poor thing must be terrified." I thought swiftly. "Can I take him home with me?" I glanced at my watch. "I can go down there right now and pick him up. He knows me, and Althea even has a cat carrier in the hall closet I can carry him in. I used to take him to the vet for her."

"I'd take him, but I'm allergic to cats," Chantel said. She treated Rafe to a dazzling smile, hoping for a response. Chantel is never happy unless she's the center of attention, and I knew she was trying to worm her way back into the conversation.

"But you're certainly not allergic to dogs," I said snarkily, thinking of how she'd bonded with Barney the Ghost Dog, who had appeared in the studio yesterday.

"Well, not really," she sniffed. "How sweet of you to remember."

Rafe reached for his cell and flipped it open. "Maggie, if you can take care of the cat, that would be great. I'll call down there to the detectives, and they'll let you in the front hall. They can put him in the carrier for you. I don't want you contaminating the crime scene." He smiled at me. "Thanks for offering. That's one less thing I have to think about."

The good thing about living in a small town is that everything is close together. I zipped out to the WYME parking lot, and ten minutes later, I pulled up in front of the historical society. There were two uniformed cops standing at the entrance, and I gave a little shudder when I saw the ME's van parked in the lot behind the building. *Poor Althea is still in there,* I thought with a pang. I tried to will the thought away, without much success.

"Dr. Maggie?" one of the uniforms asked. I nodded and he burst into a wide smile. "My wife is a big fan of your show. Do you think I could trouble you for an autograph?"

An autograph? Another perk that comes with living in a small town is that people roll out the red carpet for local media personalities. Because of my little gig at the radio station, I'm often treated like a major celeb. As a psychologist in Manhattan, I was invisible.

I quickly scribbled my name on the back of a WYME business card and handed it to him.

"Mr. Big?" I prompted him.

"He's right here, all set to go." I stepped into the front hall and saw the cat carrier with Mr. Big inside. He was meowing indignantly and scratching on the mesh door, trying to escape. I spoke soothingly to him and took a quick glance around the hallway. It looked just the same as it had last night; it was hard to believe that a tragedy had taken place. I thought about Althea. I knew she'd been murdered upstairs in her apartment. I gave a little shudder when I remembered how she'd died.

I picked up the carrier and turned to leave when something struck me. Something felt a little bit off, a tad different. What was it?

I glanced into the front parlor. The same oppressive drapes, heavy furniture, and tired Oriental rugs. Crime scene techs were wandering around dusting for fingerprints and probably looking for trace evidence like hair and fiber samples.

And then it hit me. It wasn't the parlor that was different; there was something about the front hall that wasn't quite right. But what was it?

My eyes roved over the grouping of paintings hanging on the burgundy-colored walls. They were an uninspiring collection of faded portraits and muddy landscapes, nothing memorable. Just like the ones I'd looked at last night. And the same pile of paintings was still on the floor, the ones Althea hadn't decided what to do with.

I took another look at the wall. Suddenly I knew what was wrong and gave myself a mental head slap. The Joshua Riggs was hanging in a different place. It had been switched with a delicate watercolor of a pond scene. Interesting. It used to be to the right of the watercolor and now it was to the left. I wondered why Althea had moved it. She'd told me she'd planned on getting it reframed. She obviously hadn't gotten around to it.

I held my breath while my brain arranged the data. I felt certain the painting was another piece of the puzzle but I had no idea how to fit it in. I heard the techs coming down the stairs just then, so I grabbed the cat carrier and decided it was time to make my getaway.

I dropped Mr. Big off at the town house and locked him in my bedroom with a plate of tuna fish, a water bowl, and a cardboard box with shredded newspaper. That would have to do until I had a chance to buy some kitty litter for him. Pugsley came running over to greet me when I came in the front door, but when he spied Mr. Big in his carrier, he stopped dead in his tracks, his tiny feet skidding on the wood floor. He flared his nostrils, probably getting the full scent of Mr. Big.

His joyful expression immediately changed to a look of stark betrayal, his dark eyes filled with reproach. Pugs are masters at this. Something about the dark eyes and the intelligent expression makes you cringe with guilt.

You brought a cat in here? he asked silently. I rubbed his head, promised him a Frosty Paws treat after dinner, and dashed back to the station.

I wondered what Vera Mae had decided on for the afternoon show. The truth was, I'd be happy with anything except Chantel and her spirit guide. I was relieved to see my producer standing in the lobby, talking with Mildred Smoot, the librarian whom I'd chatted with at the séance last night.

Vera Mae looked at her watch and raised her eyebrows. "Cutting it close, as always, Maggie."

I grinned at her. "I knew you'd pull a rabbit out of a hat for me. You always do."

"Well, here's your rabbit," Vera Mae said. "Mildred was a good friend of Althea's, and she knows a lot about the historical society. She's agreed to be your guest today."

"That's wonderful, Mildred," I said warmly. "I know you'll have a lot to share with the listeners."

"I've never been on the radio before," Mildred said in a quavery voice. "I hope I don't freeze up. I'm only doing this because I feel I owe it to dear Althea. What if I suddenly go blank?" She looked pale, and I knew her anxiety was cresting.

Uh-oh. I've learned the hard way that when a guest tells you they're going to be nervous on the air, it often turns out to be a self-fulfilling prophecy.

"Oh, I'm sure that won't happen." I gave her my standard spiel, the one I give to reluctant guests. "Just pretend you're talking to a friend," I said, walking her back to the break room. I was happy to see the break room was empty, because it would give me time to calm Mildred down. I knew Rafe had left the station because I hadn't seen his car in the parking lot and there was no sign of his faithful sidekick, Officer Brown.

"So that's the secret to doing a radio show?" she asked tentatively. "Pretend that I'm talking to an imaginary friend?"

"Well, it works for me," I confessed. "Just act like you're chatting with someone you enjoy talking to, and everything else will fall into place." I didn't tell her that I've never had stage fright in my life, so my situation was a little different from hers.

I always felt a little buzz of excitement as Vera Mae counted down the seconds before we went live, but I've never felt the tiniest bit nervous. Just happy and excited, eager to start the show.

She heaved a little sigh, and her green eyes moistened over. "I hope you're right, dear. I know I have to do this for Althea." She tightened her lips, drawing them inward for a second before releasing them. "I told Candace Somerset I was doing the show today, and she was pleased."

"Candace Somerset?"

"Althea's sister. She's coming to town to settle Althea's estate." She paused and wiped a tear from her eye. "Anyway, I have to pull myself together. It's the right thing to do."

"That's the spirit." I felt a wash of relief. I could see that Mildred had some steel reinforcement under her mint green pantsuit and ruffly schoolmarm blouse. I made her a cup of tea and offered her a jelly doughnut. I figured the sugar and carbs might help to calm her nerves a little, and it would keep her occupied for a few minutes.

She seemed to relax as she sipped her tea, although her hands still trembled a little as she brought the cup to her lips. I decided it was better not to draw her attention to it.

"I feel a little better," she said gratefully.

"That's good. Just sit here and relax for a few minutes, Mildred. Try to think of your favorite memories about Althea and the historical society. That's the kind of thing the listeners love to hear. Vera Mae will come and get you when it's time to do the show."

"All right," she said. "I'll do my best." Her voice was tremulous, but she managed a faint smile. I wondered whether she was going to be a total disaster on the air but decided it was too late to do anything about it.

I glanced at the clock. We were already counting down to showtime.

Chapter 9

Chantel left the station in a huff, right before airtime. Vera Mae told me Chantel had made a last-ditch effort to ingratiate herself with Cyrus, pleading to be on today's show, but he wasn't having any of it. Apparently he'd told Chantel in no uncertain terms that we'd scheduled a memorial show for Althea today and that we already had a full roster of guests.

This was music to my ears. The last thing I needed was a pushy medium hijacking my show on a day like this.

Mildred was already settled in the studio when I breezed in to do my afternoon show. Vera Mae was in the control room, watching from the window, holding up two fingers. I knew the drill. *Two minutes till airtime.*

I sat down next to Mildred and was pleased to see that all the lines were already lit up; it looked like plenty of listeners wanted to share their memories of Althea and the historical society. Vera Mae lowered one finger, curling it toward her palm. Okay, we had one minute to go. I slapped on my headphones and smiled at Mildred.

"Live in ten!" Vera Mae opened her mike. "Stand by!" Her scratchy voice ricocheted around the studio, and Mildred gave a little squeal, jumping in alarm.

"Five, four, three, two," Vera Mae yelled and then mouthed "Go!" as she pointed her finger straight at me.

We were live. Showtime. I slid into my standard opening ("You're on the couch with Maggie Walsh") and then read a quick intro that Vera Mae had written. It was a nice tribute that described Althea's life, how many people she'd befriended, and how she'd played an important role in the town's history.

And of course, it mentioned her lifelong devotion to the historical society. I fervently hoped that we could concentrate on Althea's life and not get bogged down in the grisly details of her death. I knew a lot of people had loved Althea, but sometimes the public has a morbid curiosity when it comes to violent crime. I wanted to make sure today's show was a tribute, not an exercise in voyeurism.

"We have Karen on line one, Maggie," Vera piped up. "She wants to know if Althea had planned to take part in the time capsule celebration." Vera Mae extended her hands, palms up, and gave a little shrug as if she wasn't sure of the answer.

"Oh, yes, she was looking forward to it very much." Mildred said, leaning in toward her mike. Then she looked flustered and said to me, "I'm so sorry. I shouldn't have jumped in like that. Was it my turn to speak?"

"Go right ahead, Mildred." I was glad to see she'd recovered from her bout of nerves and actually seemed to be enjoying herself sitting in front of the console, her headphones clasped over her tight gray curls.

"Karen, to answer your question, Althea talked about the time capsule ceremony all the time." Mildred's voice grew stronger, more confident. The best way to get over stage fright is to concentrate on the task at hand, and that was exactly what Mildred was doing. "In fact, we used to try to figure out what was inside it." She gave a girlish little laugh. "I have to confess, we came up with some pretty outlandish suggestions. Maggie, do your listeners know the history behind the time capsule?"

"Just a little. We've been running some promos about it," I told her, "but why don't you fill us in on what you know. I'm sure they'd like to get an inside track on the story."

"Well, here's what I can tell you. The story goes that Ronald Paley is supposed to have placed several important documents inside the capsule." She had leaned in too close to the mike, and it made a harsh popping sound when she said "Paley." I angled the mike away from her and she continued. "You're new here, Maggie, but you've probably heard that the Paleys were very important people in Cypress Grove history, and Ronald Paley was one of the town's founders."

I nodded, trying to look suitably impressed.

"Excuse me, but my daughter's writing a term paper on the time capsule," the caller cut in. Either she was bored by Mildred's trip down memory lane or she just had one of those unfortunate whiny voices. "She's having a heck of a time trying to dig up information about it. What's the big deal, anyway? What did this Paley guy put in it, and why's it such a big secret?" Her voice raked across the line, gritty with impatience.

"Oh, I'm so sorry to hear that," Mildred said, all apologies. "It's not a secret at all, but perhaps you didn't know there was a huge fire at the courthouse that destroyed a lot of important documents. The old courthouse building on Elm Street was burned right to the ground. And of course, this was before the days of computers and the Internet, so people had no way to salvage all the information that was being stored there."

"So a lot of history is missing."

She gave a little sigh. "Births, deaths, marriages. It's sad to think that priceless memories and documents are gone forever, but that seems to be the case. I've been researching Ronald Paley for the past few months, and I've come up with a few interesting tidbits, but not as much as I'd hoped."

"Really? What have you found?" I asked, curious. The main thing I knew about the Paleys was that the town's founder was fond of naming parks and streets after himself.

Mildred waited a beat before replying. "There might be a few surprises when the time capsule is opened." She spoke slowly and precisely, as if she was weighing her words with care. "I think a few townspeople might get more than they bargained for, but I suppose I shouldn't say anything else." She exhaled audibly. "It will all come out soon enough."

Vera Mae raised her eyebrows and locked eyes with me. Vera Mae and I worked together so closely, I could guess what was going through her mind. *What will come out soon enough? Is there a story here? Is this something we should be pursuing?*

"What about the local newspaper?" I asked, thinking of my reporter friend, Nick Harrison at the *Gazette*. "Surely they'd have records going back to that time, wouldn't they?"

"You'd think so," Mildred offered. "But the newspaper building also burned to the ground in 1970. It was just an odd sequence of events, or some people would say, a strange twist of fate. It's all very perplexing. We're left with a giant puzzle, it seems."

"Like a jigsaw puzzle with some of the pieces missing," Vera Mae said.

"Exactly," Mildred agreed. "But all is takes is one piece to complete it."

We went to break then, and it gave me a few minutes to mull over what Mildred had told the listeners. Ronald Paley had placed some important papers inside the time capsule, and Mildred had hinted that a few citizens would be surprised (or maybe shocked?) at what would be revealed. But of course Ronald Paley was dead, and there was no way to ask him.

Althea may—or may not—have known something about the contents of the time capsule, and now Althea was dead. And Althea was supposed to have been present at the time capsule celebration. Could this be significant? Was someone afraid of what she might say or do at the unveiling?

Michael—if you believe in ghosts—had appeared during the séance to warn the townsfolk that there was danger afoot. He'd hinted that there was an evil presence in Cypress Grove, and Althea was murdered sometime after the séance. Of course he hadn't specifically said "murder," but he was planting the suggestion that something awful was about to happen.

And Althea was at the séance—not only present in the room, but up onstage with Chantel. Was this significant, or just an odd coincidence? Another point: Chantel had specifically requested that Althea join the group at the table even though it was pretty obvious that Althea was reluctant to do so. Was this important, or just another coincidence?

I remembered that Sigmund Freud said "There are no coincidences." So going along with his theory, these two facts must somehow be connected.

And then there was the question of Michael the spirit guide. Was Michael just part of Chantel's usual shtick, or had she dredged him up last night to increase her book sales? I'd seen Chantel on a couple of television talk shows, and from what I could recall, she always spouted messages of doom and gloom. The audience ate it up; it was part of her standard act.

It probably makes for better theater, I decided. Just one

of the basic laws of entertainment. If you're going to have
someone from the spirit world communicate with mortals,
it's more effective if the spirit says something startling, not
mundane. You get more attention if you up the ante and act
like something really important is at stake. A life-or-death
issue, for example. An evil presence, unknown dangers lurking, ready to pounce on unsuspecting folks. Think about it.
"Beware the Ides of March" sounds a lot more compelling
than "Annual White Sale This Thursday."

The other possibility, of course, is that Chantel really *does*
know something about a few dark secrets buried in the town's
past, and she invented Michael to pave the way for her "reve-
lations." She'd probably spring them on us when she decided the time was right.

The moment the show was over, I thanked Mildred and
called Nick Harrison at the *Gazette*. We agreed to meet for
an early dinner at Gino's, my favorite Italian restaurant in
town. Lark was taking Mom to a yoga class, so there was no
reason for me to hurry home. Too many thoughts were swirling in my head, and I knew I needed to run them by someone
cool and objective.

Gino's is an Italian restaurant close to WYME that I discovered when I was new in town. It's a little kitschy, with its
red-and-white checked tablecloths and photos of long-dead
opera singers lining the walls, but I wouldn't change a thing
about it. The food is good, the prices reasonable, and the
service fast, perfect for the business crowd.

Nick was already waiting for me, sitting at one of the
outdoor patio tables. He had the remains of an antipasto
plate in front of him (a dish that the menu claims serves four
to six people), and I could see that he had nearly polished
off the whole thing.

"Hey there," he said by way of greeting when I sat down. He was talking around a mouthful of marinated artichokes. "I did a little snooping around on Madame Chantel." He patted a thick file on the chair beside him. "You were right to be suspicious. She's a piece of work." He looked thoughtfully at the demolished antipasto plate and popped a giant stuffed olive in his mouth. He practically inhaled it and generously nudged the lettuce-lined plate toward me. "Help yourself," he said with a grin.

"Thanks. I think I'll pass." I nudged the plate back at him.

Nick is a good-looking guy, tall and athletic with a boyish smile and dirty-blond hair worn on the longish side. Today he was wearing what I call Cypress Grove casual: a snowy white golf shirt, pressed khakis, and loafers with no socks.

There's enough of an age difference between us that Nick thinks of me as an older sister, not potential date material. We bonded when I first came to town and sat through a rubber chicken dinner at the Cypress Grove Press Club. You would think Nick and I would be rivals, but we're not; he's not really interested in the pop-psych field, and I have no interest in covering arts and entertainment. Actually, Nick doesn't either, but he knows he has to stick with this gig until something better opens up.

"So tell me," I demanded, after ordering a roasted veggie plate and iced tea from the server. She smiled at Nick the whole time I was talking to her, and she got my order wrong. Twice.

"Well, for starters, her name isn't Chantel Carrington. It's Carla Krasinski." He waited a beat. "From Duluth."

"She's Carla Krasinski from Duluth?" My voice spiraled up a few decibels, and a man reading the *Economist* at the next table turned to glare at me. "That's a hoot," I said, reining in my amusement. "On her business card it lists Paris, London, and New York as her residences."

"I think it also says she's an oracle," Nick said thoughtfully. "She sent along one of her cards with a press packet on her new book. So she fudges the truth a little."

"Some oracle." I snorted. "She only has one shtick. She predicts dark and dangerous deeds, along with some evildoings."

"Dark, dangerous, and evil?" Nick parroted.

"Yeah, she sounds like an ad for a Kevin Williamson flick."

"And—"

"And what?" I picked through some lifeless lettuce on the platter, looking for a sliver of heirloom tomato or a bit of red-skinned onion. Maybe even a hot pepper or two. Nada. Nick was unbelievable; he really *had* eaten the whole thing.

"Maggie," he said, leaning across the table, looking intently at me, "you know what happened shortly after she made these predictions."

"Oh. Well." I stopped to think. "Althea was murdered, if that's what you mean."

"Exactly."

"Don't be too impressed. Chantel says this sort of thing all the time. She's bound to be right occasionally. Even a stopped clock is right twice a day, you know."

Nick shook his head. "You're quoting Sigmund Freud again?"

"No. That was Dr. Phil."

Chapter 10

"Tell me what else you dug up on Chantel," I said, eyeing the fat folder he'd plunked down onto the tabletop.

"There's a lot here." He glanced up abstractedly as the server put his Heineken down in front of him with a blinding smile. She'd already told us her name was Lori. Three times, actually. She was very pretty and made a big show of fiddling with the coaster, eyeing Nick like he was Robert Pattinson. She slapped my iced tea in front of me with no fanfare at all and hightailed it back to the kitchen.

"She's been on the move her whole life, never really settling down anywhere."

I nodded. "Interesting." I sipped my iced tea and wondered whether I dared try to flag Lori down and ask for a slice of lemon. "Where has she lived?"

Nick put on his reading glasses to scan the sheaf of papers. The rimless glasses gave him a "hot young professor" look, and I couldn't resist a grin. "San Diego, San Francisco, New York, Montreal, New Orleans. She's bounced back and forth all over the place. And she must be smart, because she didn't leave much of a paper trail. Smart and very cunning, a dangerous combination. Sometimes she didn't even seem to have an address, so I assume she stayed with friends in the area. Also no credit card history. She must have used cash or maybe mooched meals off people."

I shook my head, trying to wrap my mind around what Nick was telling me. "I don't get it. Those are expensive cities. Even if she was invited out to dinner a lot, she must have had some source of income. How did she support herself?"

"The séances, I guess. Don't forget she's been doing them for a long time. It's only in the past year or so that she's actually gotten these book deals, and that's what gave her a platform. The séances, the books, the personal appearances— they all work together; they drive each other. I'm pretty sure she was scrounging for years and years before her career took off." He held up a newspaper clipping. "This appeared in the arts and entertainment section of the *Dallas Morning News* twenty years ago. So it predates the Internet. Chantel was giving séances for wealthy Dallas women in their homes and it made the society column. Someone faxed it to me, or I never would have had access to it."

Predates the Internet. Never would have had access to it. Yowsers. I suddenly remembered what Mildred had said on my show today. It was time to shift gears. "Nick, forget about Chantel for a moment. There's something else I need to tell you."

He patted the folder and pretended to look aggrieved. "Forget about her—you're kidding, right? After all my hard work?"

"I think I'm on the wrong track. I heard something today that was disturbing, and I don't know what to make of it. At least—" I paused, my mind whirring, adrenaline pumping. "Tell me if I'm on to something here."

My thoughts were coming so fast, the words were tumbling out over one another like popcorn kernels in a popper.

I quickly filled him in on what Mildred had said about the courthouse burning down and the newspaper offices being destroyed in a fire, all those years ago. "She said that tons of records, decades of history, have disappeared. They're gone, vanished forever. The only way to reconstruct them would be to search birth and death registers at the local churches. Or maybe check family Bibles, that sort of thing. It would be a huge undertaking. Some really important information would stay buried forever."

He nodded, as if this was old news to him. "It's true. A big chunk of Cypress Grove history is gone. That's probably why there's so much interest in the time capsule celebration. We're running a three-page spread in the weekend edition."

Like WYME, the *Cypress Grove Gazette* had been promoting the time capsule ceremony every chance it got. The mayor was scheduled to attend, along with all the local politicians, and the movers and shakers. And of course, the media would be out in full force. With any luck, some of the bigger regional newspapers, like the Fort Lauderdale *Sun Sentinel* and the *Palm Beach Post*, might be there, too.

"But I think there's more to it than that," I said. "Mildred hinted that there's some big secret involved with the contents of the time capsule. Something that goes way beyond historical interest."

"Yeah? A secret? This is the first I've heard of it." Nick automatically patted his pocket as if he hoped to find his notebook tucked away there. When he came up empty, he grabbed a paper napkin and a ballpoint pen Lori had left on the table. "Tell me everything you know."

He wrinkled his brow in concentration, his voice low and intense. I had the feeling Nick figured this was the scoop that would catapult him into the major leagues. I hated to disappoint him, but I was as much in the dark as he was.

"Here's the problem. I don't know very much," I admitted. "Mildred just said she'd been researching the topic for weeks and that she'd found out something important."

"Something important?" He stopped writing and stared at me. "That's pretty vague, Maggie. That could mean anything."

I nodded. "I know, but I couldn't get any specific details out of her. Believe me, I tried. I have the feeling she had access to something very sensitive, something that would cause shockwaves if it ever became public."

"I don't know. It's not much to go on." He heaved a sigh, doodling on the napkin, lost in thought. "There's got to be some other avenue to explore. I'm drawing a blank."

Lori reappeared with Nick's dinner just then and flashed him a blinding smile as she put the plate in front of him. Too bad the toothy grin was completely wasted on him. She stood there for several seconds, one hand on her hip, chest jutting out, still hopeful. When she finally realized he preferred doodling on the napkin to drooling over her, she stomped away.

"Yes, it's discouraging. She said just enough to tantalize the listeners, and then she clammed up. It was frustrating."

"Maybe she's a tease." Nick eyed the heaping plate, practically salivating. He looked ravenous. "Um, do you mind if—"

"Go ahead and start," I told him. He immediately plunged into his dinner, scarfing down a huge forkful of pasta. Nick always acts like he hasn't eaten in a month.

"You said Mildred was a tease?" I thought of Mildred in her polyester pantsuit and orthopedic shoes and giggled. "I think that's a bit of a stretch." The idea of Mildred being a tease was about as likely as her becoming a Hooters girl.

Nick grinned. "You know I didn't mean that kind of a tease. I meant maybe she's just trying to drum up some interest in the time capsule. After all, when does a librarian get a chance to be the star? She probably knows more about Cypress Grove history than anyone else in town. This could be her big moment to shine. Or maybe we're both reading too much into this."

"We'll see," I said grudgingly. I sat back in my chair while Lori slapped my roasted veggie platter in front of me. It was loaded with eggplant, leeks, and three kinds of sweet peppers.

"Watch out for the tray, hon. It's right out of the oven," she said in a bored tone. "It's really hot."

I poked my dinner with my fork, spearing a piece of egg-plant.

Really hot? No worries on that score, hon.

It was barely lukewarm.

It was dusk when I arrived back at the town house and spot-ted Ted Rollins arranging the sprinklers on the front lawn of the Seabreeze Inn. A dozen or so guests were milling around on the wide-planked porch, enjoying the night air and the complimentary wine-and-cheese party that Ted hosts every evening.

The way Ted keeps up the place, you'd think *Architectural Digest* was planning to use the Seabreeze for a photo shoot. It's a charming Victorian with a bright yellow exterior and glossy white gingerbread trim, and it looks more like a private house than a B and B. Colorful bougainvillea and night-blooming jasmine bushes in the garden make it smell like paradise. Baskets of lush ferns hang from the rafters, and porcelain pots of lipstick pink primrose are artfully ar-ranged around the chairs. It's on the historic register and always looks camera ready.

Ted hurried over when he saw me crossing the lawn, gath-ered me into a brotherly hug, and kissed me on the cheek.

Ted would like to be more than a friend—what can I say? He's the proverbial nice guy, the kind your mom and all your friends wish you would marry. Lola always says that if I don't marry Ted, she will. I think she's only half kidding. Tall and ruggedly handsome with sandy brown hair and a terrific smile, he's quite a catch, by anyone's standards.

Can I help it if I'm attracted to bad boys, the kind the nuns always warned me about? The kind of men who exude danger and excitement (think Rafe Martino) and can make my pulse jump with one sultry look?

Ted and Rafe are on opposite ends of the continuum. Ted is steadfast, loyal, and reliable. Rafe is none of those things. Rafe is the kind of guy who exudes heat, magic, and raw masculinity. He's wild and unpredictable, and you feel like anything can happen when you're around him.

Rafe is the guy who makes my heart go pitter-patter right before he breaks it. Ted is a warm and cuddly big-brother type who brings me homemade soup when I'm sick, bought a doggie birthday cake for Pugsley, and offered to power wash my deck.

Naturally, I picked Rafe over Ted. Go figure.

"Maggie, good to see you! Have a glass of white wine," Ted urged. He took my arm and steered me toward the guests mingling on the front porch. "Terrible news about Althea," he said, his voice laced with concern. "It must have been very hard on you, doing today's show. I happened to catch it. You were wonderful, as always. It was a beautiful tribute to her."

"Thanks, Ted," I said, giving his hand a little squeeze. See what I mean? Ted listens to my radio show every single day and compliments me on my performance. The only other person who routinely listens to my show every day is Lola. And Lola doesn't count, because after all, she's my mother.

"Hey, Maggie, there's someone I want you to meet," Ted

said, breaking into my thoughts. He waved at a tall guy in his late forties and motioned for him to join us.

"Trevor! Come on over here for a sec. I need to talk to you." The man put down his drink, and Ted did the introductions. "Maggie Walsh, this is Trevor McNamara."

"Nice to meet you, Maggie." His accent was cultured, and his crisp white shirt and perfectly pressed pants were expensive. Ditto the buttery leather Italian loafers. I guessed from his cultured accent that he was from the northeast corridor. Maybe somewhere near Boston? He struck me as a fish out of water here in the little backwater town of Cypress Grove.

"Maggie's a radio talk show host, Trevor. You're new in town, but her show is really popular. She's a celebrity." Ted is always a little over-the-top when he talks about me. Lark tries to explain it by saying he's madly in love with me, and I hope for his sake she's wrong.

"I'm not a celebrity." I smiled and extended my hand. "Ted just likes to pretend that I am. Are you here on vacation?"

As soon as the words popped out, I knew the answer would be no. Trevor didn't look like the kind of guy who'd be doing a garden tour of south Florida, and I couldn't imagine him whiling away his day fishing for grouper from the pier.

I pictured him in Miami, making deals at the Delano, or churning through Biscayne Bay in a cigarette boat stocked with a couple of supermodels.

"Actually, it's a business trip." He had piercing green eyes, and he held my hand just a second too long. "I'm a real estate broker and I'm thinking about investing in some properties in Cypress Grove."

"Really? Commercial real estate?" I immediately pictured

a string of tawdry strip malls and big box stores, urban monstrosities that would ruin the small-town feel of the place. But something about the idea didn't ring true.

He shook his head. "Oh no, nothing like that. I'm interested in vacation properties." He glanced out at the quiet street, the tall palms and lush foliage making a postcard-pretty view against the evening sky.

I must have looked doubtful, because he felt compelled to explain himself. "It's a nice climate here," he said, spreading his hands out in front of him. "And you don't have the traffic congestion and hassles of some of the big resort cities. I'm thinking Cypress Grove could be a great place for family vacations."

"Family vacations?" If I sounded incredulous, it's because I was.

"Sure, this would be the perfect spot. No casinos or nightlife, just a quiet town with warm weather, great restaurants, and some interesting sights." He quirked an eyebrow ever so slightly, and I wondered whether he was flirting with me. "And of course, friendly people," he added. "People I'd like to get to know better."

I was silent for a moment. Nothing he'd said made sense. Why would anyone want to vacation in Cypress Grove? It was one thing to live here, grow up here, surrounded by friends and family, but there was no way Cypress Grove could compete for tourist dollars with places like Orlando and Miami. You could see the whole town in half an hour, and then you were back on I-95, heading north toward Palm Beach or south toward Fort Lauderdale.

Even a three-day weekend here would seem like overkill.

"The chamber of commerce will be thrilled to hear you like this place so much," I told him.

I thought about Cyrus, my station manager at WYME,

who would be absolutely salivating over Trevor and his plans to inject money into the town. "The folks at the chamber are always eager to meet developers." I paused, still trying to make sense of what he'd told me. "You know, I'm really surprised the bigger cities haven't courted you. We might have a sort of Mayberry charm, but the major resort areas have a lot of attractions that our little town can't offer."

"I told Trevor that I'd help him line up some vacation rentals," Ted said, always the Boy Scout.

"Vacation rentals? Does Cypress Grove have any?" As far as I knew, Ted's place was the only decent B and B, and outside of the big chain hotels next to the interstate, there wasn't much to choose from.

"There's the Regal Palm Hotel downtown," Ted said uncertainly. "We send our overflow there when things get busy."

"I'm not really interested in rentals. I'd rather line up some sale properties for my clients. I'm looking for multifamily houses," Trevor said quickly.

"Multifamily houses?" I nearly laughed. "Well, good luck with that. I don't think there are any. I managed to find a town house when I moved here a few months ago, but it was sheer luck. There wasn't much to choose from."

"I thought some of those big Victorians on Main Street might be available as sale properties," Trevor said vaguely. "I might knock on a few doors and see what I come up with."

Ted and I exchanged a look. The Victorian mansions in town are owned by longtime residents, people who never would consider turning their homes into a condo or a B and B in a million years. These are the kind of grand old homes that stayed in the family for years, passed down from one generation to the next. It would be unthinkable that an owner would sell one to an outsider. And sell to a developer? Never!

Trevor must have picked up on the negative vibes, because he said quickly, "Well, I've just started my search. It's still early in the game. Nice to meet you, Maggie." He checked his watch. "Catch you later, Ted. I'm running late for an appointment in town." And with that, he took off down the wide expanse of lawn, heading for his car.

I looked at Ted for a moment. "That was odd. I don't think he's looking for rental properties at all."

Ted smiled and tousled my hair in a big-brother way. "You know what your problem is, Maggie? You think too much."

"Get me a white wine and maybe I'll think a little less," I teased him.

Chapter 11

I zipped into the station early the next morning to help Vera Mae with the time capsule promos. I'd left Mr. Big dozing happily in my bedroom with a fresh litter box, a full dish of Meow Mix, and a water bowl. My beloved Pugsley had been banished to the den sofa last night. I'm sure he and Mr. Big will reach a detente eventually, but I figured it was a good idea to keep them separated for a week or two.

I found Vera Mae in her cluttered office chatting with Kevin, who'd been assigned the task of writing and producing a series of thirty-second spots on the event. She waved me to a box of fragrant apple cider doughnuts balanced on top of her printer. "Help yourself, Maggie. They're fresh from Wilson's Bakery."

"Wilson's Bakery. I always like it when they send their account exec over here."

"Well, take what you want. Once Big Jim spots them, they'll be history."

I grabbed a doughnut, moved a pile of papers and files from the molded plastic visitor's chair, and plopped myself down. Vera Mae and Kevin were deep in conversation about the best way to run a contest and what sorts of prizes would rope in the most listeners.

I let my mind wander back to Althea Somerset and the picture in the front hall of the historical society. Was it an important clue? Or a blind alley? Maybe there was a perfectly ordinary explanation for why it was hanging in a different place.

I figured I had two choices: I could tell Rafe my suspicions right now, or I could try to track down some information on the painting myself. (And then tell him my conclusions, like Hercule Poirot does. I could even adopt that slightly supercilious manner, which was bound to annoy Rafe and would be enormously satisfying.)

But I needed some leads and I wasn't sure where to start looking. Would Mildred know why the painting had been moved? I remembered she'd made some disparaging remarks about it the night of the séance. I made a mental note to check with Mildred as soon as I got the chance.

As far as I knew, the police still didn't have any leads on who the killer might be, and what the motive was.

Motive, means, opportunity—it was all still up for grabs.

"Maggie, what do you think about the contest?" Vera Mae asked, breaking into my thoughts. "We can do this a couple of different ways. Should we ask the viewers to *guess* what's in the time capsule, or should we ask them what item*s they'd* put in a time capsule?" Vera Mae was chewing on a pencil, decked out in one of her crime-of-fashion outfits: a bright blue sleeveless blouse over shocking pink capris.

"Why not do both?" I said idly, still thinking of Althea. "Asking them what they'd put in a time capsule is a little subjective, though. I like the idea, but how will we decide on the winner? There won't be any right or wrong answers. I guess you'd want to preserve whatever you think is important, and that's a very personal thing."

"That's exactly what I thought, Dr. Maggie," Kevin piped up. "I think maybe we could go for the most original suggestion—"

"But who's to decide what's the most original?" Vera Mae interjected. "It's a matter of taste, isn't it? What appeals to me might not appeal to you. And some people might not have any ideas at all. They don't know anything about time capsules or why people bury them in the first place. Whatever the contest is, it has to have broad appeal. We want to have the maximum number of entries because that means we'll have more people tuning in every day, to see if they've won."

"I wonder if anyone knows where the idea first started," I said.

Kevin jumped in. "Time capsules go back at least five thousand years to Mesopotamia," he said.

I practically reeled back in shock. It seemed Kevin was a boy wonder. Who knew?

"People buried time capsules in vaults and hid them inside the city walls. And more recently, there was a famous time capsule at the 1939 World's Fair. They put some crop seeds and a microscope in that one, and I think they even included a newsreel." He scrunched up his face, deep in thought. "Let's see. I believe there was a dictionary, an almanac, and a Sears, Roebuck catalog in there, as well." He gave a bashful smile. "I'm afraid that's the best I can recall off the top of my head. But I can check this all out, if you'd like."

Vera Mae and I stared at each other for a moment.

"Like? I'd like that very much. Kevin, you are amazing," she said, clasping him by the shoulders. "I wish we could hire you full-time, right this minute."

"Well, thank you, Miss Vera Mae, but you know I have to go to broadcasting school first." His face lit up in a smile. "Maybe you can keep me in mind when I graduate, though. I'd love to come back here to work. I'd be part of the WYME family." If Kevin had been wearing his trademark Larry King suspenders today, I think he would have snapped them at this point.

I had a brainstorm. "Kevin, how would you like to do a preinterview with Dr. Grossman, the history professor? It would be good practice for you, and I bet you could ask him all the right questions."

"You want me to do a preinterview?"

"Yes, that's what they do on all the big talk shows. The national ones. You just have a mock interview, like you were on the air with the guest. Once you hear what he has to say, you can weed out all the boring stuff and get the guest to concentrate on three or four really good stories. That's all you need for a great interview. That's what they used to do on the Johnny Carson show."

"Golly, Dr. Maggie, I'd love to do that." Kevin broke into a wide grin. "And Professor Grossman is really well-known, isn't he?"

I nodded. "He's an expert in his field. I bet he knows all about how people first came up with the idea of time capsules and why they're still around in the twenty-first century. He's got all the book smarts and he knows amazing facts and figures."

"The audience would probably like that," Kevin offered.

"But here's the problem, Kevin." I paused. "And it's a pretty big one."

"Problem?" His face clouded, his eyes focused on my face.

"The facts and figures aren't going to be enough. He's

going to need direction. A *lot* of direction. And I'm counting on you being able to guide him toward the interesting stuff." I gave him a meaningful look. "Interesting, not boring. That's what we're looking for."

"Oh, yes, I see what you mean. The good stuff."

I smiled. "That's it, Kev, the good stuff. You know, the audience would really eat it up if you could get him talking about some juicy tidbits associated with time capsules. Maybe he can think of some scandals associated with them. Or maybe dark secrets came to light, or a big surprise was revealed. That's the kind of thing our listeners want to hear. Everybody loves a mystery."

"I can do that," Kevin said. He immediately grabbed a legal pad and started making notes. "Scandals, secrets, surprises. Got it. The good stuff."

"That's exactly what we're looking for."

"And here's another good angle," Vera Mae jumped in. "Get him talking about what sort of things people tuck away in them. That would go along with the contest we're running. Like Maggie said, you might have to sift through a lot of boring academic stuff to get to the juicy tidbits."

"Juicy tidbits." Kevin actually wrote that phrase down and circled it. And added two stars next to it.

"I have to warn you, Kevin," Vera Mae went on. "I've heard Professor Grossman speak at the Rotary Club, and take it from me, this guy is as dry as dirt. He knows his stuff, though. So if you can convince him to jazz it up a little, that would be great. You'll have to do it tactfully, of course."

"Tactfully." Another circle and stars. "I'll do my best," Kevin said. "Has anyone contacted him yet?"

"I have a call in to his secretary. She said if he can cancel one of his classes he'll be here for part of the show tomorrow." Vera Mae looked at her clipboard and heaved a sigh.

"As it stands, we're going to go with Chantel today. I didn't have a choice."

Chantel! I didn't say a word, but she must have caught my expression, because she glanced into the hallway and then lowered her voice to a near whisper. "You know, listeners have been calling in every day, asking when she's going to guest host the show again. I don't think Cyrus is that keen on her, but he can't ignore the phone calls and e-mails. He has to give the listeners what they want." She gave Kevin a little nudge and made a little lip-zipping gesture. "This is strictly confidential. You didn't hear that from me, sonny."

"Yes, ma'am, Miss Vera Mae. I didn't hear a thing." Kevin's eyes were wide and his Adam's apple was bobbing up and down. Even though Kevin is an intern, he'd have to be as thick as a brick if he hadn't noticed how everything at the station revolves around ratings. Cyrus has to keep the sponsors happy, and the only way to do that is to keep the ratings up. It's just a matter of dollars and cents.

"So what's the topic for today?" I decided to snare another doughnut before the rest of the staff found out Vera Mae's secret stash.

"It's a little woo-woo." Vera Mae said, wrinkling her nose. "Not my cup of tea, but these shows are always popular, and Chantel will be in her element."

"Woo-woo?" Kevin raised his eyebrows.

"Supernatural. Paranormal. Things you can't explain. Crop circles. Satanic bar codes. Government plots. Space aliens. It was Maggie's idea. I ran it past Cyrus and he loved it."

"Oh, you mean like things you read about in the *National Enquirer*."

Vera Mae laughed and slapped Kevin on the back. "Ain't that the truth! But Cyrus likes to pretend we're in the news and information business, Kev, so don't let him hear you say that."

"I came up with the idea, but I don't really know anything about conspiracies," I protested. "I really need time to read up on it."

"Oh, don't you worry, now, Dr. Maggie," Kevin said. "You know you don't need to read up on anything. Miss Chantel will talk enough for both of you. I guarantee it."

Truer words were never spoken.

"Sandra on line one wants to know about crop circles," Vera Mae said into her open mike. We were only five minutes into the show and the switchboard was lit up like a Christmas tree. It seemed our listening audience just couldn't get enough of things that go bump in the night; we already had eight callers on hold.

"Crop circles? I'll take it!" Chantel sang out. "This is one of my areas of expertise, Maggie." *Areas of expertise? You'd think were talking about gene splicing.* "You don't mind, do you?" she asked, sliding over the fact that it was, after all, my show. The woman was as slick as extra-virgin olive oil.

"Be my guest." I tried not to grit my teeth, reminding myself that jaw clenching led to a bout of TMJ, a painful condition that requires me to wear a bite plate every night.

"I've heard they're a sign from space aliens." Sandra's voice raced across the line. "But if they're smart enough to make those circles, wouldn't you think they'd know enough to leave a message in English, so we really know what they want? As far as I can tell, all they do is flatten down a whole bunch of wheat or barley to make a circle design. I could do that myself with a weed whacker, but why bother? Why would aliens zip down to earth from another planet just to do that?"

Chantel gave a little tinkly laugh. "I see your point, my dear, but you have to remember, space alien culture is completely different from our own. And when you say 'circles,' you have to remember that some of these designs are quite intricate. Have you ever seen the double triskelion in Milk Hill, England?"

"I can't say that I have," Sandra said.

"Well, it's a work of art, my dear. It took four hundred and nine circles to make the design."

"Wow, I didn't know that," Vera Mae offered. I looked up just in time to see her wink.

Chantel must have caught the wink, because she shot a dagger glare at Vera Mae. "You have to remember, Sandra, whoever made those circles—and I firmly believe it was made by our alien friends—communicate through symbols. They may not have a recognized spoken language. So the symbol, the circle, is highly significant to them. It's up to us to come up with the correct interpretation."

Chantel looked pleased with herself. I was surprised she had all this information on tap, but apparently she did. "There's a message there. We just need to be sensitive enough to understand it."

"And what might that message be?" Vera Mae asked from the control room. Her voice was as sugary as maple syrup, but Chantel raised her eyebrow, refusing to take the bait. I'm sure Chantel runs into a lot of nonbelievers in her line of work, and she's probably figured out the most effective way to deal with them.

"I hope you can tell us what it is," Sandra piped up. "If space aliens go to all the trouble of flying down to earth and making these circles, I'd be interested in hearing what they have to say."

Chantel stiffened. I knew from her other appearances on my show that she hated to be put on the hot seat and she knew how to wriggle her way out of difficult questions. "I can understand your feelings, Sandra," she said, oozing empathy. "But it's a complex issue. No one knows for certain what the message means," she said, hedging her bets. "They could be saying 'we come in peace,' or 'join us in harmony,' or—"

"Or we're gonna eat you alive?" Vera Mae chuckled. "Remember that billboard that caused such a ruckus in California? It was advertising a local gym. The picture showed an alien that looked like he was straight out of Roswell with a big head and bulging eyes. The caption said, 'When they come, they'll eat the fat ones first.' People got so upset over it, they took the billboard down."

Chantel threw Vera Mae a death glare. "That's simply outrageous, and ridiculous." She was practically bouncing out of her seat in indignation, her bracelets clanging together, playing havoc with the volume meter. This time I didn't bother pointing it out to her; I decided to just sit back and enjoy the show.

"I have never sensed any malevolent vibes from space aliens." She'd turned an unhealthy shade of beet red and her voice was shaky. "Not the slightest. Never!" Her voice cut through the air like a knife. "And I've been researching this issue for several years."

I wondered what kind of research Chantel could be doing on the topic of space aliens but decided to let that one ride. We were on a roll, it seemed. Vera Mae's prediction was right on target; the audience couldn't get enough of this stuff.

The very next question was about Area 51, the famed "alien body" site in southern Nevada. If you believe the hype, extraterrestrials crash-landed in Roswell, and their remains were taken to Area 51, which is actually part of a military site, for examination. Some theories insist that none of the aliens survived the crash and that autopsies were performed on their bodies. Other versions claim that a few space aliens survived and joined with the United States to work together on research projects.

Our next caller seemed unable to make up her mind what she really believed. "Just help me figure this out," Darlene from Boca pleaded with Chantel. "If there really was a massive government cover-up, I want to write to my congressman. Unless he's a space alien himself, of course."

The first hour passed quickly. Chantel sidestepped a question on supermarket bar codes. It seemed half the audience thought they were satanic and the other half thought they were part of a government plot to control our minds. Chantel left the answer open and promised to ask Michael, her trusty spirit guide, for some information.

We were nearly into a break when Lurleen from Darien asked about telekinesis. "I wonder if it's a trick, or if some people just have learned a way to control objects," she asked. "I think I may have a poltergeist in my house because things are moving around all the time. Sometimes it's big things, like a chair, and sometimes it's something small, like a salt and pepper shaker."

"Telekinesis is a respected area of scientific research," Chantel said. "Of course, movies have blown the idea all out of proportion, and a lot of these poltergeist claims are false. They make for good entertainment, but they're not scientifically valid."

"You know, a lot of studies show that a child or adolescent is often behind these incidents," I broke in. "The parents refuse to believe that their little darling is acting out to get attention, and the next thing you know, they've hired a team of psychic investigators to rig up cameras and audio equipment throughout their house. The results are always inconclusive. But once you remove the kid from the home, the events magically stop. I think that says it all."

"That's sometimes the case," Chantel acknowledged. "And it's unfortunate that the whole paranormal field is tainted by these charlatans. It casts aspersions on all of us. There will always be gullible people, very suggestible, who buy into hoaxes and scams."

"So are you saying there is such a thing as telekinesis? Has anyone ever proven it?" Lurleen huffed.

Chantel was silent for a moment. "I can assure you, it's a very real phenomenon." She turned to stare at me. "And I can prove it, if you just give me a moment."

Vera Mae raised her eyebrows. Her hand had been hovering over the button that would launch the next commercial, but she drew it back, her eyes wide.

"Do you see that ballpoint pen, Maggie?" Chantel gestured to a pen lying on the console between us.

"Yes, of course." I wondered where she was going with this.

"Am I touching it in any way?"

"No, you're not." I was starting to feel a little foolish, like I was David Copperfield's assistant, a foil for whatever trick Chantel was going to try to pull off in the studio.

"I want you to watch it carefully. And once I begin, I will need complete silence. Try to keep your mind a blank, so you don't interfere with the process."

The process?

And then Chantel's expression changed imperceptibly, almost as if she were a shape-shifter, ready to take on a new persona. It was like someone had paralyzed every muscle in her face, and her eyes suddenly became dilated, giving her a slightly crazed look. She stared straight ahead, looking like a wide-awake corpse in a zombie flick.

I waited, watching.

She sat perfectly still for several seconds, with her nostrils quivering like a Thoroughbred's. Then she inhaled a deep breath that seemed to come from somewhere in the depths of her being.

"Are you ready?" she asked in a flat voice. Her right hand was lying flat on the console, the fingers splayed, wide apart. For one crazy moment, I thought I felt heat waves, like little bolts of energy, darting out from her fingertips. But that was just my overactive imagination at work, right?

I gave myself a mental head slap. *Get a grip, Maggie!*

I smiled. "Ready for what?" I asked in my most professional voice. I caught a flash of movement, and my heart stuttered. *The pen! What was going on with the pen?* "The pen," I said stupidly. "I think . . . I mean, it can't be, but it looks like it's—"

"Holy moley, it's moving!" Vera Mae yelled from the control room. I stared at her through the glass, and her mouth was open wide, like she was one of those characters in an Edvard Munch painting.

And then I looked back at the pen. It *was* moving. No doubt. It was moving! Slowly, at first, but then it seemed to gather speed.

I still had my eye on the pen when it skittered across the console, wobbled back and forth on the edge for a long, heart-thudding moment, and then dropped straight into my lap.

The pen. In my lap. As if a ghostly hand had placed it there.

I gasped out loud, just as we went to commercial break.

Chapter 12

"How in the world did you do that?" Vera Mae flipped open her mike to talk to us. I flinched as a new House of Beauty commercial, complete with cheesy jingle, floated through the studio. "Be kind to your hair, because it's hair today, gone tomorrow." There was a syrupy version of the theme song from *Doctor Zhivago* playing in the background. The ad copy made absolutely no sense, but with Irina, it doesn't have to.

Note to self: remind Cyrus to hire a real copywriter. Soon.

Chantel stared at Vera Mae through the window and shrugged. "How did I do it?" She gave a little toss of her head and inspected her long, talonlike fingernails. "I don't know what to tell you. It's a power, a gift."

"It's pretty impressive, but I sure wish you could explain it to me," Vera Mae persisted.

"I'm in the dark as much as you are, Vera Mae. I don't really do anything, you see. I just concentrate and allow things to happen. That's the key to understanding the workings of the universe. I am but a channel, a vessel."

Chantel put her right hand on her ample bosom and looked skyward. She either had heartburn or she was contemplating the mysteries of the intergalactic system. "I am but a drop in the ocean of life."

Okay, I get it. *She's only a channel, a vessel, a drop in the ocean.* I felt a bubble of irritation rising in me at her mock-humble act. She was being as cryptic as Michael the spirit guide had been at the séance. What was her shtick for today? Chantel the wisewoman? Or maybe she was in her guru-oracle-psychic-medium mode. Chantel seemed to be a jack-of-all-trades in the metaphysical world, the ultimate multitasker.

I picked up the pen and turned it over in my hand a few times, taking a close look.

"It's an ordinary pen, right, Maggie?" Chantel had her Cheshire cat face on, her enormous eyes focused on me. I wished I could figure out a way to unmask her, but nothing came to me. I was tempted to pocket the pen, but I didn't dare. That would be too obvious. Better to play dumb for the moment and act like I was going along with her.

"Yes, it certainly seems to be"—I waited a beat—"perfectly ordinary." I shifted the pen from one hand to the other, sure that I was missing something.

The only thing I noticed was that it felt a little heavier than most ballpoint pens, but other than that, I couldn't see anything different about it. I took a closer look. It had an attractive silver-colored casing; maybe that was what added the weight. In any case, I bit back a sigh. I was forced to agree with her; it looked completely normal.

"Do you think I could learn to do that?" Vera Mae asked from the control room. "I'd sure like to wow the girls at the next Beef 'n' Beer down at the fire hall."

Chantel wrinkled her nose. "I doubt you have any teleki-netic powers, Vera Mae. It's something you're born with. If you haven't noticed a sensitivity to paranormal events up to now, it's fairly certain that you don't have the gift. As I like to say, 'when you have the gift, you feel it in your gut.'"

"Oh, darn. Well, I was afraid you were gonna say that," Vera Mae said. Her face sagged for a moment, and then she brightened. "It looks like I'll just have to get through life without the gift."

Vera Mae is an incurable optimist and never stays discouraged for long. She had one hand on the dial and one eye on the clock, ready to whisk us back to the second hour of my show. "You know," she said in a chatty tone, "I always did like that old TV show *Bewitched*, with Elizabeth Montgomery. It's still going strong in reruns. I wish I could just twitch my nose like Samantha and—oops, here we go, Maggie. We're live!" she said suddenly, pointing at me.

"And we're back," I said quickly, sliding right into the next round of callers. It's funny—once the show starts, you get into a sort of rhythm and you can practically go on autopilot. Most of the calls were for Chantel, and I hate to admit it, but she did a good job fielding them. She knows a lot of paranormal mumbo jumbo and has a knack for coming across as warm and insightful with the callers. The listening audience couldn't seem to get enough of her; the lines were jammed the entire time.

I managed to look interested during the second hour, nodding and making the appropriate noises while I zoned out. I let my mind play over Althea's murder. How sad and senseless it all was. Who had killed her, and why? Probably the first thing to decide was whether the killer was someone she knew. An intruder? Someone who had a grudge against her? A random act of violence?

It seemed like it was unplanned, a crime of opportunity. After all, the killer hadn't brought a weapon to the scene, and poor Althea was bludgeoned to death with her own fire-place poker. It made me shudder just to think of it.

That would surely indicate what the profilers call a disorganized crime scene. If someone was breaking in to rob Althea, wouldn't they have brought a weapon? Or something to restrain her with?

What was the motive? There couldn't be much of value in the historical-society building. I wondered whether the killer had bothered to wipe up his prints, or whether he'd left trace evidence at the scene. If the crime scene was disorganized, as I suspected, that meant the killer had been careless and could have left DNA evidence scattered all around.

But back to the killer. It appeared that Althea had opened the door to let him in, because there was no sign of forced entry. But that didn't necessarily mean that she knew him. Cypress Grove is a small, friendly place. When I first moved here from Manhattan, I was shocked to discover that a lot of people don't bother to lock their doors. Day and night. So it wouldn't have been unusual for Althea to open the door to a complete stranger. He might have pretended that he wanted to visit the historical society.

Or the killer might have been hiding inside, waiting for her to return home. Maybe he'd been stalking her, and followed her home? I wondered whether Rafe had managed to track down Althea's movements that day. It would be interesting to know where she'd gone and whom she'd talked to. And I wondered if she'd been killed very late at night or in the early-morning hours.

I suddenly thought of Trevor McNamara, the real estate developer I'd met at Ted's. I was positive that he was hiding something, and he'd specifically mentioned knocking on the doors of the old Victorian mansions downtown. But if he'd been involved in Althea's murder, why would he broadcast the fact that he'd been in the area? That wouldn't be a very smart move on his part, and I had the feeling Trevor was a shrewd guy.

I was getting nowhere with this train of thought, and I forced myself to concentrate on Chantel, who was taking a call about supermarket bar codes. It must have been a doozie of a question, because I could see Vera Mae allowing herself a small eye roll in the control room.

If you haven't heard the controversy about supermarket bar codes, here's the CliffsNotes version: a tiny, demented group of folks think that bar codes actually contain hidden Satanic messages. The first time I heard this, I felt like I'd officially entered the Twilight Zone.

But wait. There's more. Another group of conspiracy theorists claim the bar codes are part of a giant government plot to control our lives. How? This part gets sticky, and I've never fully understood it. I think it has something to do with mind control and the power of suggestion. There might be other, equally wacky bar code conspiracy theories out there, but these seem to be the two most popular ones.

It was scary to think we were giving them some validity by even discussing them on the air today. This was surely a new low in my show's history, and I thought of Kevin's comment about the *National Enquirer*. Maybe that was where we were headed. Tabloid on the air.

The trend seemed to be headed for the lowest common denominator—the more sensationalistic the topic, the better. I felt my spirits plummet, realizing that schlock sells. Today's ratings would probably be through the roof. And Cyrus would be delighted. Not with me, but with Chantel. What implications would that have for my *On the Couch* show? They certainly couldn't be good. I bit back a sigh.

The rest of the show zipped by quickly, and before I knew

it, I was reading a thirty-second promo for the upcoming time capsule ceremony and thanking Chantel for being my guest.

"I'd love to come back and take more questions from your listeners. Anytime," she gushed.

I just bet you would! I was sure she was angling for her own show on WYME, and if Cyrus thought the ratings would support it, he'd hire her in a minute. Did the station really need two afternoon talk shows?

I had no job security, and I was already halfway through my yearly contract. If Chantel really wanted to cut into my territory, there was no way to stop her. She said she'd come to Cypress Grove for seclusion to work on her next book, but maybe there was more to the story. She seemed to love the attention of being a local media star, and maybe she figured a WYME gig was a stepping-stone to bigger things.

Moments later, I was heading to the break room, when Irina stopped me in the hall. She was glowing with excitement as she introduced me to a young man wearing khakis and a white long-sleeved shirt.

"My English teacher," she said proudly. "Mr. Simon Brent. This is Dr. Maggie Walsh," she said formally.

"Nice to meet you," I said, eyeing Simon Brent. *Her English teacher?* A little bell went off in my head. He was an attractive guy, broad shoulders, great smile, but he didn't look like an English teacher. He was male-model good-looking, like an English teacher you might see on a CW show. And since when was Irina attending classes at the local university? This was news to me.

"I had no idea you were studying literature, Irina." The thought of Irina tackling the complete works of Dostoyevsky or Henry James boggled the mind. I wondered whether her instructor had ever read any of her House of Beauty commercials.

"Oh, no, it is not the literature I am studying. I am taking the English as a third language class." Irina giggled and clapped her hand over her mouth. "Wait—I mean second language. English as the second language, as they say." She nudged Simon playfully on the arm. "But Simon—I mean Mr. Brent— thinks my English is so perfect, there is no need for more of the instruction."

"An ESL course. How interesting." I raised my eyebrows, and Simon Brent shifted his stance, looking distinctly uncomfortable. "And how amazing to think that you don't need any further instruction. That's really remarkable. You must be a very quick study, Irina."

"Yes, Maggie, is true, I swear. Mr. Brent says I speak just like a savage." Irina's voice trembled with pride. She nodded her chin up and down like a bobble-head doll. A slow red flush crept up her finely chiseled features, and her eyes were dancing with excitement. "Can you imagine, Maggie? I speak like a savage! Is high compliment—that is for sure. My grandmother back in Sweden would be so pleased."

"You told her she speaks like a savage?" I thinned my lips and gave Simon Brent the hairy eyeball. Let Mr. J.Crew try to talk his way out of this one.

"I'm afraid there's been a slight misunderstanding." Simon Brent crossed his arms over his chest and gave a deep chuckle, managing to flash an adorable dimple. Very Mario Lopez. "I didn't say a *savage*, Irina. I said a *native*. You speak like a *native*. Remember, we talked about that in class the other day? Someone who is born in this country is called a native." He paused, watching me. "A savage is something else entirely," he concluded lamely.

"Why didn't you tell us you were studying English, Irina?" I asked. "We could have helped you with your lessons."

"But I wanted to make the big surprise to you," she said,

her plump lips turning downward. "At end of four weeks, you will think I am living here the whole of my life."

"Amazing," Vera Mae cut in. She'd been standing in the corridor, following the whole conversation. "How is that possible? You must be a heck of a teacher, sonny."

"Er, actually, Irina's a very good student," Simon Brent said in a strangled voice. "I really can't take credit for her, um, remarkable progress."

Irina pursed her lips, her eyes dreamy. "I remember first day of class. You tell me that I speak English with perfection. But just one big problem. Americans do not seem to understand me when I speak English. That is true, right? You explain it all to me. You say it is all their fault if they cannot understand own language. Too bad for them, you say."

Simon Brent glanced down at the tile floor as if he wished it would part like the Red Sea and swallow him whole. "Well, it's a little more complicated than that, Irina." He gave a nervous chuckle, and I saw a thin film of perspiration sprouting on his upper lip. "That's not quite what I said. I think you might have taken it the wrong way." He was clearly backpedaling as fast as he could, without much success.

"So now I am giving Mr. Simon Brent tour of station," Irina continued. "And I saved the least for last, Maggie." Her voice was brimming with pride. "Dr. Maggie Walsh and her *On the Couch* show."

Saving the least for last? Gee, thanks a bunch. Irina must have caught my expression, because she quickly corrected herself. "No, I am not saying that right. You are not the least. You are the best. We saved the best for last."

"So did you like the show?" I asked, curious what his response would be.

"It was wonderful," he said, looking deeply into my eyes. "You have so much energy and enthusiasm. I can see why your show is so successful." I had the feeling he was thrilled to change the subject. "Actually, I have a favor to ask. I was hoping I could have a moment with your cohost. Do you think that would be possible?"

"My cohost? Oh, you mean my guest." I squeezed out a good-natured laugh. "I think Chantel is in the break room grabbing a coffee right now. I'm sure she'd be happy to chat with you. Irina can take you back there right now, if you have a minute."

"I'd like that," he said, grabbing Irina by the arm. "Nice to meet you both," he added, hurrying away.

"Well, if that don't beat all," Vera Mae said the moment they were out of earshot. "You know, that young feller is no more an English teacher than I'm a supermodel."

"I know. The whole thing is bizarre. Something just doesn't smell right."

"I've had the feeling all day that something real bad was about to happen," Vera Mae said ominously. Since Vera Mae has these feelings of foreboding at least half a dozen times a week, I tend to ignore them.

"What else could go wrong?" I asked her as we made our way down the corridor to her office.

Kevin was waiting for us inside Vera Mae's cubicle. He looked pale under the fluorescent lights and had a stricken expression on his face. "Dr. Maggie, Ms. Vera Mae." There was a note of urgency in his tone, and I felt the first twinges of foreboding go through me. A little shiver tickled my spine. "I'm afraid I've got some real bad news for you." I noticed his lower lip was trembling, and he grabbed the desktop for support.

"Well, for heaven's sake, what is it, Kevin? Spit it out." Vera Mae said. She stopped dead in her tracks and tossed a bunch of files on her desk before she turned to face him.

"It's Miss Mildred." A couple of seconds of silence and then, "You know, Miss Mildred Smoot, the librarian." His voice stuttered to a stop, and he swallowed hard. Vera Mae and I exchanged a baffled look and then stared at him.

"What about her, Kevin?" My heart jumped into my throat, and I tried to swallow it, before touching him lightly on the shoulder. "Did something happen to Mildred?"

Kevin took a deep breath and blew it out slowly before answering. "There's no easy way to say this, Dr. Maggie. Miss Mildred is dead." He widened his eyes, and his fist involuntarily flew to his mouth. "I can't believe it, but it's true. She was murdered late last night. They just found her body."

Chapter 13

For a second, I felt like my heart had stopped. Mildred dead? It seemed impossible. I could barely wrap my mind around it, and I sank like a stone into Vera Mae's visitor chair. Two deaths in our tiny town; it seemed like a macabre joke. But from the ashy gray pallor on Kevin's face, I knew it was all too real.

Vera Mae pushed Kevin into her own swivel Aeron chair. "Sit down, boy. You look as pale as a ghost." She reached into the tiny fridge she keeps under her desk and grabbed a can of Dr. Brown's cream soda. She popped the tab and handed it to Kevin. "Drink this. It'll put some color back in your face." She waited while he took a few sips. "And then tell us what you know, when you feel ready."

"Yes, ma'am," he said slowly, taking a sip. "I just found out a few minutes ago. Detective Martino called for you, Dr. Maggie, but I told him you were on the air. He wanted to talk to you right away, and I think he only told me about Miss Mildred because he wanted me to know how important it was."

"It's very important," I agreed. I felt tears springing into my eyes when I thought of Mildred on my show, how nervous she had been, and how she'd rallied, so eager to talk about Althea's work with the historical society. I blinked a few times to make the tears disappear. This was no time to cry.

I had to figure out what had happened to her. Althea Somerset and Mildred Smoot. Both had been struck down with no warning. Were the two murders connected? How could they not be? One small town, two old ladies. There had to be some common thread, right?

"Rafe said you can call him on his cell," Kevin said, breaking into my thoughts.

"Use my phone, hon." Vera Mae's eyes looked troubled. I knew she was having trouble dealing with this second death, as well.

I picked up the handset on Vera Mae's desk and punched in Rafe's number, but it went straight to voice mail. "It's me," I said tersely. "I just heard about Mildred. Catch you later."

Vera Mae said, "Cyrus is going to want to run a news piece on this right away." She flipped open her desk calendar. "Big Jim is covering a game over in Lakesville. Maggie, do you suppose you can get some information from the desk sergeant at the police department? Or even call up Nick?"

"I'll try. I'll call you the minute I know something." I decided the best thing would be to go directly to the PD and hope to see Rafe or, at the very least, get some concrete information from one of the investigating officers. I hurried to my own office, grabbed my purse, and was sailing through the lobby when Irina called to me. She was back at the reception desk, and there was no sign of her hunky instructor.

"Maggie, you have message," she said, waving a piece of paper at me.

"Can it wait?"

"Is sort of urgent," she replied. She glanced down, probably trying to decipher her own handwriting. "About a man."

"A man?"

"Mr. Big. A woman called, and she said she wants him back." She gave me a sly smile. "Maggie, I think you have been very naughty girl—"

"It's not what you think," I said, grabbing the paper out of her hand.

I skimmed the note as I dashed through the parking lot behind WYME. The message was from Candace Somerset. *Candace Somerset? Why did that name sound familiar?* I gave myself a mental head slap. Of course. Althea's sister. Mildred had told me that Althea had a sister who was flying in to handle the estate.

And now it seemed she was here in Cypress Grove.

And she wanted Mr. Big.

Rafe was strolling through the lobby when I flew in the double glass doors to the Cypress Grove PD.

"Maggie," he said, grabbing me lightly on the upper arms. "I got your message. We need to talk."

I nodded as he motioned me to follow him back to his office. The moment we were inside, I sat down, feeling like my knees were ready to buckle. "What happened to her?" I asked, feeling a bubble of anger rising in my chest. "Who would hurt someone so sweet, so helpless? And coming right on the heels of Althea's murder," I rushed. "The two murders are connected, right? They have to be."

Rafe silently handed me a cup of the brown sludge that passed for coffee in the department. I wrapped my hands around the cup, feeling oddly comforted by the warmth. I felt chilled to the bone inside, and my thoughts were scrabbling through my head like manic squirrels.

"We don't know much yet," he said, sitting across from me. "The CSIs are combing the place for clues. All we have so far is the murder weapon."

"The weapon?"

"An antique silver letter opener. And it was left at the crime scene, the Cypress Grove Library."

A letter opener. I winced. "Just like the poker was left at Althea's," I pointed out. "You see, they have to be connected!"

"It's too early to tell. We've got a long way to go to make that assumption. None of the forensic evidence is back yet. This isn't *CSI Miami*, you know."

I nodded. Law enforcement guys always get a kick out of the "*CSI* effect." Audiences are so used to crimes being solved in the space of a one-hour TV show, they tend to forget that real investigation and evidence gathering can take weeks and months.

"So you don't have any credible leads? Even a wild hunch or two?"

"Nothing I'd want to talk about."

Here's something else I've noticed about Rafe. He can clam up like a sphinx when he wants to, and he makes it a rule never to jump to conclusions. We have totally different personalities. I rely on instinct and snap decisions; Rafe is calmer, takes a more measured approach. I like to trust my gut feelings, and he relies strictly on the hard evidence.

He doesn't believe in hunches or educated guesses; he deals only in facts. I like to tell him that he was Joe Friday in another incarnation. *Just the facts, ma'am. Just the facts.*

"But there is one thing the crimes have in common. It's the séance," I said flatly. "There's no way to ignore that. That's the link that ties everyone together."

"Go on." He took a big gulp of his coffee and didn't even

grimace. Besides having an analytical mind, he must have a cast-iron stomach.

"Don't you see? Mildred and Althea were both at the séance that Chantel held at the historical society the other night. And now two people are dead. Chantel predicted something like this would happen."

He gave me one of those "And your point is?" looks. I think you have to have Mediterranean heritage and dark eyes to really do it justice. Rafe has it down to an art form.

"Mildred. Althea. Chantel. Don't you see? Three women. Somehow they're all connected. Think about it, Rafe. A phony psychic blows into town, and all hell breaks loose. First Althea is murdered, and now Mildred is killed. Maybe this sounds irrational, but I have the feeling none of this would have happened if Chantel hadn't come here."

Did I sound bitter? Probably. Not an attractive quality, but there you have it.

"Chantel did say there was a curse on Cypress Grove," Rafe said, lost in thought. "Nick reported it in that piece he wrote for the *Gazette*."

"Oh, I don't mean the part about the curse," I said. "That was sheer hype. She just said that because she's trying to pimp her new book." *And take my job at WMYE,* I added silently.

"You're not seriously suggesting that Chantel would kill two people to promote her book, are you?" From the look on his face, I figured he considered it a pretty far-fetched theory, even for me.

"I suppose not," I said grudgingly. "But nothing else is really going on in town. Both these women have lived here for half a century—" I stopped suddenly. Half a century. I had just insisted that nothing else was going on in town, but that wasn't quite true. There was plenty going on in town. The time capsule was going to be unearthed. Bingo. Somehow I'd have to factor that into the equation. "And there's something else—"

Rafe must have read my mind. "The time capsule," he said slowly. "I thought of that angle, too. Both Althea and Mildred probably know more than anyone else in town about the town's history. They had access to information that was lost in the fires all those years ago. But where does that leave us?" He swirled the last of the coffee in his cup before pushing his chair back and standing up.

"That leaves us back at square one. Unless . . . you think some long-buried secret might emerge when they dig up the capsule."

"It's possible." He shrugged and looked at me. "At the moment, that's all we have to go on."

Something nudged my mind, and I remembered the call from Candace Somerset, Althea's sister. "She called me because she wants Mr. Big," I explained. "She's staying in Althea's apartment at the historical society. I guess she'll be in town long enough for the funeral and to take care of Althea's things."

"Why not drop the cat off with her," Rafe suggested, "and stay for a while and try to chat with her. Try to get a feel for her relationship with Althea. She's the only surviving heir, you know."

I bet my eyebrows shot up into my forehead at that one. "She is?" I swallowed hard. "I didn't know Althea had any heirs. I just assumed there wasn't any inheritance. I figured Althea was as poor as a church mouse. She lived so frugally, I thought she pumped the little money she had into the historical society."

"Appearances can be deceiving. Althea made some shrewd real estate investments over the years, and she didn't get hit by the recession. Let's just say she had considerable assets." He paused, watching me. "Althea was a very wealthy woman, Maggie." The words hung in the air between us.

"And now Candace is going to be wealthy," I said softly. I mulled that for a couple of seconds. *Interesting.* "Nice for her, isn't it?"

"My point exactly." He gave me a sidelong glance. "As I said, see if you can find out what she thought about Althea. Find out if anyone in town knows Candace or if she's come back to visit very often. Maybe you'll learn some other information as well. This town is full of surprises."

I nodded, my thoughts swirling like scrambled eggs. Chantel, Althea, Mildred, and Candace. Two of them dead and perhaps the other two were suspects? It wasn't much to go on, but what other leads did I have? And there was the time capsule, looming over everything. Just a few more days, and it would be unearthed.

Rafe crossed around the desk so we were standing very close to each other. My heart did a familiar little flip-flop when he put his finger under my chin, tipping my face toward him. His expression changed; a smile took over his mouth. "And there's something I want you to keep in mind." He gave me a level look, his voice low and husky.

"What's that?" I asked a little breathlessly. I always feel a little buzz of attraction when I'm near him, like a shot of pure adrenaline going through me. His black eyes were piercing into mine; we were so close I could see the little golden flecks in them. "While you're out there digging up clues—"

"Yes?" I took a breath. He leaned toward me, brought his face near me, his lips brushing my ear.

"Be careful, Sherlock," he whispered. "I don't want anything to happen to you."

I wanted to shut my eyes and melt into him, but the next thing I knew, he'd opened the office door, and we were heading down the hall.

Classic Rafe behavior.

Chapter 14

"That was so sweet of you to rescue Mr. Big," Candace Somerset said to me half an hour later. I'd stopped by my place, grabbed Mr. Big, who'd been napping on my bed, and drove to the historical society with him.

"Althea adored this cat, and I know she'd be happy that you took such good care of him. I hate to think what might have happened when those police officers were going through the house." She gave a little shudder. "Poor Mr. Big might have run out in the street and been lost forever."

"I was happy to do it." I smiled at her and accepted another cup of tea. We were settled in the front parlor of the historical society, and Mr. Big was stretched out on the Oriental rug, sound asleep. Whoever called a cat "a pillow that eats" must have known Mr. Big.

I think he was glad to be back home. I'd done my best to keep him comfortable in my town house, but Pugsley had turned out to be more territorial than I'd realized, and his constant barking had threatened to turn the placid Mr. Big into a head case.

"So you have your own talk show?" Candace asked.

"That must be very exciting." She was younger than Althea and smartly dressed in a tailored beige suit with an apricot shell and understated gold jewelry. She was tall and willowy, like Althea. Her blond hair was streaked with expensive highlights, and she was wearing designer peep-toe pumps.

"Some days it is." I gave her an Idiot's Guide explanation of how I had given up my Manhattan psychoanalytic practice and moved to Florida to become a radio shrink for WYME. I'd told the story so many times, I had it down to a science. A few people think I was crazy to give up my practice ("all that education and training!"), but most folks are fascinated by my new job and think that I struck a good bargain.

"I know there's been a lot of media coverage about Althea's passing," she said in a low voice.

"Not as much as you might think," I replied. I wondered whether it would be greedy to reach for another buttery jam tart and took one anyway. "The police really haven't said much about the details of the"—I paused, searching for a word—"investigation, so there hasn't been too much to say."

"I'm glad to hear it. It seems awful to think of people gossiping about . . . you know, how she passed. As if her last few moments on earth were more newsworthy than all the years that went before."

Candace's eyes clouded for a moment, and I suddenly realized that she wanted to be assured that Althea's life and achievements would be honored. That the details of her death wouldn't be sensationalized and overshadow everything else about her. Of course, there really isn't any way to guarantee this in a murder case. The public seems to have an insatiable appetite for violent crimes. That's true whether you're in Cypress Grove or Manhattan.

"Will you be in town long?" I wondered whether she minded staying in the large Victorian mansion where her sister was murdered. It seemed macabre to me, and I had to repress a little shudder.

"Just a couple of weeks. There are the funeral arrangements to attend to, and I need to decide what to do about her things."

Hmm. No mention of the sizable estate she was going to inherit. "I wondered what you think of the place. A little town like Cypress Grove must seem like the boondocks to you. Althea mentioned to me that you lived in Boston."

She narrowed her eyes. "You know I'm from Boston? Word travels fast, doesn't it?" There was a sharp edge to her voice, and I could tell she wasn't pleased that I knew any details about her personal life. I wondered why. Did she have something to hide?

"It goes with living in a small town," I said, spreading my hands in a "don't shoot the messenger" gesture.

"Yes, well, I suppose I do like it here." She smoothed her skirt and forced a slight smile. "I haven't really spent much time in Cypress Grove over the years, if that's what you're really asking." She waited a beat. "Althea and I had a complicated relationship. We were certainly fond of each other, but you know how it is with some relatives. You do better if you only see them occasionally." She gave an uncertain little laugh. "But you're a psychologist, so of course, you already know all about these things."

I made a small, noncommittal sound. "I've seen that happen, yes. Family relationships can be complex." I glanced at my watch. I couldn't seem to get a handle on Candace Somerset, and I wondered where to steer the conversation next.

"Terrible about Mildred Smoot," she said, surprising me.

"Did you know her?"

"No, but Althea mentioned her to me several times. Even though I didn't visit much, Althea and I stayed in touch through e-mail. She had considered Mildred a dear friend. And they had a lot in common. They both loved Cypress Grove and were dedicated to its history. There's probably nothing that went on in this town that they didn't know about." She paused. "Who would think that they would both fall victim to a serial killer," she said with a sad shake of her head. "It's shocking."

"A serial killer?" I had to bite back a laugh. Was Candace serious? "Is that what you think happened to Althea and Mildred?"

"Well, yes, of course I do," she said without missing a beat. "What else could it be? There certainly wouldn't be any motive for someone to just randomly kill two women in the same week. Especially in such a tiny town," she added.

She must have read my expression, because she said, "Isn't that what you think happened? An attack by a serial killer? I heard that you used to be a forensic psychologist. So I'm sure you know much more about the criminal mind than I do."

Not if you have firsthand experience. Not if you had something to do with your sister's death.

I took another sip of tea, wondering how much to say, what cards to lay on the table. There was no point in showing my hand to Candace. In the space of a few minutes, she'd somehow managed to turn the tables and was grilling me for information. But why? Was it morbid curiosity or was something else going on?

I had the feeling that Candace had a secret agenda and simply wanted the murder investigation to just go away. "No, I'm afraid I can't agree with you on the serial killer theory," I said finally. "Mildred and Althea simply don't fit the victim profile of any serial killer cases I've studied." I waited for a couple of seconds. "There were similarities, of course.

The crimes were committed where the victims worked, and the weapon was left at the scene. And of course they were both elderly women."

"A random act of violence, then?"

"In Cypress Grove?" I shook my head. "I don't think so."

She gave an exasperated little sigh. "Well, what do you think happened to my sister? And to that poor librarian?"

Her voice crawled over my skin, and I felt myself recoiling a little. I had the feeling she was holding something back and was playing with me, trying to ferret out information.

"What do I think happened? I think someone wanted them dead."

It was nearly ten thirty when I zipped down the corridor of WYME the next morning. I noticed that Vera Mae had a visitor in her office. I was planning to scoot right past to my cubicle, but she spotted me and stepped out into the hall. "Cyrus told me to give this guy the VIP tour," she said under a breath. "He's probably going to buy a lot of ad time on the station. So Cyrus figures big bucks. In other words, play nice." She winked at me.

She pulled me into her office and introduced me to her guest. "Mark Sanderson, Maggie Walsh," she said. There was no place to move in her cramped office. We smiled and shook hands awkwardly over the top of a file cabinet. There was absolutely no place to sit; every available surface was covered with piles of papers and unopened mail.

I felt a sudden wave of claustrophobia wash over me, and my heartbeat ratcheted up a notch, like I was trapped in a phone booth.

"Mark's a real estate developer from Georgia, and he plans on spending a lot of time in our little town." Vera Mae gave me a meaningful look. I got the message. "Mark, you've probably heard of Maggie Walsh. She's our star. She's the host of *On the Couch*."

"Not a star by any means," I said.

"I heard your show when I was driving into town yesterday. Very nice." He was attractive, early forties, and looked buff, like he worked out every day.

He was wearing a snowy white knit shirt with a Lakeview Golf Club logo. A golfer; I should have known. Probably good for business. Cyrus always says he makes half his business deals on the links.

"I'll get Kevin to rustle us up another chair," Vera Mae said vaguely, reaching for her phone.

"That's okay. I really can't stay, but it's nice to meet you, Maggie." He dug into his pocket, pulled out a business card, and handed it to me. "I know your schedule is probably jammed, but if you ever have time for coffee or lunch, I'd love to talk to you."

I glanced at the card. "Sanderson Properties," I said slowly. "Why does that ring a bell?"

"Mark was on the *Today* show last week. Remember that feature they did with Barbara Corcoran? Mark's got a big development project planned for Cypress Grove." Vera Mae was frowning, glancing around the office as if she could magically make a chair appear.

Of course. A visiting developer. No wonder Cyrus wanted us to treat him like a visiting celebrity. *Ka-ching, ka-ching.*

Mark nodded. "We're doing a condo project on the grounds of the old courthouse."

"The old courthouse?" I was puzzled. As far as I knew, there was only one courthouse, the one right on the town square.

"Well, I mean the present courthouse," Mark said hastily. "We're going to raze it in the next couple of months and then start construction on the Royal Palm Towers. We're planning on twelve stories, and we'll have studios, as well as one-, two-, and three-bedroom units. And of course, a fully equipped state-of-the-art gym. We're offering furnished and unfurnished units and low maintenance fees."

I wouldn't have been surprised if he'd whipped out the blueprints and shown them to me on the spot. Instead he reached down into his briefcase and handed me a full-color brochure.

"Looks impressive," I said idly. I was being polite. Judging by the artist's rendition, the building was bland and uninteresting, a tower of tan brick with small windows.

"The interior shots are from a place we did up in Jacksonville. The furnished units will be very similar. As you can see, the living room and kitchen area are quite large by industry standards."

"Ah, yes, I see." I tried not to wince; the interiors looked like they were straight out of a Holiday Inn. I thought how lucky I was to have snared my hacienda-style town house in its beautiful garden setting. If I had to live in a place like the Royal Palm Towers, I might as well have stayed in New York.

"Who are you hoping to attract?" I asked. "Cypress Grove is a small town."

Mark nodded. "But it's perfect for a bedroom community. We can beat the big-city condo prices, and commuters can just zip home from work on I-95. They'll save a bundle." When I didn't say anything, he pressed on. "The units are going fast, so if you know anyone who happens to be in the market—"

"I'll be sure to put them in touch with you." I paused, frowning. Something was tickling the edges of my mind. Some memory about the courthouse. "There's just one thing. Maybe I'm mistaken, but I thought—"

"What's that?" Mark shot me a keen glance, and I noticed his eyes were very blue, piercing into mine.

"Oh, it's nothing. I'm probably getting the facts mixed up. I thought the courthouse was on the historic register, or something like that. You know, designated as a building that has to be preserved. But apparently, I was mistaken."

"That was the old courthouse you're thinking of," Vera Mae cut in. "The one that burned down all those years ago. Mark's talking about the current courthouse, the one standing on the town square right now. That was a gift from old man Paley. Ronald Paley. He gave the county the land for it. He owned practically all the land around here, acres and acres of it."

"Vera Mae, you amaze me."

She grinned. "I read up on all this because we're having a history professor on the show today."

Mark checked his watch. An expensive Patek Philippe, I noticed. "Got to run, ladies, but I hope we meet up again. Cyrus invited me to play a few rounds of golf with him, so I'll be in town for a while."

"Sounds good." I kept my voice deliberately neutral.

"Why the thoughtful look?" Vera Mae asked after Mark Sanderson had left. "He seems like a nice guy. A little pushy maybe, but that's to be expected. He's got to sell those concrete boxes"—she gave a disdainful little sniff—"and he's got his work cut out for him. I wouldn't have one of those things for free."

"Neither would I. I'm just thinking that it's a little odd. He's the second real estate person I've met this week. The other guy says he's buying up vacation properties."

"Vacation properties? Here in Cypress Grove?" Vera Mae sniffed. "That doesn't pass the smell test."

"That's exactly what I thought."

Chapter 15

Professor Grossman was waiting in the break room for me, loaded down with books, folders, and legal pads. I took one look at the mountain of papers sitting in front of him and my heart sank. Whenever a guest comes armed with a ton of notes, it doesn't bode well.

Why? It usually signals a lack of confidence. Meaning the person isn't quick on his feet and won't be the least bit spontaneous or entertaining on the air.

A lack of spontaneity makes for a very dull guest. I introduced myself to the good professor, ushered him into the studio, and then made an excuse to zip outside for a moment. I ran down the hallway, looking for Kevin, and found him filing press packets in an empty office.

"Kevin," I whispered. "How did things go with Grossman? You were supposed to do a preinterview with him, remember? I wanted you to get some short, snappy stories. I think he's dragged half a research library into the studio."

"Yes, ma'am, I sure do remember, Dr. Maggie." Kevin scrambled to his feet, a stricken look on his face. "I tried to do exactly what you said, but I had a devil of a time getting him to loosen up, you know? He kept staring at the ceiling and talking really slow. And most of it wasn't very interesting. It sounded like he was giving a lecture to some of his grad students. It nearly put me to sleep."

"That's just what I was afraid of." I bit back a sigh. "He gives new meaning to the term 'dry,' doesn't he?" I shook my head. "I should have known he'd be a tough nut to crack. Did you manage to get anything interesting out of him?"

"There's not much to work with, I'm afraid."

"Meaning—"

Vera Mae brushed by me, heading to the studio, and gave me a friendly nudge. "Live in five, girl!" she yelled over her shoulder. "Time to hustle!" I nodded and turned my attention back to Kevin.

"Meaning he rambled on for about twenty minutes or so, telling each story," Kevin continued. "And to be honest, Dr. Maggie, I didn't really get the point of any of them. I think I may have dozed off for a few minutes."

"Twenty minutes? Kevin, this is live radio." I snapped my fingers. "He's got to be quick, compelling, on the mark. We're talking sound bites here."

"I understand, Dr. Maggie. I did the best I could."

Kevin looked so crestfallen, I patted him on the shoulder and managed an encouraging smile. After all, we were talking about Professor Grossman. You don't usually hear the words "Bernard Grossman" and "fascinating" in the same sentence, I thought drily.

Maybe I was asking for the impossible. The whole concept of live radio was probably completely foreign to an academic like Professor Grossman. "It's okay, Kevin. I'm sure you did the best you could. Maybe he'll surprise us and be a terrific guest, you know? Maybe he'll be bright, witty, and loads of fun."

Or maybe not.

The first twenty minutes of the show plodded by as Professor Grossman fiddled with his notes and textbooks, giving way too much information. The topic was fairly interesting, but he didn't have any idea how to cull the material, giving the audience the most compelling tidbits.

"Laura from Dania is on line two," Vera Mae cut in. "She wants to know about the most interesting thing people have tucked away in time capsules."

"The most interesting?" Professor Grossman repeated. I knew the body-language clues by now. First a sage nod of the head and then straight into Lecture Land. Think of the most boring textbook you've ever read, turn it into an audiobook, make it human, and you've got my guest.

"Well, I'd have to say I think the most interesting things are the predictions people make about the future. In 1963, a time capsule was buried in San Diego. It was to be opened exactly one hundred years later, in the year 2063."

"Really? That's fascinating." I sounded as bubbly as a game-show contestant. "And what was the most surprising thing about this particular time capsule?" I nudged him.

"That's a tough choice." He allowed himself a scholarly chuckle. "They asked the leading scientists, astronauts, politicians, and military commanders to make some predictions about the future. All their comments were stored in the time capsule for future generations to ponder."

"Amazing," I murmured. "That would certainly be something to . . . um, ponder." I wondered how much pondering my listeners were doing, or if everyone had changed stations by now. Or fallen asleep.

Vera Mae caught my eye from the control room and held up one of her famous hand-lettered signs, "MIAB," which means "Move it along, buster." (She has another sign for women, "MIAS," which means "Move it along, sister.")

I think of Vera Mae as my own version of a Greek chorus. She has a variety of these signs and holds them up at key points through the show. She twirled her index finger in a "let's hurry it up" gesture and pointed to the clock. I knew we weren't far from a commercial break, and we always try to end on a cliff-hanger before we slide into a commercial. It keeps the listeners tuned in and pumps up their interest. At least that was the theory.

But Professor Grossman, it seemed, was not to be hurried.

"That certainly sounds interesting," I said brightly. I'd bet that Laura, my caller, was hoping for something juicier than this. "What sort of predictions did they make?"

"A few startling ones," Professor Grossman said, stroking his white goatee. "I believe I have a copy of the booklet somewhere in my notes." He fumbled around with his folders, scrabbling through sheaves of yellowed papers covered in tiny handwriting. "Naturally, they kept a copy of the booklet they put into the time capsule."

"Naturally." I wondered whether there was any way to light a fire under him. Uh-oh. He was pulling out a wad of papers the size of the Manhattan telephone book. "You can just give us the gist of it," I pleaded. I could hear a note of desperation creeping into my voice. This guy needed media training. Badly.

Vera Mae made a throat-slitting gesture in the control room and then closed her eyes and let her head flop to one side in her famous dead-producer pose. The woman would have been brilliant as a stand-up comic, but I wasn't chuckling.

"Oh, no, I couldn't do that," my guest chided me. "Accuracy is key when you're dealing with historical matters." He gave me a stern look over his horn-rims as if daring me to disagree with him.

But this is entertainment! I felt like shouting. Maybe he thought this was the History Channel.

He locked eyes with me and tapped the folder with a self-important air. "These are the predictions, and I daresay your listeners will be astounded when they hear them. Shall I share them with your listeners?"

"Yes, please!" I urged him, glancing at the clock. I crossed my fingers. Maybe there'd be a couple of juicy tidbits in there. Miracles do happen, right?

"The famous astronaut John Glenn predicted that we would discover an antigravity system." He read slowly, enunciating every word, and raised his eyebrows when he finished. Maybe he was waiting for a round of applause.

I blinked twice and stared at him. *That's it?*

"Ah," I said, trying to sound suitably impressed. "Antigravity, imagine that!"

I wasn't sure what an antigravity system was, but it sounded like a big deal. I thought of those boots that were popular in the seventies that allowed you to hang upside down. Weren't they called antigravity boots? Or was it gravity boots? I didn't dare admit my ignorance because I knew he'd launch into a half-hour lecture if I asked for an explanation.

"Interesting," I murmured. "Anything else?"

"Here's another prediction that made it into the time capsule." He put on his Ben Franklin glasses to peer at a jumbo index card. "William Pickering, the well-known astronomer, predicted that we'd be traveling to nearby stars—at the speed of light! It's certainly possible, but Pickering predicted it positively. Imagine that!"

His eyes lit up, and he leaned forward into the mike. Oh,

dear. All those p's were wreaking havoc with the sound system. It sounded like someone had turned on a popcorn popper in the studio.

I saw Vera Mae waving her hands from the control room. I reached over and adjusted the mike so the professor was talking at an angle, and not directly into it.

"That's it?" Laura, the caller, broke in. Her tone was annoyed, challenging. "That's the most interesting thing that anyone's ever put into a time capsule?" It was clear that Laura had no interest in scientific breakthroughs, amazing or not.

"Well, yes," Professor Grossman said, clearly surprised that she didn't seem to share his enthusiasm. "Here's another one that might catch your fancy. Have you heard of Fred Whipple?"

"Can't say that I have," Vera Mae said from the studio. "Unless he's Mr. Whipple from those 'Don't Squeeze the Charmin' ads." She glanced at me. "That was before your time, Maggie. We're talking twenty-five years ago."

Professor Grossman frowned at her. "Fred Whipple was an astronomer who predicted the control of fusion. That was certainly a major prediction." Dead silence from Laura. She'd either hung up or fallen asleep.

I was about to break in when he continued, "And he also predicted that the use of ordinary hydrogen in 1995 would lead to a comparatively infinite supply at relatively low cost."

Aha. Stunning news. I wasn't sure why I needed an infinite supply of hydrogen. Did I dare ask? The silence stretched out for another beat, and I spotted Vera frowning as checked the screens.

"And now it's time for a word from Slim's Auto Repair!" Vera Mae sang out. A jingle filled the studio, and I leaned back in my chair. I motioned to Professor Grossman that he could take his headphones off. "We've got a five-minute break," I told him. "They do the local news and weather, so if you want to get up and stretch your legs, or get a coffee, now's the time to do it."

"Thank you. I think I will," he said, getting to his feet. "I think that went rather well, don't you?"

"Brilliantly." I put my head in my hands the minute he left the studio.

My mind was reeling. I had brain freeze from listening to Bernard Grossman, and we were barely twenty minutes into the show. There were only a couple of lights flashing on the phone; the call-in lines were nearly dead. My listeners had already tuned out—literally.

All because of my guest professor, who was probably listed in the Guinness book of world records—as the Most Boring Human Being in the Western Hemisphere.

"Girl, we've got to do something. And we've gotta do it quick!" Vera Mae yanked off her headphones and tore out of the control room into the studio.

"I know we have to do something, but what? I'm out of ideas."

I felt hopeless, helpless, and powerless—a classic case of what the shrinks call "learned helplessness." That's what happens when you're trapped in a completely impossible situation and you think you're powerless. It's the sinking feeling you get when you're up against a brick wall—you've run out of options and there's no way it's going to end well.

"Well, we just have to take charge, here," Vera Mae said. "Right off the top of my head, I can think of a couple of things that will help." She glanced at the clock. "We have four minutes and counting till we go live again."

"What sort of things?"

She held up her index finger for silence and then picked up the intercom and paged Kevin to the studio. Stat. I raised

my eyebrows. Then she paged Chantel to the studio. *Chantel?*
I hadn't even realized Chantel was in the building.

"Chantel? I don't get it. What are you up to, Vera Mae?
And what's My Favorite Psychic doing here today?"

"Chantel came in to do some promos for the time capsule
ceremony," Vera Mae said in a panicked staccato. "And it's a
good thing she did, because we can use her right this minute. She's our ace in the hole."

"You're putting Chantel on my show?" Now I really did
feel like putting my head down on the console and crying.

"Desperate times call for desperate measures, sweetie."
She pointed to the phone lines, and I followed her gaze. Not
a single line was lit up. "Look at that. They've all switched
to another station. Cyrus is going to have a conniption, that's
for sure."

"I know things look bad, Vera Mae, but I'm really not
comfortable with the idea of calling in Chantel." I tried to
put a little backbone in my voice, but it was hard. Deep down,
I knew that Vera Mae was right.

"You're not *comfortable* with that?" Vera Mae's shrill
tone reminded me of the time I dropped a fork into the gar-
bage disposal while it was running. "Did I hear you cor-
rectly? You're telling me you're not *comfortable*?"

I probably should explain that Vera Mae goes ballistic
when I slip into what she calls "shrink speak." And the word
"comfortable" nearly always sends her round the bend. ("How
do you feel about that?" is another dangerous thing to say
around her.) It was time for a quick backpedal, but Kevin
was already racing into the studio, and I could hear the clip-
clop of Chantel's Birkenstocks in the corridor.

She sounded like an eager Clydesdale heading back to
the barn. My barn.

"We're not talking about comfortable," Vera Mae said, her hands on her hips. "We're talking about life and death."

"We are?" *Life and death?* I wondered where she was going with this.

Vera Mae nodded, her towering beehive slipping slightly. "We're talking *ratings*, Maggie. Ratings! And ratings trump feeling comfortable any day, in my book. I don't need a PhD in psychology to figure that one out, now, do I?" She paused, drawing in a deep breath. She leaned closed to me. "At this very moment, we're running neck and neck with *Bob Figgs and the Swine Report.* Do you want Billie Bob to jump ahead of us?"

Bob Figgs and his pigs. He'd dropped the Billie from his on-air name because he wanted to sound more professional.

Vera Mae knew my Achilles' heel, and I had to admit she had a good point.

"Maggie, it's your decision. Shall I bring Chantel into the studio or not?" She gave me a long, meaningful look, like an actor in a soap opera. My breath caught in my throat, and I blinked as her eyes drilled into mine.

I was in the throes of an existential dilemma. What to do? Stand for my principles, or cave? I blew out a long breath. Caving can be a good thing, I told myself. (Rationalization is also a good thing. Freud said it's a classic defense mechanism.)

"You win. Bring her in," I said weakly. I leaned back in my chair, limp with defeat. If Chantel could save the day and boost the ratings, then I'd just have to deal with it. The thought of Bob Figgs and his Swine Report had taken the fight right out of me.

Chapter 16

Okay, true confession time. It's galling to admit this, but Chantel knows her stuff. Even though she could win a lifetime achievement award for being annoying, the woman seems to be a walking Google, a font of information on arcane subjects.

Maybe she'd been reading up on time capsules because she knew we were doing a series of promos? Or maybe time capsules were one of her pet interests? An odd choice, but anything was possible. Or maybe she was just a quick study.

In any case, she "took the ball and ran with it," as Big Jim Wilcox, our sports announcer, is fond of saying. Not only did she run with it, but she scored a virtual touchdown. She jumped into the fray, leaving poor Professor Grossman out of the game and sulking on the sidelines.

Bernard Grossman, by the way, wasn't quite the mannerly gentleman I'd thought him to be. He wasn't at all gracious in defeat. "Who took my briefcase, my books, my notes?" he bellowed, returning to the studio and pounding his fist on the console. "I left them right here!"

Vera Mae opened her mike with a *tsk-tsk* expression on her face. "Sit down, Professor. We can worry about that later. Trust me. They're tucked away someplace safe. A man with all your education and fancy degrees shouldn't need all that stuff anyway. You should have all that information stored up here." Vera Mae tapped her head and flashed a fake smile at him.

"This is outrageous!" Professor Grossman opened his mouth and shut it abruptly, suddenly noticing Chantel, who was sliding into the chair right next to mine. "What are you doing? That's my chair!"

"Oh, for heaven's sake, take the other one!" Chantel hissed. It was true. We'd played a little musical chairs number on him. Professor Grossman's chair was pushed farther down the line, like a second-rate guest on a late-night talk show. He had a set of headphones in front of him, but the mike was clearly angled toward Chantel. He stared at the microphone for a few seconds, and I could almost see the wheels churning in his mind, his mouth turned downward into a scowl.

I think he realized he was benched for the rest of the game.

"What have you covered so far?" Chantel asked. She was all business, the consummate professional. She was wearing another muumuu creation, a pale yellow cotton plastered with pink hibiscus blossoms. Her gaze briefly met mine, then flicked away again to the phone lines. "Looks like the lines are dead. It must not be a hot topic," she added with a snide smile at Professor Grossman.

"We've just started taking calls on time capsules," I said, trying to marshal my thoughts. "The callers seem interested in hearing about time capsules from the past, what happened when they were opened, what they contained, that sort of thing." I would have liked to add that Professor Grossman had run that topic into the ground with his incredibly boring answers, but I figured Chantel could guess that from the dead phone lines.

"There are loads of fun stories about time capsules," she said confidently. "The kind of thing your listeners will really eat up."

"Fun stories?" Professor Grossman groused. "I thought this was going to be a scholarly exploration of the topic."

You did? I longed to ask.

"Live in ten!" Vera Mae hollered. She put her headphones on and began twirling the dials, her brows knitting together in concentration.

"We could run a contest right now," Chantel suggested. "We can give away copies of my book as prizes. That would bring some calls in right away."

"A contest? Well, I don't know . . ."

"A contest? Love it. It's a great idea," Vera Mae cut in. "Live in five!" she yelled before I could object. Then she pointed to me and we were live once again.

I opened the show, mentioned that we had a new guest, and then abdicated my power, like a Latin American dictator. The board lit up the moment my listeners realized that Chantel was on the air, and the calls started flooding in, just as she'd predicted.

"So the thing to remember," Chantel was saying in her melodic voice a few minutes later, "is that the objects in a time capsule should reflect the spirit of the present. It's actually a rather Zen idea. It's all about being in the moment and being aware of what is unique about today." She paused and looked at me, probably wondering why I was sitting there like a mute.

The fact is, I had nothing to say. She was handling everything well. Too well.

"Can anyone tell me what's the largest item ever found in a time capsule? We're offering a free copy of *I Talk to Dead People* to whoever can answer this question. C'mon, guys, you know you want to read my book. Why not get it for free? I'll even autograph it," she wheedled.

Like magic, the board lit up. Chantel couldn't resist tossing me an "I told you so" look.

"Cindy from Hialeah thinks she knows the answer," Vera Mae said from the control room. "Line four."

"Is it a horse?" a raspy voice asked. "I thought I read somewhere that a person buried a horse in a time capsule."

"Well, if they did, it's news to me," Chantel said smoothly. "Maybe you're thinking of that woman in Wyoming who asked to be buried with her horse. The horse died three years after she did, and I think they had adjoining graves." She paused. "But let's get back to the time capsule. Here's a hint: I'm thinking of four wheels and bucket seats. Does that help?"

A car? Vera Mae mouthed from the control room. Chantel nodded. Okay, it was a car. I had no idea, but apparently my listeners did, because all the lines lit up like fireworks. "Take line one. It's Leslie from Fort Lauderdale," Vera Mae said.

"I think I know the answer! I know it! I know it! Oh, my God, I think I'm going to faint!" Leslie was so excited she was practically hyperventilating as her voice raced over the line and spiraled into a high-pitched squeak.

"Slow down, Leslie," Chantel said good-naturedly. "We're not going anywhere. Now, take a deep breath and give it your best shot."

"Okay," she gulped, "I'll try." A long pause, a noisy breath, and then, "It was a car. It was a brand-new Chevy Vega! Some guy in Nebraska put it in a vault and then buried and sealed it. That was back in 1975, and he buried it in front of his furniture store. Don't ask me why—who knows why people do what they do!" Leslie gave a nervous laugh, and I realized that she sounded like someone on the edge of hysteria. You'd think she was competing for a trip to Puerto Vallarta, not a copy of Chantel's new book.

Chantel raised her carefully plucked eyebrows. "You are absolutely right, Leslie. I'm impressed. So tell me, how did you come up with that so fast?"

"My son's writing a term paper on time capsules," Leslie panted. "I was helping him with it last night, and it's sitting right here on the kitchen table in front of me."

"Nice work," Chantel said.

"Did I win?"

"Yes, you certainly did. If you'll just call back the main number and leave your address with the receptionist, I'll make sure that an autographed copy gets to you."

"Oh, thank you. Thank you! I am so excited. I've never won anything in my whole life."

"Well, now you have, my dear." Chantel glanced at me, her lips twitching in amusement as she gave a tiny eye roll.

For a moment, I almost felt myself liking her. After all, we were partners in this crazy business.

She leaned into the mike, and her tone turned brisk. "Now, let's get back to some other questions, shall we?"

In the next half hour, Chantel asked the audience what Nicolas Cage movie featured time travel (*Knowing*), and the lucky listener won a copy of her book. The phones lines were jammed. I could see Vera Mae frantically pushing buttons, putting a few callers on hold, and generally trying to manage the chaos.

Chantel asked whether anyone knew about the location of the time capsule that was buried for the 1970 World's Fair. As soon as the words were out of her mouth, someone called in with the right answer (Osaka).

How do people know this stuff? Either all my callers are geniuses or they're quick with Google.

"What's the best way to make sure someone will actually be able to find the time capsule?"

Hmm, I'd never thought of that angle. From the look on Professor Grossman's face, he was drawing a blank as well. An excited caller from Miami had the right answer "That's easy. Just write down the GPS coordinates."

When the show was over, Professor Grossman beat a hasty departure out of the studio. Kevin had returned his books and notes to him at the last break and had been rewarded with a stony stare.

"Well, that's a wrap," Vera Mae said, taking off her headphones. "Nice work," she said to us. I nodded, feeling more than a little embarrassed. It was obvious that Chantel had saved the day, and I still was baffled by the depth of her knowledge. Maybe she wasn't as superficial as I'd thought.

Another thought occurred to me. It was odd that Chantel knew so much about time capsules and she had showed up in time just for our big time capsule unveiling. Coincidence? Or something sinister?

Cyrus bounded into the break room a few minutes later as I was pouring coffee for Chantel and Vera Mae. He was rubbing his hands together, his jowly face red with excitement. "Terrific job, everyone! Now, this is the kind of show we should be doing every day. Vera Mae, make a note of that."

"Oh, no need to write it down. I'll just keep it up here in my steel-trap mind," Vera Mae said drily. She tapped her temple with her index finger.

Cyrus sat down and reached for a doughnut with a sheepish grin. "I was going to start Atkins today, but I think this calls for a celebration." He wolfed down a jelly doughnut in three bites before reaching for a glazed bear claw. "So how many calls did we get today? Was anybody keeping track?"

I shook my head, and Vera Mae stepped in. "More calls than I could keep up with, Cyrus. The lines were pretty much jammed after the first commercial break, and they stayed that way for the rest of the show."

She flashed me an apologetic look, and I shrugged. Ratings are ratings; this was no time for hurt feelings. My name is on the show, so spectacular ratings make me look good, right? (Freud would say this was rationalizing, but I wasn't in the mood for psychoanalytic ramblings at the moment.)

"I knew it!" He reached over and gave Vera Mae a triumphant fist bump. "Wait till we get the ratings at the end of the month. We're going to top every station around—I can't wait." He was looking longingly at a lemon-filled doughnut when Vera Mae and I stood up, ready to make our way back to our offices.

When he realized we were leaving, Cyrus suddenly scooted his chair close to Chantel, oozing charm. "Can you stay and talk for a minute? There's something I want to run by you." He let his hand rest lightly on her wrist, and she smiled at him.

I took a good look at his face and nearly giggled. I don't think he had the slightest idea that he had a big smudge of confectioners' sugar right smack on the middle of his nose. He leaned close, locking eyes with her like he thought he was Johnny Depp.

Vera Mae nudged me at the doorway. I lingered for a second, just long enough to hear Chantel purr, "Of course I can stay and talk with you, Cyrus. I always like to hear good news."

Good news? How did she know it would be good news? Oh, yeah, she's psychic. Silly me.

Chapter 17

I did a few errands after work, picked up some veggie stir-fry at Johnny Chan's for dinner, and pulled up in front of the town house around six thirty. I was surprised to see an elderly Ford Focus with a bad paint job parked outside, right next to a flowering hibiscus bush. It had a WYME parking tag on the rear bumper. *Irina?*

Baffled, I let myself in the front hallway as the mellow sounds of Jimmy Buffett drifted out to greet me. Jimmy was singing about cheeseburgers and the joys of paradise. This is an ongoing debate here in south Florida: the constant pull between developers and local preservationists. The builders argue that their projects bring money and jobs to the area, but the locals are protective of their town and prefer that things stay pretty much as they always have been. As a newcomer, I'm somewhere in the middle. I can understand the developers' point of view, but I was drawn to Cypress Grove because of its rustic charm, and I'd hate to see that disappear.

If you took a picture of Cypress Grove today and compared it to postcards from the sixties, the only difference would be the cars. The storefronts, the stately palms, the concrete pots filled with bougainvillea and vinca, are just the same as they were fifty years ago.

I stopped for a moment as a sudden thought swirled around my brain and then surfaced like a message in a Magic 8-Ball. Mark Sanderson was a developer, and his towering condo project would change the character of downtown Cypress Grove forever. The concrete building would clash with the Mayberry charm of the downtown area, and Cypress Grove would end up looking just like any other Florida city.

The tinkle of glasses and Mom's throaty laughter brought me back to the moment, and I tossed my car keys on the hall table. Music and drinks? Were we having a party?

"Oh, here you are, darling! Look who stopped by, and look who she brought with her," Mom added archly. Yep, it was Irina. With that English teacher. I scrambled to remember his name. Simon something. Simon Brent.

"Irina," I said, managing a little smile, "what brings you here?"

"Well, we really shouldn't have intruded," Simon interjected smoothly, "but Irina and I were going out to dinner, and she insisted on bringing you this fruit basket. Someone sent it to the station for you."

Pugsley was dancing around my feet, and I scooped him up for a quick hug before examining the ginormous fruit basket that was sitting on the coffee table. He immediately curled in next to me and licked my chin. I made a note to buy some doggie breath mints for him.

"A fruit basket?" After today, I doubted I had any fans left. This was a fancy one with all my favorites: ripe mangoes and jicama packed in tightly with star fruit and kiwi. I could see a box of Godiva chocolate peeking out at the top. A very generous gift. I looked at the note. It said, *Thanks so much, Candace.*

"Is from Candace Somerset," Irina explained. "It came in

about half an hour ago for you. She called first to get address. She wants to thank you so much for taking care of the cat Mr. Big."

"It was nice of you to bring it over, but you certainly didn't have to," I told her. "I could have brought it home with me tomorrow." I put Pugsley down on the floor, and he wound himself around my legs, his own subtle way of telling me that I wasn't giving him enough quality time.

"Oh, no, I had to save it for you," she said, her blond head bobbing up and down. "There would be nothing left of it by tomorrow. Lots of people at the front desk when it came in. Big Jim read the note to us," she said, *tsk-tsk*ing disapproval. "He was giving it the ear, you know."

"The eye," Simon said. "You mean he was giving it the eye." Funny, he was smiling, but I thought I heard a note of irritation in his voice.

Just for a microsecond, I felt a flash of suspicion. Wouldn't an ESL teacher be used to these sorts of mistakes? I felt a telltale prickly feeling on the back of my neck. There was something about this guy that wasn't quite right. Nothing I could put my finger on, but I knew it was there. There was something a little too slick about him, from his puppylike enthusiasm to his penetrating stare.

"Yes," Irina agreed with a giggle. "I am meaning the eye. You are so right, as usual," she said, leaning into him a little. "Is a good thing I bring it here to you, Maggie. Big Jim would have eaten the whole thing, and the night staff would have helped him." She made a little dismissive motion with her hands. "They are pigs. Pigs at the trout."

"Trough," Simon corrected her. "Pigs at the trough. A trout is a fish." This time I caught a distinct note of exasperation. I wished I had Cal Lightman from *Lie to Me* on speed dial; he'd know whether Simon Brent was telling the truth.

"Yes, trough. Anyway, you know how the radio staff loves the free food. Nothing is safe there." She turned to Simon, her eyes wide with amusement. "One time they are eating the dog food. No joke. Remember the doggie yummies, Maggie?"

"Yes, I do," I said, reaching down to pat Pugsley's head and nudge him toward his Abercrombie & Fitch plaid doggie bed. "That was actually pretty funny." Lark poured me a glass of iced tea, and I took a long swallow. "A client sent me some gourmet doggie treats from Switzerland for Pugsley. The writing on the bag was in French. I left them on my desk, and the next day they were gone. Vanished."

"The evening staff *ate* them," Irina explained when Simon still looked puzzled. "I am telling you the truth. Night staff is like bottomless pit. Any food they see, they suck it up like a vacuum cleaner. Like this, whoosh!" Irina did a passable imitation of a Hoover, and Lark grinned.

"Speaking of food, is that from Johnny Chan's?" Mom asked, eyeing my takeout bag.

"Veggie stir-fry. And some egg rolls."

"Oh, we should go. You are planning the meal," Irina said, moving to the door. "I didn't mean to interrupt you. I just wanted you to have the fruit."

"Wait a minute," Lola spoke up. "Why don't you join us for dinner? I'm sure there's plenty."

"Is trouble for you, I think." Irina cast a hopeful smile my way, and I could see she wanted to stay. A delicious aroma was wafting out of the Johnny Chan's take-out bag, and she licked her lips.

"It's no trouble," I assured her. "I bought plenty of stir-fry, and Lark always makes her own wild rice to go with it. We can combine it with the white rice from Johnny Chan's, so there'll be more than enough to go around. The portions are huge."

"Done!" Irina clapped her hands together and beamed a worshipful smile at her ESL instructor.

Simon was an entertaining dinner guest, and he knew exactly how to wrap Lola around his finger. To my amazement, he'd actually seen some of her movies, and she loved talking about "the old days" in Hollywood with him. Of course, she never makes them sound too far in the past, because that would date her.

Lola likes to remain au courant, as she says, and can talk knowledgeably about all the young stars from Robert Pattinson to Lauren Conrad. So unless you had access to her birth certificate, you'd never know her biological age.

"Tell me how you landed the part in *Night Vision*," Simon asked. "I bet that was really something. Wasn't that movie shot somewhere in North Africa?"

"Well, the principals were"—she quickly corrected herself— "I mean, some of the scenes were shot there." A nice save. If she didn't include herself with the principal actors, Simon would realize that she'd had a very minor role in the film.

I happened to know that her character didn't even have a name. Lola played a part that was described in the cast list as "Airline Reservations Clerk." It was a step above an extra because she did have a line or two, but nothing to brag about. Knowing Lola, she'd figure out a way to put a good spin on it.

"As it happened, my scenes were shot right in Hollywood on a sound stage." She paused, lost in thought. "They also did some exterior shots in California. You know that stretch of the Pacific Coast Highway that they used in the opening shots of *M*A*S*H*? They did a few shots out there."

"That's a great stretch of highway," Simon said. "Who did you play? I only remember a few people from that film."

"My character's name was . . . Karen," she said quickly.

"A small part, more of a character role, I'd say." *Karen? How about Ms. No-Name Ticket Agent.* Lola has a vivid imagination. She smiled and quickly changed the topic. "But no more ramblings about Hollywood. Tell me what it's like being a language instructor. It must be fascinating."

Lola rested her chin on her hand and gave Simon her best sultry stare. She was at full throttle, looking deeply into his eyes and using her smoky Kathleen Turner voice. She's a born flirt. A few days ago, I caught her telling a portly middle-aged guy at Starbucks that she'd always been fascinated by life insurance and how she'd love it if he could explain the difference between whole life and term insurance to her. *Huh?* I couldn't believe the guy fell for it, but he did and promptly asked Lola to lunch (she declined).

When I asked her later why she'd been practically throwing herself at him, she clued me in. "Oh, so embarrassing! He's a dead ringer for an indie film producer I worked for a long time ago. By the time I realized my mistake, he was smitten with me. What can I say?" She made a little moue of disgust. "So I had to pretend to be intrigued by life insurance before I could make my escape."

After dinner, we all sat around the kitchen table sharing a lime cheesecake (one of Lark's specialties, made with soy cheese) and coffee. Simon seemed particularly interested in hearing more about Chantel, and my antennae were up. I remembered that he had asked to meet her the other day at the studio. Was it possible that he was a fan?

"Are you interested in the occult?" I smiled to show him the question wasn't entirely serious.

Simon leaned back in his chair and nodded when Lark offered him another slice of cheesecake. "Well, if you mean demons and vampires, no," he said affably. "But I think there's something out there, you know? Chantel's predictions can't all be lucky guesses. So I guess I'd say I'm neutral on the whole idea of the paranormal. I'd like to find out more information before I make up my mind. I guess you could say I'm open to the idea."

I was tempted to tell him that the *National Enquirer* had run a piece detailing Chantel's predictions and the outcomes. She was accurate less than thirty percent of the time. I'd probably have the same track record, if I bothered making predictions. But I decided to keep my snarky thoughts to myself. After all, I was still reeling from Chantel's performance on my show today; it would be mean-spirited to criticize her. And worse, it would make me look like sour grapes. Never an attractive quality, and as a shrink I should know better.

"Chantel seems to have popped up out of nowhere," Simon said idly. "I wonder what her background is." He paused. "Does anyone know if that's even her real name?"

"Didn't she give you a copy of her press kit? She passes them out like candy."

Simon laughed. "Yes, as a matter of fact, she did. But I don't think you can really tell much from a press kit, do you? Some publicist has been paid to gloss over the real facts and give a wildly flattering picture of the celebrity."

"Interesting, I've never thought of it that way," Lark said. Lark always sees the good in everyone and never believes that someone might have an ulterior motive or a hidden agenda. We're polar opposites. I'm the cynic, always ready to see the worst in human nature. You'd be surprised how many times I've been right. As Vera Mae says, "I always go by first impressions. It saves a whole lot of time."

"You could do the Google on her," Irina said, trying to be helpful.

"That's a good idea," Simon said politely.

I could tell his heart wasn't in it, and I had the sneaking suspicion that he'd already tried it. I knew, of course, from my reporter friend Nick Harrison, that Chantel's real name was Carla Krasinski, but I had no intention of sharing that information with Simon. I wondered why an English-language instructor was so interested in Chantel. I couldn't imagine him as one of her devoted followers, and he was asking entirely too many questions. What was really going on behind that handsome *GQ* exterior?

"Maggie, does Chantel make you think of someone else?" Irina said suddenly. She snapped her fingers. " 'Remind'— that's the word I mean. Does she remind you of someone?"

"No, I don't think so. Do you mean a movie star, or someone like that? Who does she remind you of?"

"No, it is not me who says that. It is Vera Mae. She says it twice. That Chantel reminds her of someone, but she can't put her hand on it."

"Can't put her *finger* on it," I said automatically.

"Do you mean another celebrity?" Simon asked excitedly. "Or someone else? Maybe someone Vera Mae ran into in broadcasting?" His whole face lit up, blue eyes glittering, as eager as Pugsley with a new chew toy.

"It's certainly possible."

"Then that makes it even stranger," Simon said, stirring his coffee. "She's quite the mystery woman, isn't she? Chantel told me she'd never been to Cypress Grove before."

"Chantel told you that?" I remembered how Simon had insisted on talking to her that day Irina was giving him a tour of the studio.

Simon flushed. "We were chatting." He spread his hands on the table and took a breath. "I was just making conversation. I thought I might be able to persuade her to come to my class to give a presentation. I figured my students would really enjoy it." He glanced down and away as he said this, and a little muscle jumped in his jaw. A sure sign he was lying, as any fan of *Lie to Me* would tell you. In any case, it was one of the lamest answers I had ever heard.

"What did she say about speaking to your class?" I asked, putting him on the spot. I was pushing a little too hard, to the point of rudeness, but I didn't care. I wanted to get a handle on this guy.

He colored slightly. "Well, she said she'd love to, but she was terribly busy at the moment. You know, the séances, the talk show, and of course working on the book."

"Of course," I said with more than a touch of irony. "After all, according to Chantel, that's the reason she came here in the first place. For a little peace and quiet to work on her book."

"I'm surprised to hear it, because I never thought of Cypress Grove as a writer's retreat," Lola said, sipping her coffee. "Lots of writers live in Miami and South Beach. Loads of color and excitement, always something going on." She sounded a little wistful. "I'm more of a 'bright lights, big city' girl myself." She grinned at Simon, probably hoping to switch the subject back to herself, but he toyed with his spoon and didn't answer.

"It does seem like an odd choice," he said finally. "But who knows what drives the artistic temperament. Maybe this is the ideal spot for her to work on her memoirs."

"So many sad things have happened since Chantel arrived in town," Lark said slowly. "Two people have been murdered. I can hardly believe it." She must have caught my look, because she added, "Not that she's responsible. I just meant it's a strange coincidence." I was about to remind her about

Freud's comment that "there are no coincidences," when she let out a little sigh. "Maybe it's bad karma. In any case, it's very sad."

"Oh, yes, quite sad," Simon agreed. His tone was perfunctory, and I found it hard to believe he actually cared one way or the other about Althea and Mildred. After all, he was new in town himself, and the women were just strangers to him.

We spent another few minutes talking about the murders and the fact that the Cypress Grove PD seemed to have no leads. Irina reminded me that Althea's funeral was tomorrow morning, and I felt my spirits sink even further. There wouldn't be a funeral service for Mildred; her relatives were planning to hold a wake and burial out of state. I made a mental note to make a donation to the town library in Mildred's name.

To my surprise, Simon mentioned that he planned on attending Althea's funeral. Odd, right? Why would you go to the funeral of someone you've never met? I remember Rafe telling me that sometimes killers like to show up at the funerals of their victims, but I found it hard to imagine Simon Brent as a murderer. On that note, Simon and Irina left, and after taking Pugsley for a quick walk, I turned in.

Chapter 18

I tossed and turned for at least an hour, my brain whirring with possibilities. My thoughts were muddled; everything was unresolved. I felt "stuck," as the shrinks would say, my mind running in an endless loop, like a gerbil on a treadmill.

I finally switched on the light, grabbed a legal pad and a ballpoint pen, and decided to go over everything in detail. Writing always helps me focus my thoughts, separating what I know as cold, hard fact from my hunches or intuitions. Pugsley gave an annoyed little yip when the light hit his face, but I patted him and he went right back to his doggie dreams.

What I knew for certain was very little. Two elderly women had been murdered within the same week, both longtime residents of Cypress Grove. What did they have in common? Althea was murdered where she lived and worked; Mildred was murdered where she worked. In both cases, the murder weapon was left at the scene.

After that, everything gets murky, and I found myself drifting into the realm of pure conjecture. Was it significant that the weapons were left with the victims? Possibly. It might have meant that both murders were crimes of opportunity and not planned. If they were impulsive acts, did that mean that anger or revenge was the motive? Or was it a home invasion gone wrong? That might have been a possibility in Althea's case, but I couldn't imagine anyone wanting to steal anything from the Cypress Grove Library, where Mildred was murdered.

Both the library and the historical society were registered as historic buildings in Cypress Grove, but I didn't see how that was relevant.

On to another question. How were the victims related? Two points of similarity jumped out at me. The victims knew each other, and they both knew a lot about Cypress Grove. Interesting, but what did it mean? What could I do with that information? Did that suggest that one killer had committed both crimes? Did the physical evidence collected by the CSIs point to one killer or two? I wrote the names "Althea" and "Mildred" and drew lines between them, noting all the connections.

When I worked as a forensic psychologist for the DA's office back in New York, my boss always told me that a single fact didn't mean much. You had to see the big picture and figure out where that fact fits in. He always taught me to think of a case as a jigsaw puzzle and to look at a fact as a puzzle piece. Maybe the piece fit right in the center of the puzzle, or maybe it was a bit of the background, something at the edges of the puzzle. You never knew how important a single piece might be, until you had the whole puzzle assembled.

A nice analogy, but I knew I didn't have all the pieces for this one. From the looks of things, neither did the Cypress Grove PD. Radio silence from Rafe, and even Nick couldn't get them to cough up any new leads.

I kept going back to the notion of one murderer or two.

Either Rafe was keeping quiet about any trace evidence, or the Cypress Grove PD hadn't come up with anything. I knew Nick was desperately trying to get some information for his *Gazette* articles and coming up dry. He'd left a message on my machine earlier that day, asking whether I'd heard anything new about the case. He promised he wouldn't quote me and would use me as "deep background."

I left a message saying I was as much in the dark as he was and that I hoped we could touch base at Althea's funeral the next day.

Look for means, motive, and opportunity. Rafe always tells me that's the hallmark of any successful murder investigation. I wondered whether he was drawing as much of a blank as I was. Who would want to murder Althea and Mildred? The motive in Althea's case might have been robbery, but Rafe had told me that she'd been wearing an expensive antique watch when her body was found. If robbery was the motive, why had the killer left it? How could I explain that?

And he said that a ring had been pulled off her finger, but it was a cheap costume piece, with no monetary value. Of course, it was possible the murderer didn't realize the vintage watch was valuable, and maybe he figured the ring was a real gemstone. So was he a thief who didn't have a good eye for jewelry? That was certainly a possibility.

My gut feeling told me that Althea or Mildred (or both) had some information that someone wanted suppressed. Something that would be devastating if it came to light. But what? Mildred had hinted on my show that there would be some big surprises when the time capsule was unearthed. She seemed to be suggesting that she had special knowledge no one else had.

During her séance, Chantel had hinted that there was evil afoot in Cypress Grove. So, there was innuendo, but nothing firm to grab on to. That reminded me of another point of similarity. Both Althea and Mildred had been present at the séance. I drew a third line between the two names. So far this was all circumstantial, tenuous connections that might not be significant.

I ran down the list of suspects, feeling more frustrated by the moment. Chantel Carrington was the first name that leapt into my mind. Why did I think of her as a suspect? I wrote down everything I knew about her. She was here in town under an alias, her background was murky, and somehow she'd made a name for herself in the motivational field.

If Nick had uncovered her real name and her origins, then surely it was just a matter of time before TMZ, Gawker, and all the big entertainment sites blared out the truth. This was the kind of thing you couldn't keep a secret for long. Could Mildred or Althea have suspected who she really was, or maybe they uncovered some dark secret from her past? Did they threaten to reveal it? I thought of Althea and Mildred. I couldn't picture either one of them as a blackmailer.

Irina said that Vera Mae told her Chantel reminded her of someone. Did she mean a celebrity? Or someone close to home? Could Chantel have relatives living in the area? Maybe there was a family resemblance that Vera Mae picked up on? It was a possibility, but I had no idea how to investigate it further. My best hope was to find someone else who'd lived here a long time and ask them whether they thought Chantel looked familiar.

Why had Chantel come to Cypress Grove? Yes, I knew the standard answer, but I didn't buy it. My gut instinct told me she would never choose Cypress Grove as a place to kick back and pound out her memoirs. She'd lived all over the country, and I found it very hard to believe that she'd chosen our little town as a retreat.

Unless she had some big business deal planned in Miami? Maybe some media opportunity that Cyrus never suspected? What if she wanted to put together a kick-ass demo tape at WYME and then head for one of the big stations in Miami? That was certainly a possibility, but I didn't see how could it be connected with the two murders.

I put a star and a question mark next to her name. Chantel was still in the running, even though I was drawing a blank as to her motive.

I was more convinced than ever than Simon Brent, Irina's English teacher, had something up his sleeve. And why was he so interested in Chantel? It seemed odd that he turned up in town at the same time Chantel did, and that he was so determined to meet her and talk with her. *Note to self: ask Nick to find out more about Simon Brent.*

Trevor McNamara, the guest at the Seabreeze Inn, certainly aroused my suspicions with his bogus story about scouting out vacation properties in Cypress Grove. At least, I think it was bogus. A few calls to the chamber of commerce would probably tell me what I needed to know. I'd have to ask Ted Rollins, the innkeeper, if Trevor was still in town.

And Mark Sanderson. Was he reconsidering his choice of Cypress Grove for his towering condo project? The town seemed like an odd match for his real estate venture. Could he bail out? But it was too late—the deal was already in the works, right?

Surely they'd done some feasibility studies. A high-rise condo building just didn't fit in with the small-town feel of the place. I wasn't at all sure people would be willing to live in his condos and commute to metropolitan areas, as he'd suggested.

I could probably find out more about Mark Sanderson from Cyrus. Offhand, I couldn't imagine any reason Mark

Sanderson would have for killing either Althea or Mildred. He'd turned up in town around the same time they were murdered, and that hardly was enough to make him a viable suspect.

Candace Somerset stood to inherit a small fortune from her dead sister's estate. She didn't seem like a killer to me, but money can make people do strange things. Following the money is always a good idea when you're looking into murder. I'd learned that back in my days doing forensic psychology in Manhattan. I added her to the list as well.

There was a good turnout for Althea Somerset's funeral the next morning. It was cool and drizzly as Vera Mae and I drove west on Porter Street to the edge of town. Althea had left instructions with her attorney, opting for a short religious service graveside followed by burial at the old Cypress Grove Cemetery.

The minister, Reverend Appleton, kept his remarks brief, and the service took less than half an hour. The minister mentioned that Althea was "taken from us suddenly" and mouthed a few platitudes about the brevity of life, but apart from that, he made no mention of the murder.

Not that I'd expected him to, but it must have been in everyone's thoughts. I didn't do a head count, but it looked like about seventy-five people were huddled under umbrellas, a few sniffling into handkerchiefs. It was a somber scene, and I was eager to pay my respects and get away from the cemetery.

Nick stood next to me, taking notes. I glanced over and saw him listing all the town dignitaries who were in attendance: the mayor, the leaders of the town council, and of course, the board of directors of the historical society. Candace Somerset, Althea's sister, thanked everyone for coming and invited the entire group back to the historical society for a light repast.

I turned questioningly to Nick. *A light repast?* Those words must have been music to his ears. Like every reporter I've ever known, Nick is not one to pass up free food. Ever. And he seems to be perpetually hungry. "Are you heading over to the society for the reception?"

"You bet. I'm on it," he said, snapping his notebook closed. "I might get a couple of quick quotes, you know, something to fill out the article," he added. "Catch you later."

Rafe caught up with me as I was walking back to my car. He came up silently behind me, pantherlike, and touched my shoulder. "Maggie," he said. Only Rafe could manage to make one word sound as sexy as hell.

His lips twitched when I gave a little startled noise and whirled around to face him.

"I didn't know you were here," I said breathlessly. My heart tripped into a familiar double-time beat, and I told it to calm down.

"I just came in a couple of minutes ago with Brown." He nodded toward a black-and-white parked on the shoulder of the winding road. Officer Duane Brown was standing next to it, his arms crossed in front of him like he was posing as a rookie state trooper for a Don't Drink and Drive billboard. He looked serious, but very young, and the freckles didn't help.

"So," Rafe said, his eyes roaming over my face, "what have you been up to? Anything you want to tell me?" We paused for a moment, standing at the edge of the cemetery, and he ducked under my umbrella. He closed his hand over mine for a moment to steady it, and my heartbeat kicked up another notch at his touch.

Anything I want to tell him? This was a loaded question. Rafe and I have a sort of unspoken agreement on my detective work. He pretends to believe that what I do is sheer nonsense, absolute psychobabble with no scientific basis and no evidence-based research to back it up. *Ooo-kay.* I let him think that way, because it's silly to argue. I know how valuable good police work is, but I think psychology has something to offer as well.

I also know that this is an argument I'm never going to win.

"I'm still in the dark," I admitted. I suddenly remembered what he'd said about the crime scene at Althea's looking staged. "Anything new on your end of things?"

"Nothing."

"What about the crime scene? You said you thought maybe it was staged to look like a home invasion. Do you still feel that way?"

He smiled. "That was just a hunch, a gut feeling. I don't have any hard evidence that it was staged to look that way, except that no valuables were taken. That could be significant, or maybe he was interrupted and had to flee the scene." He rubbed his chin with his hand, and I noticed he had dark circles under his eyes. Apparently the double murder investigation was taking a toll on him. I caught myself wanting to touch my hand to his cheek, which was so unprofessional, I gave myself a mental head slap.

"So you still have no idea whether the two murders were connected?" That was obviously the place to start, as far as I was concerned.

"Nada." He shook his head. Either he really didn't have any information or he was a terrific actor. "Althea and Mildred were just taken"—he snapped his fingers—"like that. No trace evidence, and nothing as far as motive. Both crimes seem to have been unplanned."

He gave me a thoughtful look, his dark eyes flashing with

interest. "Unless you've discovered something?" I shook my head, but he moved a little closer, his eyes locked on mine. "You're not holding out on me, are you, Maggie? If you've found something, I need to hear about it. This is no time to play games."

"Play games?" *Ouch.* "I'm not playing games. I found out that Candace Somerset, Althea's sister, stands to inherit a small fortune. That's all I know." I felt a little flash of white-hot anger go through me. Rafe knows exactly how to push my buttons, and trivializing my profession is one of the best ways to do it. No matter how many times I tell myself not to get annoyed, I do.

"And that's a hard fact, as you would say. Not a psychological interpretation," I huffed. It's very hard to be angry with Rafe because he's so damn attractive, but I had to at least defend my profession.

"Oh, don't be so oversensitive, Maggie," he said, breaking into a grin. "It's just an expression. You shrinks are all alike, you know. It kills me the way you analyze everything to death." He broke away when we reached the edge of the grass, tossing a rakish smile over his shoulder. I watched him walking toward the squad car, his movements fluid, determined. Rafe is sure of himself, with an icy resolve that would bring a criminal to his knees.

Do I really analyze everything to death? Funny, but Vera Mae has told me the exact same thing. Many times.

Chapter 19

"I can't believe you're checking your BlackBerry at a funeral reception," I sniffed at Nick half an hour later. We were sitting in the front parlor of the historical society, and Nick had both thumbs on his BlackBerry, texting away. We'd found a quiet corner with two wingback chairs nosing up to a lovely Queen Anne coffee table facing the fireplace. Nick had stashed a towering plate of finger food on an end table, and amazingly, it was untouched. For once in his life, Nick was more interested in texting than eating.

I was intrigued, my antennae quivering. Something big must be up.

"You know, Nick, checking your messages all day long is looking a bit obsessive to me," I said. "I'm concerned about you. And I say that not only as a shrink, but as a friend—"

He frowned, annoyed, and held up a finger to silence me, never taking his eyes off the keys. I let out a noisy sigh, nibbled at a pimento cheese puff, and took a quick inventory of the guests. Most of the people from the graveside service were there, plus a few elderly women I didn't recognize. I pegged them as neighbors or friends of Althea's, women in their eighties who were probably too frail to make it to the cemetery on a rainy day. They were talking in hushed voices, looking sad and dejected as they exchanged hugs. I remembered again how much good Althea had done for the town and how much everyone had loved her.

Not *everyone*, I reminded myself. One person had killed her. Maybe someone in this very room.

I watched Candace, Althea's sister, as she flitted around the parlor. She was charming and hospitable, greeting each guest at the door with a warm welcome and then dashing off to make sure the platters were refilled with goodies. Candace looked very urban and quite sophisticated in her Armani linen suit and strappy Jimmy Choos. I had the feeling she paid more for her caramel highlights than I paid for my rent every month.

She looked out of place at the historical society. I wondered again about her relationship with Althea. As she'd said, it was "complicated." *Complicated?* What relationship isn't? That could mean anything, I mused.

"This is unbelievable," Nick said softly, yanking me back to the present. His eyes were still riveted on the BlackBerry. He shook his head as he glanced at the screen, then punched a button and slid it into his pocket.

"What is?" I waited while he grabbed a miniature crab cake and swallowed it whole like he was a seal at SeaWorld. Then he took a very long swig of iced tea while I drummed my fingernails on the table. He was about to reach for another crab cake when I grabbed his right hand. "Tell me," I demanded. "Now!" His eyes strayed to a tiny sausage biscuit just inches away, teetering on the edge of his plate. I increased the pressure on his fingers. "You can eat later."

"Ow," he said pulling away. "You've got a grip like steel. You're stronger than you look." He shot me a dark look and rubbed his wrist. "You must have been zeroing in on a pressure point."

"Krav Maga," I said, taking a deep breath. It was satisfying to know that all those practice sessions with a personal trainer in the Bronx had paid off. "Three years."

He raised his eyebrows. "Isn't that the martial arts training method they use in the Mossad?"

"Yes. And unless you want to find yourself pinned on the floor in a spectacular takedown in the next two seconds, you'd better tell me what you've found out. I know it's something big."

"It is big, or at least it could be. My source managed to dig up some intel on Chantel. It seems she might have been here before." He glanced over his shoulder as if he feared the flamboyant medium might materialize at any moment.

For a moment, I was puzzled. "She was here? *Here*, as in another lifetime?" I knew that Chantel believed in reincarnation, but I didn't think Nick did.

Nick snorted. "Hardly. I'm talking about *this* lifetime. I found someone at the high school who thinks she remembers her.

"So Chantel might have lived here when she was young?"

"Maybe. She would have been a teenager. But we don't know this yet, not for sure."

This was interesting idea, and my mind scrambled to make sense of it. "You sound like you believe it." I knew Nick had excellent sources, but this really seemed like a stretch. If Chantel had been born and raised in Cypress Grove, why was she keeping everyone in the dark? Unless, of course, she'd come back here for some dark, ulterior reason.

"That's what my source says. I'm surprised no one in town has picked up on it, though."

"Maybe someone did," I said, remembering Irina's comment. I watched as Nick devoured a shrimp toast, his brows knitted in concentration. "Vera Mae thought she recognized her." Maybe what I thought had been a chance comment was actually a bombshell.

"She thought she recognized her?" Nick reached into his pocket for his notebook. "From where? What name was she using?"

"I don't know. It wasn't that specific, just an offhand comment." I gave a little dismissive wave of my hand. "I figured Vera Mae meant Chantel reminded her of someone she'd seen on television or in the movies. You know, a celebrity. It never occurred to me that she meant a real person, living here in Cypress Grove." I made a mental note to ask Vera Mae for an explanation as soon as I got back to the studio.

Nick squinted at his notes and frowned. "This isn't much to go on, but I can try to dig a little deeper." He looked around the crowded parlor. "If Chantel really did live here before, wouldn't someone here recognize her? How much could she have changed over the years?"

I shrugged. "If Chantel is really in her mid-forties, it might have been thirty years ago. And we don't even have a name to go on. That Carla Krasinski name could have been an alias." *Just like Chantel Carrington is an alias,* I thought. Trying to get a handle on Chantel was like trying to pin Jell-O to a wall.

"So what's next?" Nick said, his words wrapped around a mouthful of flaky cheese biscuits. I was surprised to see that he'd already scarfed down half of the hors d'oeuvres on his plate. "I can ask my friend in L.A. to go deeper, but it might take a few days."

"A good turnout for poor Althea," an elderly woman murmured when I stood up to get another cup of tea. She looked like half the women in the room, probably mid-eighties, with tightly curled white hair and glasses.

"Did you know her well?"

"Oh, yes, my dear," she said, laying her hand on my arm for a moment. "I've always admired the way she kept this place going." She glanced around the room, taking in the old-timey furnishings and knickknacks. "She's kept it just the way it was when it was built. Quite an achievement."

"Yes, it was." A lightbulb went on over my head, and I thought about the Joshua Riggs painting. "You've visited here a lot, right? I mean, to the historical society?"

"Yes, of course," she replied, looking puzzled. "Dozens of times, why?"

"I need to ask you something." I guided her toward the front hall. "Take a good look around." She raised her eyebrows, and I said quickly, "I know this sounds silly, but just bear with me. Does anything look different to you?"

She peered at the heavy mahogany Parsons table, the porcelain umbrella stand, the dried-flower arrangement. "I don't think so," she said slowly. "Not much has changed in this front hall in fifty years. I told Althea she needed to thin out these paintings. It's hard to appreciate them when she has so much wall space covered. All the way from the floor to the ceiling." She allowed herself a small chuckle. "Althea wouldn't hear of it, though. She had her own way of doing things. Some people called her obstinate, but I think of it as being principled."

"Take your time," I pleaded. "Take a good look."

Then she spotted it. "Oh, yes, I see it now. It's this landscape." She pointed her finger at the painting that was hanging right above us. "That's what's different."

"Are you sure?"

"I'm positive. Althea had very definite taste in art. She loved watercolors and she was quite fond of landscapes, but not dark, dreary ones." She took a step closer. "Someone's switched the paintings, you see." She pointed to the Joshua Riggs. "This one used to be on the right of the pond scene. Now it's on the left."

Bingo. That was just what I'd thought.

"Are you sure?" I could hardly keep the excitement out of my voice.

"I certainly am." She wrinkled her nose in disgust. "This dreadful thing should be banished back to the basement."

"What do you know about this painting?" I said, pointing to the muddy landscape.

"Well, I'm surprised that Althea would move it. She liked everything in its place. Very persnickety. She talked about getting it reframed. I know that was on her to-do list." She paused. "Odd that she would move it, though." She took a step back and studied the wall. "Maybe she was trying to get a different feel with the arrangement. I don't think she succeeded, though. Now the whole collection looks unbalanced."

"Very odd." My mind was whirring with possibilities. "If she did have it reframed, where would she go? Someone local, or would she send it out?"

"Oh, there's only one place in town to go. Chris Hendricks on Water Street does all the framing for the historical society. He knew her taste. She liked simplicity, clean lines, nothing ornate. But I know she didn't get it reframed. This is the same dreadful frame as before." She hesitated, glancing over my shoulder. "Is there anything else you'd like to ask me?" She flashed an apologetic smile. "Because I see that my ride is waiting for me."

"You've answered all my questions. Thank you so much. You've been wonderful, very helpful. May I write down your name and phone number?"

"Here, take a card, my dear. I'm Lucille Whittier."

"Maggie Walsh." I scrambled for a card, but she stopped me.

"Oh, I know who you are, dear. I love your show. I listen to it every day." She gave a fluttery little wave and joined another woman in a pastel pantsuit who was moving toward the front door. "If you have any more questions, just call me. I'm home almost every day."

"Thanks. I'll do that."

I took a quick look around the dimly lit hall. It was dark and oppressive, and the massive furniture didn't help lighten the atmosphere. I glanced at the Parsons table. It looked like it needed a good dusting, and the lace doily on the top had a grayish tinge around the edges. Odd to think that someone might have crocheted it a hundred years ago. It moved slightly when I touched it, and some flakes of blue confetti inched out onto the dark wooden surface. Strange.

I thought about the conversation I'd just had. So Lucille Whittier was convinced that the painting had been moved to another spot on the cluttered wall? I felt that this could be the clue I'd been waiting for, but the trick was knowing what to do with it.

I wandered back to the wing chair to ponder my options when an overbleached blonde sidled up to me. She was mid-thirties with big hair and a great set of veneers and was wearing a mint green and hot pink Lily Pulitzer. She looked vaguely familiar, and I thought I might have met her before at a literacy fund-raiser at the public library.

"Maggie," she said, her voice tentative. She held out a hand with a flashy yellow diamond the size of a walnut. I half stood up to shake hands with her, and she immediately sat in the wing chair across from me. "Shalimar Hennessey. We met at that book event at the library, remember?"

I managed to smile. "Yes, of course." She treated me to a

blinding Hollywood smile, and as my synapses connected, I did a quick mental rundown her.

Social butterfly and ace tennis player. Rich, very rich. Bobby Hennessey's net worth was rumored to be the same as the GNP of a small Latin American country. Vera Mae had described her as one of the "ladies who lunch." Apparently, the biggest decision she has to make every day is whether she should play golf or tennis. Live-in help and a beach house in St. Thomas. (I stopped doing an inventory at this point. I was getting too depressed.)

The most notable thing about her (besides her bank account) was the fact that she was married to Bobby Hennessey, a big shot in all the town's civic groups. Bobby plays golf with Cyrus, our station manager, and I wondered whether Shalimar was going to hit me up for a donation. Bobby is on the board of a dozen different nonprofits. Or maybe she just wanted some publicity for her favorite charity?

From the looks of her expensive dress, shoes, and jewelry, her pet cause was probably herself.

"Were you a friend of Althea's?" she asked. I had the feeling she was only saying that as an icebreaker and was biding her time, waiting to get to the real reason for chatting with me. She was perched on the edge of the wingback chair, like a bird of paradise in her colorful dress.

"More of an acquaintance," I said. "She was very kind when I first moved here, helping me get to know the town and find my bearings." I smiled at the memory. Althea had brought over a homemade veggie casserole for dinner and a box of liver treats for Pugsley. Anyone who goes to that kind of trouble for a perfect stranger is a rare find, in my book.

"Oh, yes," Shalimar said quickly. "She was very kind. A lovely person."

I nodded, waiting. She paused, the way my patients used

to do when they were revving themselves up for a big revelation and wondering how to make the segue. She nibbled at
her lower lip for a moment, a small frown marring her finely
chiseled features.

She bit back a little sigh, and I stood up, ready to head
out. She noticed me reaching for my purse and blurted out,
"Actually, if you have a second, there was something else I
wanted to talk to you about."

I sat back down. "Sure, go ahead." I gave her an encouraging smile, and she flushed a little. She was definitely anxious or embarrassed about something, but what?

"I'm . . . um . . . I'm just fascinated by the time capsule
ads you're running at the station. And you've had some great
guests talking about the event. I caught your show with Professor Grossman. It was brilliant."

*Time capsules? She's fascinated by time capsules? And
she thinks Grossman is brilliant?* I was taken aback but kept
my expression neutral. "I'm glad you're enjoying them. The
time capsule shows have been a big hit at the station. We've
gotten a lot of calls from listeners, and there are some positive responses on the WYME message boards. It seems this
topic has really struck a chord with everyone."

She widened her hazel eyes a little, still focusing on my
face. It was a little unnerving, but she seemed to be waiting
for me to say more, so I went on. "I think it's a really popular subject right now, with all the talk about whether or not
the town should go in for expansion or preservation."

Shalimar blinked twice. "I don't quite follow you." She
was no Einstein, I decided. "Expansion? Preservation?"

I took a quick peek at my watch. I really needed to be
heading back to WYME to get ready for my afternoon show.
"Local development. I just meant that the time capsule repre-

sents what life was like in Cypress Grove half a century ago. Life was quieter and simpler back then. And if you read the editorials in the local paper, you know that a lot of folks would like things to stay that way."

"Really? I'd never thought of that angle. I think progress is good, but maybe some people are locked into the past." A long beat while she inspected her apricot, too-perfect-to-be-real fingernails. "So have you come up with any inside information about what's inside the time capsule? Did anyone think to keep a list of the contents when it was buried?"

I breathed out a little sigh. "I wish they had. We certainly haven't been able to locate one. It would be wonderful if we could find one somewhere. As you know, all the courthouse records and the newspaper files are gone from that time. Everything was destroyed in a fire. So it's pretty much guesswork, trying to imagine what's in there."

She nodded. "Yes, I heard. Tragic about the records," she added. "All that history down the drain." Another pause. "What's going to happen to the items in the time capsule? When it's opened, I mean."

"I have no idea. I suppose if there's anything of real value, it will be returned to the proper owner, or their family. And I guess the rest will be put on display, maybe here at the historical society."

"Sorry to interrupt. I left my BlackBerry here." Nick smiled and reached down to retrieve the BlackBerry from the end table.

"Nick Harrison, right?" Shalimar asked in a throaty voice. She stretched her arm straight out and extended her hand like she was Scarlett O'Hara and Nick was one of the Tarleton twins, coming to call on her.

"Er, yes," Nick said, looking surprised. He shoved the

BlackBerry in his pocket, ready to take off. He shook hands with her and then stood there, awkwardly shifting from one foot to the other.

"Shalimar Hennessey." She flashed him a high-beam smile, and her lips quivered like Pugsley's do when he sees a liver snack. "I just love your articles. They're the first thing I read in the *Gazette* every day."

"Well, um, thank you. That's good to hear." Nick shot me a "What's going on here?" look.

"Shalimar is quite the history buff, and we were just talking about the time capsule ceremony." I raised my eyebrows to let him know I didn't buy it, either.

"Ah," Nick said, clearly stalling for time. "The time capsule ceremony."

"I'd love to hear your theory on what's inside it," Shalimar gushed. "I bet you have some wild ideas, being an investigative reporter and all."

"Actually, Maggie has done more research on it than I have," Nick said, passing the buck. He sneaked a peek at his watch. I knew he was on deadline and needed to get to the *Gazette* as soon as possible. "I'd love to stay and chat, but duty calls—"

Shalimar waved her hand. "Oh, I know what it's like. You reporters are always running here and there." Nick smiled and started to edge away, when Shalimar put out an arm to stop him. "I have a great idea. Why don't you and Maggie come out to the house for dinner tomorrow night?" Her tone was soft and wheedling as she twirled a lock of flaxen hair around her finger.

Is she flirting with him? Is she up to something? I wondered. Nick cut his eyes to me, and I gave a tiny nod. Why not go and see what it was all about? I knew he was tempted by the idea of a free dinner, and I'd heard the Hennessey mansion outside town was a showplace. I wouldn't mind seeing it.

"Then we can kick back and talk with no deadlines hanging over you. Wouldn't that be fun? Bobby can fire up the grill, and I make a mean margarita."

"That's very nice of you," I said. I gave her a wide smile. "Nick and I can drive over there together."

"Wonderful," Shalimar said, clapping her hands together. "Tomorrow at six?"

"We'll be there," Nick told her.

I grabbed my purse, and Nick filched three ginormous brownies from the buffet table when he thought nobody was looking. As soon as we were out the front door, he leaned close and said in a low voice, "What the hell was that all about?"

I shook my head. "I have no idea. But Shalimar wants something. I'm sure of it."

"More than my charming company?" Nick said.

"Count on it."

Chapter 20

It was nearly one o'clock by the time I got back to the station, and my first priority was to talk to Vera Mae. To my surprise, I spotted Chantel in the break room, drinking coffee and reading the *Palm Beach Post* as I hurried down the hallway. She lifted a hand in greeting and waggled her fingers at me, her gold bracelets jangling. She looked absorbed, probably trying to figure out a way to snare some more publicity for herself.

I managed a thin smile and continued straight down the corridor to Vera Mae's office. I was in no mood to chitchat about the spirit world with our resident psychic. I had some serious sleuthing to do, but first I had to find out whether Chantel was going to be a permanent fixture here.

"Hey, girl, what's up?" Vera Mae was at her cluttered desk, sorting through some promo material on the time capsule. It looked like all our local sponsors were trying to get into the act and were coming up with some wacky giveaways. "Take a look at this, Maggie. I wonder if it's legit."

She handed me a sixty-second spot for Sidney's Dry Cleaning. Sidney was offering a year's worth of dry-cleaning services to anyone who could answer a question about the contents of a time capsule buried in Peru.

"Do you suppose he's making that up? Who knows if there's a time capsule buried in Peru? And how would he know the right answer?" She gave a little snort. "If you ask me, Sidney Truett is as crooked as a pretzel. The last time we ran a contest for him, he made sure his brother-in-law won. I complained to Cyrus about it, but nothing happened."

I skimmed over the copy and handed it back to her. "I wouldn't worry about it. It's probably a trick question. The Peru time capsule probably doesn't even exist, and no one's going to bother entering. I bet everyone's on to Sidney and his games."

A sudden thought flashed through my head. What if the Cypress Grove time capsule didn't exist, or was empty? I thought of Geraldo Rivera opening Al Capone's vault all those years ago. After all the hoopla, the vault was empty. Still, it was unlikely that the town's time capsule would be empty, wasn't it? I let the thought drift away; there were too many pressing things to consider.

"You look worried, sugar." Vera Mae's voice snapped me right back to the present. She was giving me an odd look as if I'd zoned out for quite a while.

"Not worried, just thoughtful." I took a deep breath. "Vera Mae, I'd like to run something by you."

"Okay, shoot."

She passed me a bowl of M&M'S and I waved it away. "Uh-oh, this must be serious." She sat back in her chair, folded her arms over her ample chest, and pushed her reading glasses up on her head.

"It's about Chantel," I blurted out. "Please don't tell me she's doing my show today. I just saw her sitting in the break room."

"Yep, she's sitting there, big as life, hon." She sifted through the M&M'S, looking for the chocolate ones. "Is that what you're worried about? Well, I can put your mind at rest on that score." Vera Mae motioned for me to push her office door closed. She picked up a pencil from a jar on her desk and started fidgeting with it. I knew something was up, because she only does this when she's teed off about something.

"It's Cyrus," she said finally in a low voice, her mouth twisting. "He's got some darn-fool idea that maybe we should give her a regular show. Just on a trial basis, I mean. And only twice a week, not every day."

"*Only* twice a week? Her own show?" I pulled a pile of papers off the visitor's chair and sat down. "This is exactly what I was afraid of. Once she gets her own show, there will be no stopping her."

I could hardly get my mind around the notion of Chantel being a regular on WYME. I'd always suspected that Chantel was going to steamroll right over my *On the Couch* show with some talk-to-the-dead nonsense that listeners would lap up. And now my worst fears were coming true. I suppose I'd been in denial all this time, and now the truth was hitting me like a ton of bricks.

"Now, don't go getting your panties in a twist," Vera Mae cautioned. "Nothing is definite yet. This is all in the planning stages."

"She's in direct competition with me," I moaned. "How can I compete with voices from the beyond?"

"Now, that's not true at all. You're just putting a really negative spin on this, and that's not like you at all." Vera Mae grabbed a Twizzler from a jar on her desk and offered me one. When I shook my head, she went on, "You have a really loyal fan base, Maggie, and nothing's going to change that. People love your show, and you really help them. Well, some of them," she added after a beat.

"Then why does WYME need another show?" I hated the petulance in my voice, but I couldn't shake off the depressive gloom that had settled over me.

She gave a helpless little wave of her hand. "I think it's just the novelty that appeals to people. We've never had a psychic in Cypress Grove before. And somehow the time capsule is connected with it."

"I don't see how it could be." I put my elbow on her desk and cupped my chin in my hand. "The two things aren't connected, and anyway, that's not why Chantel came to town. She came to Cypress Grove to work on her book. Or so she said," I added darkly. As far as I knew, there wasn't any new book in the works. After that first pronouncement, Chantel had never mentioned it again.

Which led me to the question: why was she really here? "I wish I knew what was really going on with her."

"Well, here's the thing, Maggie." Vera Mae's cell phone chirped, and she glanced at the screen before shaking her head. "It can go to voice mail," she said coolly. "Now, getting back to Chantel. Here's the connection, at least the way I see it. The time capsule has sort of gotten people to thinking about their past, and their ancestors. They're even thinking about the town's past in a way they never have before. Brenda down at the Dollar Store said there's been a big rush on those old postcards that show Cypress Grove at the turn of the century."

"There wasn't much here then. Just swamp."

"I know, but they're still fascinated by it. Brenda said they can't keep them in stock. And they like the ones from the fifties, with those old Buicks and Corvettes. People are just eating this stuff up."

"I still don't see what any of this has to do with Chantel," I said glumly.

"Chantel is all about dead people," Vera Mae said. "You know, the past." She stared hard at me, to see whether it was sinking in. "People we used to know who have passed. Wouldn't you like to say a few words to your deceased relatives?"

"I suppose so," I said grudgingly. I thought about my aunt Arleen, who ruined every family gathering with her caustic remarks. It would be tempting to give her a piece of my mind. "I know it's impossible, though, so I never think about it."

"A few people have even called in to see if Chantel could try communicating with old man Paley and the folks who planted the time capsule all those years ago." She gave a snort. "Of course, I think they're saying that because they're hoping for a clue as to what's in the darn thing. They'd like to win that convertible that Ed Hays is offering down at the Around Again car lot."

"The Around Again car lot. Are you telling me we're offering a *used car* as the grand prize?" Ed Hays advertised with us, so I supposed Cyrus worked out a deal. A pretty chintzy deal, I thought.

"'Previously owned,' as Ed likes to call them." Vera Mae grinned. "A lot of people have called in asking if Chantel could do a reading on the courthouse grounds. Cyrus did talk about doing a live remote from out there. Chantel would work her mojo and try to pick up some clues about the time capsule." She stopped fiddling with the pencil and jammed it back into the jar. "Who knows." She let out a little sigh. "I hate to say it, but it might get good ratings, a show like that. Anytime you talk to the dead, people are interested."

"Ridiculous." I was appalled. "I hope she's not planning

on doing that on my show. My credibility will go down the drain. Remember Barney?"

"I remember, sugar." Vera Mae bit her lip as if she was holding back a belly laugh. "You know, that ghost dog sure brought in the listeners."

I was annoyed at the thought that Chantel might use her hocus-pocus on the time capsule festivities. It trivialized the importance of the occasion, made it seem like something out of a carnival. Her séances were one thing, but now she was nosing onto my turf, and my hackles were rising.

"I'm disappointed in Cyrus," I said bleakly. "I was told that I'd have creative control over my show when I signed the contract."

"Creative control? He told you that?" She paused for a moment. "Well, I'm sure he meant it, but here's the thing you have to understand about Cyrus. He's all about the ratings. We've said this before." She shrugged and stuck out her hands, palms up. "So if a lot more listeners call in, who knows what he'll decide. All you and I can do is keep on truckin', though."

"I guess," I said dispiritedly. I gave in and grabbed a Twizzler. I might as well go back to my sleuthing since I wasn't going to get anywhere fighting my rival. "There's something else I want to ask you about Chantel. Irina said that you may have remembered her from someplace. Or that she reminds you of someone. Could you tell me about that?"

"Yeah, it's true, and it's the oddest thing." Vera Mae leaned forward and cupped her hand under her chin. "It's been buggin' me ever since that first day she came into the studio. I feel real sure I've seen her someplace before, but I can't think where." She adjusted a bobby pin in her towering beehive. "I know it will come to me eventually, but right now, I'm drawing a blank. I'll let you know the second I think of it."

"Nick's found someone local who thinks Chantel might have gone to high school here."

"Really? I'll track that down, sugar. Don't you worry." She grabbed a handful of M&M'S. "Anything else?" She looked at the clock, and I knew she was thinking that it was time to get ready for today's show. But there was one more thing I needed to know. I was still puzzled over the strange conversation I'd had with Shalimar. Vera Mae knew the down-and-dirty on everyone in Cypress Grove, and I wondered whether she could fill me in.

"Tell me what you know about Bobby Hennessey," I said, following up on a hunch.

"Oh, Bobby's a good old boy. His family's lived here for generations. He's like Mr. Cypress Grove, hon. Big town booster, belongs to all the right clubs, and of course he advertises with us." She wrinkled her brow in thought. "And he plays golf with Cyrus."

"Interesting." But not very helpful. There had to be more to the story. What was I missing?

Vera Mae gave me a shrewd look. "I'd say you were hot on the trail of someone," she said. "Why did Bobby catch your interest?"

"Not just Bobby." I told Vera Mae about meeting Shalimar at the historical society and how odd it was that Shalimar acted like we were best buds. I barely knew the woman, and I was curious about her.

"Don't know a thing about her. Just that she flies up to New York three or four times a year to buy her clothes and sometimes she even goes to those fashion shows in Paris. She lives in Magnolia Hall, which is practically a mansion. Some people say it's Cypress Grove's version of the Biltmore House."

"Really? She invited me to dinner there tomorrow night."

Vera Mae slapped her thigh. "Then you are in for a treat, girl. Not that Bobby and Shalimar are that interesting to talk to, but I bet the food will be terrific. She has a personal chef, someone who went to cooking school in Paris. She serves lots of fancy stuff." Vera Mae made a face. "She sent over some appetizers once for a library event. It was raw tuna. Tuna tartare she called it. You should probably warn them you're a vegetarian, or you may find yourself staring at a standing rib of beef."

"That's okay. I'll take my chances," I said. I never expect people to make special meals for me because I'm a vegetarian. If they serve meat, chicken, or fish, I just ignore the entree and fill up on salads, vegetables, and bread. "She invited Nick Harrison, too."

"Oh, Lordy, Nick Harrison eating dinner at Magnolia Hall? That boy will be in hog heaven. His stomach is a bottomless pit." Vera grinned. "What do you want to bet he asks for a doggie bag to take home?"

"You'd win that bet hands down, Vera Mae." I paused, wishing Shalimar had included Vera Mae in the invitation. "What are you up to tonight?"

"Oh, don't you worry about me, sugar," she said, reading my mind. She pointed to a cardboard box tucked under her desk. "Miss Whittier dropped these papers off for me to read."

"Lucille Whittier? I met her at Althea's funeral," I said. "What do you suppose is in there?"

"Just some papers that Althea gave her a few weeks ago. She didn't want to return them to Candace because everything's up in the air right now."

"Anything valuable in there?"

Vera Mae shook her head. "I don't think so. Miss Whittier thought there might be some good material in here about the time capsule. You know, stuff I can use for the promos."

"Sounds good." I headed for the door. "Have fun tonight."

"Oh, I will, honey," Vera Mae promised, grabbing a pencil from behind her ear. "Just me and my Lean Cuisine."

Chapter 21

Dinner at Magnolia Hall was everything Vera Mae had predicted.

I gave a little gasp when we rounded a curve and I first spotted the antebellum mansion perched high on a hill. We made our way up a long winding road framed by live oak trees, and a pair of oversized black wrought-iron gates swung open magically for us, as if on cue. There was something almost surreal and stagey about the place, like it was part of a Hollywood set.

Tara meets Universal Studios. I could almost hear theme music playing in the background, a soulful melody with strings swelling to a climax as we pulled into the circular brick driveway.

"Wow, this is a showplace," I said to Nick. The exterior of the house looked like it was in perfect condition, even though I knew it dated from the nineteenth century. White pillars, dark old brick, and a curved flagstone walkway snaking up to the imposing mansion. The setting sun swiped golden light across acres of manicured lawn and flowering shrubs.

"Look at the lawn," Nick murmured. "It's so green, I bet

they spray paint it to get it to look that good. That color can't be natural. It has a sort of bluish tinge to it. It reminds me of that celery and kale juice you drink for breakfast."

"I think it's real. They probably have underground sprinklers. And I bet they don't worry about conserving water."

The only nod to our century was a cobalt blue kidney-shaped pool off to the left and a clay tennis court on the right. I'd heard that Bobby kept Arabian horses on the property, but the stables must have been tucked far away from the house, out of sight.

Everything about the place screamed old money, and I remembered Vera Mae telling me that Bobby Hennessey had been born with a silver spoon in his mouth. He'd made his fortune the old-fashioned way; he'd inherited it.

"Did you know it was going to be like this?" I asked Nick as he parked in the circular drive. I tried not to sound awestruck, but I was. The house was even more impressive up close, and the air was tinged with the scent of magnolia blossoms and lilac bushes.

"I checked out some pictures from the society pages at the *Gazette*," Nick said. "Shalimar throws charity events here a few times a year, and all of us scramble for an invitation. Her New Year's Eve party is always a hot ticket. I've never managed to snag one. She invites reporters from the *Palm Beach Post* and the *Miami Herald*. Nobody passes on an invitation to Magnolia Hall."

"Maybe you'll be on the guest list once she sees how charming you are," I teased him.

"I hope so." He turned off the ignition and tucked his sunglasses in his pocket. "I've been looking forward to this all day." He gave a happy sigh. "I've been pacing myself for the last twenty-four hours."

"Pacing yourself?"

Nick grinned and patted his stomach. "I haven't eaten since yesterday. Nothing but water and Altoids."

"Nick!" I had to laugh; he was incorrigible.

"I'm hoping for a nice filet mignon and maybe some lobster tails. You know, surf and turf." He stopped and glanced over at me. "Oops, sorry. I forgot you were a vegetarian."

"You can have my portion," I promised. "Unless I decide to take it home for Pugsley."

"Welcome to Magnolia Hall!" Shalimar was wearing a slinky white dress that fit her like a condom. She ushered us into the foyer, which had a mile-high ceiling and black-and-white tile floor. It was a decorator's dream.

The walls were covered with paper the color of lemon meringue pie, and Shalimar caught me checking it out. It looked like strips of pale yellow grosgrain ribbon, but up close, I could see that it wasn't ribbon at all. Someone had applied shades of luminescent yellow paint directly onto parchment to get that luminescent quality, an interesting trompe l'oeil effect that had probably cost a small fortune.

"This is gorgeous." Shalimar beamed while I stopped to admire it. "I've never seen anything quite like it. The wallpaper seems to pick up light from the chandelier." There was a ginormous chandelier hanging smack-dab in the center of the foyer. Tiny pinpoints of light slanted in the foyer, bounced off the hundreds of teardrop crystals dangling from the chandelier, and splashed onto the lemon wallpaper.

"Yes, that was the whole idea. We couldn't find anything from the period that we liked, so I sent a piece of vintage fabric to an artist in Paris and had him design something just for me. The paper is hand blocked, and then the ribbon pattern is painted on with little feathery strokes. It took ages to do, but I think it's worth it."

"I'm surprised you could find someone to willing do

that sort of detail work nowadays. It sounds pretty labor-intensive."

Shalimar led us into a library where she'd set out trays of tiny hors d'oeuvres. There were miniature quiches, crab cakes, and cheese straws, along with frosted grapes. I wondered whether Nick would wolf them down or whether he'd save himself for the main course.

There was an awkward silence for a moment as Shalimar waved us to a brown leather sofa with brass studs. She gave a nervous laugh, and then she decided to keep on talking about wallpaper. Always a safe topic. "Yes, well," she said vaguely. "It's painstaking work, but I found a group of nuns who were willing to paint the pattern directly onto the parchment paper for me. They live in a cloistered convent near Aix-en-Provence. Most of them are quite elderly, but they do excellent work. Bobby said I was very extravagant because some sections of wallpaper are already fading from the sunlight. I guess I should have them replaced. Sunlight is murder on colors, you know. It fades paint and it fades wallpaper. I guess I should have thought of that."

"I think it's beautiful." I tried not to think about a whole order of little old ladies going blind because of Shalimar. "The nuns did a wonderful job."

"They're the same nuns who made the lace for my wedding dress."

I did the bobble-head nod again, at a loss for words. Custom ordering handmade lace for a wedding dress was so out of my experience, I couldn't even imagine it. If I ever get married, I plan on buying a knockoff Vera Wang.

Something about the fading wallpaper nudged my brain, and I couldn't quite grab on to the thought. Fading wallpaper. Sunlight ruining colors. Sunlight fading paint. Why would that be significant? I tucked the question away, making a mental note to think about it later.

I was still baffled by the dinner invitation and wondered when Shalimar would show her hand. I took a peek around the library: lots of burnished mahogany, a fireplace filled with lush ferns, and an Oriental rug that was faded to just the right shade of merlot; half a dozen antique guns displayed on a sideboard. I remembered reading that Bobby Hennessey had one of the finest collections of pistols in the South.

A few glamour shots of Shalimar dotted the mantelpiece, along with a wedding picture in a silver frame. Her eyes jumped out of every photo. They were a dazzling, electric shade of green. Colored contacts? I recognized a recent one. She was draped over Bobby at a black-tie charity event just last week in Boca. She looked like a Victoria's Secret model with her figure-hugging dress and those penetrating emerald eyes.

Plus wall-to-wall books, but I suspected no one read them. They looked fake, somehow, all hardbacks, perfectly aligned, arranged by color and size. I wondered whether she'd bought them by the yard at an estate sale, or maybe they weren't real books at all. Maybe someone had just painted a picture of book spines and fastened it to the front of the bookcase. Another trompe l'oeil effect?

Nick was heaping hors d'oeuvres onto a delicate little plate just as Bobby Hennessey walked in from the patio. He was wearing tennis whites, and his beefy face was flushed as if he'd spent the day in the Florida sunshine.

"So glad you could make it," he said, giving a big, toothy smile. He shook hands with us; then he grabbed a bottle of Scotch from the sideboard and poured himself a hefty tumbler. He took a long swallow and glanced around the library.

He looked like he wanted to smack his lips together appreciatively but resisted the impulse.

He suddenly noticed that we weren't clutching cocktails. "Shalimar, where's your manners?" he barked. "No drinks for the guests?"

"Oh, sorry." She looked flustered and leapt to her feet like a well-trained seal. "I made margaritas," she said brightly. "Maggie, would you like one? And of course there's wine and imported beer—whatever you like."

"A margarita sounds wonderful. Thanks." I was struggling to come up with a conversation topic when Bobby started talking to Nick about a zoning bill that someone had introduced in the last town council meeting. Boring stuff.

I stared at the ceiling (inlaid mahogany in an elaborate geometric pattern) for inspiration. Shalimar must have been groping around for something to say as well, because she started complimenting me on my show. Again. Flattery is always nice, but this was getting ridiculous.

We chatted for a few minutes, and then a maid in a black-and-white uniform announced that dinner was served in the dining room. I wondered whether the maid was of the live-in variety or Shalimar had hired her for the evening. We sat down and started with a soup course served by another maid.

"It's cream of celery, Maggie," Shalimar said. "Just for you. I know you're a vegetarian."

"How did you—"

"That was easy. I Googled you," she said and then laughed and clapped her hand over her mouth. "Oh, I guess I shouldn't have said that." Bobby frowned at her, and she made a swift save. "I came across a piece you wrote about a veganfest back in Manhattan. You talked about the dishes and the recipes."

"So you made a special dinner tonight, just for Maggie?" Nick asked. He looked disappointed, probably figuring he was going to be stuck with mung beans on sprouts instead of his beloved beef.

Shalimar must have read his mind. "Don't worry, Nick. I've got steak and shrimp for you." She paused as the maid returned to serve green salads with cherry tomatoes and marinated artichokes. The salads were served on chilled plates, a nice touch. "So, Nick, what's new with the murder investigation? I bet you've got the inside scoop for us." She flashed a warm smile, but Nick was too busy buttering flaky biscuits to really appreciate it.

"No, afraid not." He glanced at the soup and salad plates, and then his eyes strayed to the door leading to the kitchen. He picked at the greens, clearly biding his time, waiting for the main course.

Bobby and Shalimar exchanged a look. "I thought you had some good connections," Shalimar said uncertainly. "They've had almost nothing in the paper about it. So I figured maybe you were saving everything for a big splashy story."

"A big story? Nope, not me."

"That's a little hard to believe." Shalimar played with her fork and stared at Nick. She swallowed half her wine in one gulp, and Bobby made no move to refill her glass. The tension in the air was so thick, you could have cut it with one of Shalimar's antique silver butter knives.

"Well, I do have some friends with the Cypress Grove PD, but you know how cops are—they keep a tight lid on information. It's like pulling nails out of a board to get them to say anything."

Bobby put down his fork, his face a mask. "Is that a fact? I thought for sure there'd be some interesting leads by now. Maybe even some shockers." He shot another look at Shalimar, but she kept her eyes down, staring at her plate. I noticed a faint flush creeping up her neck. Nerves? Anxiety? He poured red wine but still didn't offer any to Shali-mar. It must have been deliberate. Interesting. Vera Mae says I tend to overanalyze everything, but I can't help it. It's an occupational hazard, part of my training as a shrink. My mind scrambled to come up with an explanation for Bobby and Shalimar's odd behavior. Why did he decide to cut off her wine? Did she have a problem with alcohol? Maybe he didn't trust her after she'd admitted Googling me and he was worried that alcohol had loosened her tongue.

I decided to play along with Bobby and see where the conversation led. "Leads? What kind of leads?" I sipped my wine. It tasted cool, fruity, and expensive. Delicious.

"I don't know," Bobby said, his tone brusque. "I'm not a reporter." He glared at me. "Or a radio talk show host. I'm just an ordinary citizen trying to get to the bottom of this."

I was baffled at the sudden change in the temperature at the table. In the space of a few minutes, it had tumbled from genial to glacial. Our host seemed distinctly annoyed (or disappointed?) with us, but I couldn't imagine why.

"Who'd want to kill two little old ladies?" he went on, his tone irate. "Everybody in town loved Mildred and Althea."

"Not everybody," I said mildly. I remembered I'd caught myself saying the same thing not so long ago.

"Oh, yes," Shalimar said, looking up. "You mean that there's *one* person out there who didn't love them. Of course. The murtherer. I mean, the murderer."

She was ·slurring her words a little, and I wondered whether she'd been drinking before we arrived. The cords in her neck were taut, a muscle was jumping in her cheek, and she was blinking rapidly. And that telltale red flush was creeping up her chest. Clear signs of stress.

For some reason she was distinctly uncomfortable. Was

she hiding something? I remembered the strange conversation we'd had at Althea's funeral reception. She'd asked a lot of questions about the time capsule. Her interest had seemed phony, staged, and I remembered being puzzled over it. Her behavior tonight was equally baffling, and my BS detector was screaming *red alert*.

"That's it. And I'm not so sure that one person committed both crimes. As far as I know, the two murders aren't even connected." I paused, waiting for Nick to jump in, but he was sidetracked by the maid bringing in an enormous platter of grilled steaks. It looked like enough food for an army wintering in Siberia. Nick would certainly get his doggie bag, if he was brave enough to ask for it. "What do you think, Nick?" I nudged him.

"What do I— Oh, yes, I think it's a possibility. Definitely a possibility." He scratched his chin, and his eyes were glazing over. When Nick's eyes glaze over, it means he's thinking about food. Nick once confessed that he even dreams about food, a fact I'm sure he regrets telling me.

"So you agree?" I said, eyebrows raised. "With what?"

"With whatever you just said," he answered neatly. The man should have been a diplomat. Or a politician. His nose was literally twitching like Pugsley's does when he smells chicken from Pollo Loco.

I nearly laughed out loud. It was obvious Nick hadn't been following the conversation and had no idea what I was asking him. He licked his lips, and I could see that he was practically salivating over the aroma of the grilled meat. A giant platter of steaks was placed in the center of the table along with side dishes of au gratin potatoes and buttered asparagus.

A perfectly cooked veggie burger was placed in front of

me, garnished with grilled eggplant, zucchini, red onion, and mushroom caps and served over wild rice.

I didn't worry any more about Bobby's bad mood or the fact that he seemed less than thrilled with us.

I was in heaven.

Chapter 22

"Was that weird or am I crazy?" Nick asked a couple of hours later. We had said our good nights to Bobby and Shalimar and were peeling down the long winding driveway toward the highway. Two doggie bags (one for Nick and one for Pugsley) were sitting on the seat between us. I wasn't crazy about the heavy meat smell wafting out from the bags, but I knew one whiff would send Pugsley into pure nirvana.

"You're not crazy," I told him. "That was weird." Nick was right. This had been one of the strangest evenings I could remember. "I felt really uncomfortable with those two, and I'm not even sure why." I rolled down the window, trying to figure out what was bothering me. The night air was soft and warm, and cicadas were chirping in the trees.

"You're the shrink. You should know all about these things," Nick teased me. Nick was stating a common misconception—he thinks that since I'm a shrink I should be able to read people's minds. Not true! No matter how many times I've tried to correct him, he clings to this bogus belief. I keep telling him that if I could really read people's minds, I'd hit a poker party every Friday night or maybe the blackjack tables at Vegas.

I shook my head. "Well, I'm stumped. I can't shake the feeling that we were dragged there under false pretenses."

"It was pretty awkward, wasn't it? Especially at the end. Once we finished dinner, I felt like they couldn't wait to get rid of us. What did you make of that?"

"I think you're right. Once they didn't get whatever they were looking for, they wanted us out of there."

Shalimar had rushed us through coffee and dessert, and I'd noticed that Bobby didn't offer any after-dinner drinks even though there were half a dozen bottles of fancy liqueurs sitting on a sideboard. And I caught Bobby glancing at his watch a few times. Did he have another appointment, or was he just eager to see us on our way?

"So they didn't invite us for our charming company?" Nick took his eyes off the road to shoot me a grin.

"Afraid not. Maybe we're not that charming after all."

Nick laughed. "Maybe *you're* not," he teased. "Well, it wasn't a complete disaster. At least the food was good." He let out a big sigh. "And I have enough leftovers for tomorrow." I eyed the two doggie bags: an enormous one for Nick and a tiny one for Pugsley. *Tomorrow? Was Nick really serious? He had enough leftovers for a week.* "So, Maggie, what the hell was going on back there? What does your gut instinct tell you?"

I shook my head. "It beats me. Bobby and Shalimar were clearly uncomfortable about something, and I don't believe for a minute that they want to be friends with us. The two of them have a hidden agenda, and it didn't just pop up tonight. It's been in place for a while, and that reminds me—what was Bobby telling you in the library? I know he was bending your ear about a town-council meeting, but I couldn't quite pick up on it."

"I knew you were listening," Nick said. "You were leaning forward so far I thought you were going to topple over into the cheese dip."

I reached over and punched him lightly on the arm. "So tell me."

"Ow!" He briefly took his hand off the wheel to rub his arm. "There's nothing to tell. He was rambling on about a zoning bill. It was a snooze."

"A zoning bill? It does sound like a buzz kill."

"Yeah, I don't even know why he was interested in talking about it." He paused. "What was Shalimar saying to you?"

"Same old, same old." I rolled my eyes. "She's fascinated by time capsules, if you can believe that."

"I have trouble buying that. I figured her tastes ran more to Gucci handbags and Crystal Cruises."

"That's what I thought, too." I snorted, just as my cell phone chirped. I pulled it out of my purse, and my heart did a little bounce when I saw the readout: *Rafe.*

"Excuse me a sec." I flipped the lid open. Rafe's voice came racing over the line like a runaway train, and I felt my pulse jump.

"Maggie? I'm over at Vera Mae's place. I'm afraid we've got a situation going on over here." Uh-oh. Nothing romantic going on; he sounded dead serious. His tone was flat, coplike, and my heart went into free fall. *Vera Mae's?* I felt my stomach clench. There was no way this news was going to be good.

"A situation?" I took a deep breath, my mouth suddenly going dry. "What kind of situation? What's going on over there?" Nick glanced over at me, his eyes clouded with worry. I realized I was clutching the phone in a death grip, and I deliberately unclenched my fingers. *Deep breath, Maggie. Deep breath.*

"There's been a break-in."

"A break-in? At Vera Mae's?" My mind stuttered to a stop, and I had trouble forcing the words out. "Is she hurt?"

"She's okay. A little shaken up, that's all. She was home when it happened. We didn't get the guy. I'm not even sure she can identify him." His voice had softened; the hard edge was gone. I let out a *whoosh* of relief and muttered a quick prayer under my breath. Vera Mae was okay; nothing else mattered. "But I think she'd like you to come over for moral support."

"Tell her I'll be right there. We're on our way." A bubble of fear had been moving up my chest, and it finally started to dissolve. I turned to Nick. "You know how to get to Vera Mae's house, right? You go all the way down Pine, and then you hang a left on Cedar."

I was surprised that my voice actually sounded normal. I felt like I was on autopilot, just going through the motions, trying to tamp down the little quiver that seemed to be racing from my heart to my fingertips.

"Yes, but—" Nick shot me a puzzled look, all set to ask me what was wrong. One look at my expression and he thought better of it. "Whatever you say. We can be there in fifteen minutes."

I flipped the lid shut on my cell phone and checked my seat belt. "Let's make it in ten."

Nick nodded and gunned the engine. "You got it."

There was a black-and-white parked outside Vera Mae's along with Rafe's elderly Crown Vic, and Nick zoomed in right behind it, tires squealing. No EMT truck—that was a good sign. Rafe had said that Vera Mae was fine, I reminded myself. Just shaken up. Now that I'd pulled my heart from my throat, I could actually take a mental step back and try to analyze the situation.

Someone had tried to break into Vera Mae's. *Why?* I shook

my head in disbelief. It was odd. *Beyond odd*. I've been to her place a dozen times, and she has nothing to steal. She lives alone in a little stucco bungalow with Tweetie Bird, her parakeet, as her only companion.

The place dates from the late sixties, the kitchen and bathroom have never been remodeled, and the furnishings look like early Goodwill. Vera Mae saves all her money for a yearly cruise to the Caribbean, her one splurge in an otherwise frugal lifestyle. So money couldn't have been the motive.

Then what was? Could someone have broken in with the intent of harming her? My blood went cold at the idea. I couldn't imagine anyone having a grudge against Vera Mae. Occasionally I get hate mail at the station from disgruntled listeners who disagree with me, but it's always directed to me, not Vera Mae. I looked out into the trim little yard, bounded by magnolia bushes. It was shrouded in shadows, and I thought of all the times I'd nagged Vera Mae to put up some security lights at the front and back entrances. I was annoyed at myself that I hadn't been more persuasive.

Rafe had said that the perp had gotten away, so presumably he was still out there, ready to strike again.

Officer Duane Brown was on the front porch talking into his radio when Nick and I came up the front walk, and I noticed that the front door was cracked open. I could see Vera Mae sitting on the living room sofa with a female officer at her side. Her face was as pale as bread dough, and she had her hands clenched together tightly in her lap.

Rafe must be in another room, I decided, because it looked like the female officer was taking a statement, scribbling into a notebook. Vera Mae nodded her head a few times, her expression serious.

I always notice body language. I know from my training

as a shrink that body language tells eighty percent of the story and can give you a dead-on window into the person's state of mind. If you want to pick up on what someone's really feeling and thinking, check out the body language. It's a much more valuable indicator of true emotion than what a person tells you. Why? Words tell only part of the story, a very small part. And although people lie, body language doesn't. Trust me.

When I had been seeing patients back in my Manhattan practice, I discovered I could usually size up a patient as soon as I stepped into the office. Depressed people have very different body language than anxious people.

I shifted from one foot to the other while Officer Brown chatted away. He finally acknowledged that we were standing there, nodded, and motioned for us to go in. The second I stepped over the threshold, Vera Mae bounded off the sofa and nearly crushed me in a bear hug.

"Sugar, you didn't have to come over here, but I'm so glad you did." She held on to me, swaying a little, and I felt tears spring up in my eyes. Vera Mae is one of the most important people in my life here in Cypress Grove. Maybe anywhere. We struck up an instant friendship when I'd flown down to audition at WYME, and we've gotten even closer since then.

"Rafe told me what happened," I said, leading her back to the sofa. She was doing her best to put up a good front, but I noticed her hands were trembling. She needed a hot cup of tea or a big shot of brandy, maybe both.

The female officer stood up just as Rafe wandered in from the kitchen. He nodded at me and then took the officer aside for a huddled conversation in the tiny dining room. Nick and I sat next to Vera Mae on the sofa. I held Vera Mae's hands. They were chilled to the bone; it was like touching a corpse. I was just about to ask her whether she had some brandy stashed away, when the female cop left and Rafe joined us.

"So. Quite a night," he said, sinking into an armchair. Rafe is catnip to women. It's impossible not to pick up on his sexy vibes. I'm not even sure he knows he's giving them out. (But sometimes he tosses me a little smile, flashing his dimples, that tells me he knows exactly what he's doing.)

Nick whipped out his notebook, pen in hand. You wouldn't think a break-in would be big news, but there's not much crime in Cypress Grove, which was one of the reasons I had moved here. "Vera Mae, can you tell me what the guy was looking for? Do you have any valuables in the house?"

Before Vera Mae could answer, I turned to her. "Wait a minute. It was a guy? You're sure of that, right?"

She nodded. "I think so, but I didn't really get a good look at him. He was wearing sweatpants and a hoodie. I practically collided with him. He was standing in the living room, and like an idiot, I'd left all the lights off. I was coming in from my tai chi class—"

"You do tai chi?" Nick asked, pen poised.

"Not willingly," Vera Mae said with a chuckle. I could feel a little warmth coming back into her fingertips. "Lark gave me a month's worth of classes for my birthday. Don't put that in the paper, sonny." She waggled her fingers at Nick. "I wouldn't want to hurt her feelings."

"I won't." Nick grinned at me. I felt a little glimmer of relief. If Vera Mae could crack a joke, that meant she was back to her old self.

"Go on," Rafe urged her.

"I came home earlier than usual. I wasn't crazy about the

instructor they had tonight. And I walked right in on him. He nearly knocked me over, he was so eager to get out of here."

"You came home early," I said, thinking. "So that means that maybe he knew your schedule and he figured he'd have the place to himself?"

"Maybe." Vera Mae shrugged. "Who knows?"

"Or maybe it was just a random selection," Rafe said. "This place is an easy target, no outdoor lights, no security system." He looked at the thin door with the sixties-style diamond windows at the top and probably figured the same thing I did. The door looked paper-thin, like it was made of plywood. I bet one swift Krav Maga kick would demolish it.

But I also noticed there were no scratches on the door, no obvious signs of damage. Funny. I walked over to the door to double-check. The frame was intact and the lock didn't look like it was scratched or damaged.

I looked at Rafe. "I don't understand. There's no sign of a forced entry. How did he get in?"

Vera Mae flushed. "Well, there's a tiny chance I may have left it open," she admitted.

"You left the door open? Vera Mae, for heaven's sake. Please tell me you didn't do that deliberately." Vera Mae and I have had this argument many times before. She thinks that if a burglar is determined to get into your house he'll find a way, and I've been telling her that she's out of her mind. A robber will go for the easy score, the place with no lights, no security system, and no guard dog. Like her house.

"Well?" I demanded. She really had left the door unlocked. A bubble of disbelief rose inside me.

She didn't answer me, but a red flush began creeping up her neck. She licked her lips and kept her eyes down, playing with her watch. A long beat passed. She was stalling.

"Vera Mae, fess up. You *did* leave it open on purpose." Rafe's voice had an edge to it.

"Well, honestly, it was just for a couple of hours." She flashed an unrepentant grin. "And most folks in Cypress Grove leave their doors unlocked." She was right. This was strictly small-town America, with a low crime rate, and people tended to be trusting.

"And I left the back door open, too."

"What? Why in the world did you do that?" I challenged her.

"I was expecting a delivery." All three of us stared at her.

"What kind of delivery?" Rafe leaned forward, his brows knitted in concentration.

"Just some more papers for the time capsule celebration. Historical stuff, nothing valuable. Nothing worth stealing, that's for sure."

A little bell went off somewhere in the back of my brain. "Wait a minute. Didn't someone already give you a box of papers that belonged to Althea? You showed them to me at the station."

"Those were from Miss Whittier, Althea's neighbor," Vera Mae said. "This is a different set of papers. They belonged to Mildred Smoot."

"And someone gave them to you because—"

"Because they wanted them to be kept safe, I guess. I doubt there's anything interesting in there, just some more notes from the historical society. Maybe some newspaper clippings, that sort of thing."

"Why are the papers from the society spread around town like this?" Nick asked. "Wouldn't it be better to keep them all in one place? Like the historical society?"

"I suppose so," Vera Mae said doubtfully, "but you know how these old dears are. They take home a box or two to go through them, and they forget to bring them back. Or they never get around to looking at them. I think that's what happened with this batch. Mildred's colleague, Gina Raeburn, found these in Mildred's home. She figured there might be something interesting in there, so she dropped them off here tonight."

"You still have the papers?" I said eagerly. Maybe this explained the break-in; at least it was a good starting point.

"Yes, but I'm sure there's nothing valuable in there. Nobody would want them."

"Where are they?" Rafe stood up, looking around the room.

"Oh, I'm sure they're right inside the back door, in the laundry room. Gina said she was going to leave them on top of the washing machine."

Rafe and I exchanged a look. "Any particular reason she would do that?" he asked.

"She has a bad back and bad knees. She can barely walk up those two front steps, especially carrying a box. So she said she'd probably just go in the back door and leave them there for me." Vera Mae flushed. "So that's why I left both doors open, front and back."

Chapter 23

"Let's take a look at the laundry room, and I'll get Officer Brown to do another walk-through out back." Rafe called out to the square-jawed officer standing on the front porch. "Duane! Check the backyard again for footprints, evidence, anything you can find."

Vera Mae led the way down a narrow hallway to a small room with a washer and dryer. She flipped on the light switch and gestured to an open cardboard box filled with clippings and papers. "There they are. Gina left them for me, just like she said." She riffled through the top layer of yellowing papers and shook her head, her brows scrunched together.

"What's wrong?" I asked.

"Nothing, I guess. But I just don't get it. Nobody in his right mind would break in for a bunch of moldy old papers. He must have been after something else." She wrapped her arms around her chest as if a chill had just passed through her.

"Don't worry about the papers, Vera Mae," I said quickly. "You don't have to bother with any of this right now."

"I'll go through the box first thing tomorrow. I don't feel

like I'm up to much tonight. Feeling a bit peaked, you know?" She gave an embarrassed half laugh. "Silly, isn't it? Don't know what's come over me."

"It's not silly. You've had quite a shock," I said quietly. "It's going to take a little while to get over this. You need to take it easy for a day or two."

The shock of surprising an intruder in your own home is something that doesn't go away overnight. Vera Mae seemed to be coping well, but I had the feeling she was probably operating on autopilot.

Soon the reality of what happened would hit her, maybe over the next few days, or maybe the next few hours. She needed to be with someone who was supportive and who understood what had happened. Vera Mae had suffered a psychic wound, as the shrinks call it, and her safe world had disintegrated the moment she'd seen that burglar in the hoodie.

"Maggie's right. You need to take it easy for a while." Rafe touched her arm and then pushed open the back screen door and stepped out into the balmy night. The yard was shrouded in shadow, and the cicadas were humming in the trees. Officer Brown was walking around the yard with a flashlight, shining it over the dwarf palms and the low shrubs that bordered the trim little backyard.

"Nothing back here. No sign of footprints, no sign of forced entry." Officer Brown shook his head, catching Rafe's questioning glance. He moved toward the edge of the yard and suddenly the night air was peppered with furious barking. It sounded like a pack of wild dogs with one very loud alpha dog barking louder than the others. I flinched, expecting a group of Rottweilers to come tearing through the shrubbery at any second. Without meaning to, I took a quick step backward, stepping on Nick's foot.

"What in God's name is that noise?" Rafe asked. "It's coming from the back of your yard, Vera Mae. Do you have a dog chained out there?"

Vera Mae shook her head. "Are you kidding? I'm more of a cat person. That noise you hear is coming from Lemuel Clemson's house." Her lips were twitching, and I could see she was holding back a laugh. "Our property borders each other's. All we have is that low hedge dividing us."

"Tell me about him," Rafe said.

"He's not a friendly sort of guy, kind of paranoid, if you know what I mean." She lowered her voice. "Always suspicious, always complaining about something. He's a busybody, if you ask me."

"A busybody might be just what we need right now," Rafe muttered. "Maybe he saw something. Let's try an experiment." He called out to the officer patrolling the yard. "Duane, take a couple of steps backward. Toward us."

Officer Brown moved away from the shrubs, and the dog barking stopped abruptly. Like magic. Or like someone had thrown a switch. Funny. The sound still lingered in my brain, and I realized there was something odd about it. It was the kind of raucous barking that would make an intruder head for the hills, but it had a strange, tinny undertone to it.

And then the two halves of my brain connected and I figured it out.

"Vera Mae, there's something strange about that dog barking. Could it be a recording? It doesn't sound real to me."

Vera Mae laughed. "You've got a good ear, sugar. It *is* a recording. Lemuel sets it to a motion detector. He's always afraid someone's gonna break into his house. Although I can't imagine what he's got in there worth stealing." She shrugged, her shoulders slumping for a moment. "Funny when you think about it. I'm the one who nearly got robbed, and he's the one with all the fancy security equipment."

Fancy security equipment. I looked over at her neighbor's house. Another small stucco ranch, probably from the same era as Vera Mae's. Pastel stucco exterior, flat roof. And then I spotted lights on the back corners of his house, perched on the corners of the roof. Right next to the lights were rectangular gadgets that were aimed right at us.

"Rafe," I said, quietly, pointing to the gizmos on the roof. "Are those what I think they are?"

He followed my gaze and grinned. "Bingo. Cameras." He squeezed my arm. "Good work, Maggie." He looked at Vera Mae. "Maybe your intruder was caught on tape."

"Really?" She scowled. "I don't know if those things even work. I figured they were just for show. Like those security stickers people put on their front doors."

"We might be lucky." He turned to Officer Brown. "Get Gina Raeburn's phone number. I want to see if we can pin down what time she was here." He looked at Vera Mae. "And I'm going to pay a call on your neighbor right now and see if those cameras were turned on tonight. Maybe we just got lucky."

"Maybe you could cite him for disturbing the peace. I'm really sick of hearing that recording night and day."

It was after ten o'clock when Rafe and his sidekick, the Opie lookalike, wrapped up their investigation and left. Rafe had the video surveillance tape from Lemuel Clemson's camera and was going to look at it down at headquarters.

Vera Mae felt uneasy staying in the house after the break-in, so after she grabbed Tweetie Bird's cage and some extra bird food, I had Nick drive us both back to my place. Mom was down in Miami auditioning for yet another B movie, and I quickly set up the guest room for Vera Mae. Pugsley was ecstatic to see her and danced in circles around her ankles, hoping for a belly rub.

I made a pot of tea, and the two of us sat at the kitchen table, going over the box of papers from Gina Raeburn.

"Do you really think there's anything in here worth stealing?" Vera Mae was wearing John Lennon–style reading glasses perched on the end of her nose. "Some of this stuff doesn't even look old. She's got some of Mildred's mail in here, and look, here's an electric bill and a pizza coupon."

"And there's some personal correspondence," I said, opening a piece of pale blue stationery that was tucked inside an envelope. I looked at the postmark. Georgia. "Do you think I should read it?"

"What difference does it make now, sweetie? She's gone."

I quickly scanned the letter, written in a precise script.

"Anything interesting?" Vera Mae bent down and scooped Pugsley onto her lap.

"Maybe. It sounds like Mildred wrote to this woman in Georgia, trying to get some information on the Paley family. She was hoping to get a list of the contents of the time capsule, as far as I can tell."

"Did she have any luck?"

I shook my head. "I don't think so. The person she wrote to suggested some other contacts she could try." I put the letter down and sipped my tea. Clover honey. I warmed my hands on the cup and breathed in the sweet aroma. "Why was Mildred so interested in the Paleys? And the time capsule. Why would she write to someone in Georgia about it? I wonder what kind of lead she was tracking down."

"Maybe because she just liked to dig up facts. She was a librarian, after all." Vera Mae said. "Doing research was part of her job, wasn't it?"

"I guess so. But this seems like this is going above and beyond, doesn't it?" My mind kicked back to the conversation with Mark Sanderson, the condo developer. Wasn't he from Georgia? Was there a connection here?

"It does seem a little odd, now that you mention it." Vera Mae shrugged. "Almost something obsessive about it. All this interest in the time capsule," she mused. "It makes it seem like there's something much bigger at stake."

"Do you suppose there's going to be any big surprise when it's finally opened?"

"I sure hope so. We've been pushing it in those promos, and Cyrus is going to be disappointed if the ratings don't show it." She paused, tracing a pattern on the checkered cotton tablecloth. "It's funny, but all this hullabaloo about the time capsule has sort of taken the focus off the murders, hasn't it? It almost seems like they've been pushed to the back burner."

"I think I may have a lead," I said softly. Vera Mae raised her eyebrows, and I filled her in on what I'd learned from Lucille Whittier about the painting in the hallway of the historical society.

"It could be something important," Vera Mae acknowledged. "What are you going to do about it? Do you think you should run it by Rafe? He has resources you don't, honey. He has the whole Cypress Grove PD and the CSIs behind him."

Rafe. I hesitated, drumming my fingertips on the table. The thought had crossed my mind, but I wanted to follow through on this myself. "I think I want to talk to that picture framer first, Chris Hendricks. And then I may just call Candace Somerset and see if I can borrow a painting for a few days. The one that Althea had planned on getting reframed."

"A painting? What will you do with the painting?"

"I don't know exactly. But I think the painting is somehow involved in the murder. It goes to motive." I shook my head. "I can't be more specific than that."

Vera Mae stifled a yawn. "Then let's hope someone can help you with it," she said sleepily. "I still think you should tell Rafe." Vera Mae is a huge fan of Rafe's and always takes his side if I have a problem with him. She's a sucker for his bad-boy charm and acts like she's taken a hit of scopolamine if I remind her of his many faults.

I smiled. "I'll tell him eventually, but only if my hunch is right. Only if things pan out the way I think they should."

"Because?" she asked, a teasing note in her voice.

"Because if I'm wrong, I'll never hear the end of it."

Either Chris Hendricks had something to hide, or he was just a short, twitchy guy with an unfortunate facial tic. I decided to hit his framing shop first thing in the morning. I'd dropped Vera Mae off at the station at nine o'clock and had swung into town, figuring I'd catch him alone, before any customers arrived. As it turned out, I needn't have worried. The place was deserted; the picture-framing business must be slow.

"Chris Hendricks?" I asked. He stopped fiddling with a collection of wedding photos and stared at me through Coke-bottle lenses.

"That's me. Can I help you?" He wiped his hands on his pants.

"I hope so. I'm Maggie Walsh." I gave him my card. He peered at it and then gave me a puzzled stare. "From WYME? We run your radio commercials." Actually, we weren't running any current spots for him, but I remembered seeing his name on the traffic log a couple of months ago. Technically he was still a client.

Suddenly his mood changed. "Maggie Walsh! I know you." He came back from zombieland and pushed his glasses up on his nose. "You're the shrink lady with the call-in show." *Shrink lady?* I managed a smile as he wiped his hands on his jeans once more and then folded his arms across his chest. "I listen to your show all the time."

"Good. Glad to hear it."

A beat passed. I raised an eyebrow and waited. Here it came. "You know, you've really got some wack jobs calling in. How do you stand it?" He chuckled but he looked uncomfortable. I noticed he had trouble making eye contact with me.

"Some days it's not easy," I said. "It's all part of the job, though."

He pulled over a wooden stool and perched on it. "Usually Big Jim Wilcox stops by when it's time to sign up for some more commercials—"

"Oh, I'm not here to sell you airtime," I said quickly. "I just want to ask you a few questions. About Althea Somerset."

"Althea Somerset?" He strung out the words slowly, like they were unfamiliar to him. He gave me a passable imitation of someone who was genuinely puzzled, but he was no Al Pacino. I'd give him a seven out of a possible ten on the acting scale.

His right foot was jiggling back and forth like it had a life of its own. A dead giveaway. Nerves. Guilt. Deception. Maybe a mixture of all three?

When I interviewed convicted felons in my forensic work back in Manhattan, the foot tapping was a giveaway. One of the probation officers called it "The Jailhouse Jitterbug." These guys could look me straight in the eye and manage to keep their voices steady, but their feet told another story. One foot would be dancing away to an invisible mariachi band.

"You have heard of her, right? She was the head of the historical society?" He tore his eyes away from the ceiling and gave a shifty-eyed glance to the right and then to the left. His eyes slid right past my face.

Another long beat passed. It seemed very quiet in the shop; the only sound was the low hum of the air conditioner. Even though it was as chilly as Antarctica, Chris Hendricks was sweating bullets. I decided to press on. "She was murdered last week. You must have seen it. It's been in all the papers." Would he deny it? Unless he'd been living in a cave, he'd know that Althea was dead.

When I said the word "murder," he'd jumped as if I'd just laid a dead fish on his countertop. "Sorry. Did I say something that startled you?"

"No! I mean yes, of course I remember Althea. From the historical society." He took out a handkerchief and mopped his face. Then his expression shifted and he managed a somber look, something you'd expect from a junior undertaker. "Very sad to hear about her. Probably one of those drugged-up teens from Palm Beach with too much money and time on his hands. I hope they catch the guy."

"Is that what you think happened?" I let a little note of astonishment creep into my voice. "That she was attacked by a drug-crazed teenager?" I knew he was hiding something, and this bizarre explanation only heightened my suspicions.

"Well sure. Wilding, they call it. Isn't that what you think happened?" This time he tried for a direct look, his hand wandering over to a crowbar lying on a workbench. He was a skinny guy, but his hands looked powerful, and I felt a little chill go through me.

"I don't know." I shrugged. "I hadn't thought of that explanation." *Wilding?* That expression hasn't been used since the Central Park jogger case in New York many years ago. If had been a case of wilding, there would be several perpetrators involved, but the lack of trace evidence and fingerprints at the crime scene suggested a single killer.

Chris Hendricks was a liar, and not a very skillful one. "I really wanted to talk to you about a painting Althea had hanging in the front hall."

"Really? Which one?" He studiously kept his face a mask as he reached for a watercolor and began taking apart the framing. He caught me staring at him. "You don't mind if I work while we talk, do you? I've got a rush order on this frame." His hands were trembling, and maybe he figured it would be less obvious if he kept them busy.

"No, go right ahead." I forced a little smile, and my pulse went up a notch. This guy was definitely creeping me out.

"So which painting are you talking about?"

"It was a landscape in the style of Joshua Riggs. A very bad Joshua Riggs. It had an ornate frame, one of those gilt ones with fat cherubs playing tag with each other. It was awful. Althea wanted something simpler. I heard she was planning to bring it into the shop so you could take a look at it."

He raised his eyebrows. "Joshua Riggs. Never heard of him." He answered too quickly. He didn't even think about it; the words spilled out in a rush. If he'd been smarter, he'd have stalled, pretending to jog his memory. That would have made him seem more credible.

"But you do remember talking about reframing a painting for her? Sometime during the past week?"

He put the crowbar down and leaned his elbows on the workspace. I could see a flash of naked fear creeping into his eyes. "You know, I do remember her asking me about making a new frame for a painting. Funny, that slipped my mind." He gave a little shrug. "I've been so busy, I can hardly think straight." An obvious lie. The shop was empty, and the stock looked dusty, as if no one had touched it in a long time.

I decided to take a wild chance. "But did she bring the painting here, into the shop? Or did you go see her at the historical society?"

They call this a "forced choice" question because the person being interviewed has to choose between A and B. Once you pose the question this way, it's much harder for him to say he never saw the painting at all. You just don't give him this option, and usually it works. He has to choose A or B.

It worked. I felt a little zing of pleasure when Chris Hendricks took the bait. "She brought it in here to the shop," he said in a rush. "It was just the other day." Funny how his memory had suddenly improved.

He was getting more uncomfortable by the minute. His glasses started their inevitable downward slide again, and I jammed them back in place with his index finger.

"What happened when she came to the shop?"

"Althea showed me the painting. Like I just said." He looked at me like I was an idiot.

"The Joshua Riggs?"

"Yes." *A few minutes ago, he'd never heard of Joshua Riggs. It's always fascinating to see how easy it is to trip someone up.*

"And then what?"

"I could see what the problem was. She was right. The painting was overshadowed by the frame. It was way too heavy." He shrugged. "Some people like those Victorian frames with a bunch of curlicues and doodads, but I think it detracts from the painting." He stopped talking again, so I just stared at him.

"Althea wanted it reframed." A statement, not a question.

"Yes." He swallowed. He had a prominent Adam's apple, and it looked like a walnut bobbing up and down in his throat. "I quoted Althea a price, but she thought it was too high."

"Is that so?"

"She always thought the price was too high. You know how these old ladies are. They're out of touch with what things cost these days. Althea asked me if I could give her a discount because the historical society is a nonprofit."

"What did you tell her?" I kept my voice neutral.

He spread his hands. "I told her I'd go out of business if I started reducing my prices." He cast a pleading look my way. "A guy's gotta stay in business, doesn't he? Everybody and their brother-in-law wants something for nothing. You understand what I'm talking about, don't you?"

He'd moved away from the workbench and was giving me an aw-shucks smile. Mr. Nice Guy. *As if I'd buy it!* It was wasted on me because something else had caught my eye. I edged closer to him, still talking. I kept my voice low and conversational.

"What happened then?"

"She left with the painting. I never saw it again."

"Was it overcast that day?"

He looked at me like I was crazy. "Overcast? Yes, it was. I remember the sky was gray and it looked like it was going to rain any second. You could feel the humidity in the air. I figured there was a storm coming." The words spilled out of him like candies from a piñata. When people are lying, they tend to tell you way too much detail, and I wanted to see how he'd handle a silly question.

He handled it the way a liar would. He answered it immediately, and he told me more than I needed to know.

Something on the corkboard top of the work surface caught my attention. Tiny blue sprinkles, like confetti. Just a little cluster of them dotting one corner of the surface. Where had I seen those blue dots before?

The historical society. A memory kicked in like a freeze-frame in my mind, and it heightened my suspicions. My danger meter went on red alert, and I decided to get out of there as fast as I could.

"I know exactly what you're talking about," I said, making tracks for the door. "Thanks for your time."

Chapter 24

Vera Mae called me on my cell as I was peeling down Main Street, headed to WYME.

"Where've you been, girl?" A little edge of worry flared under her warm molasses drawl. "I've been trying to get ahold of you for the past twenty minutes."

"Sorry. I must have had the phone turned off. What's up?"

"How long will it take you to get to the station?" A sharp intake of breath and then, "Stop whatever you're doin', because you need to get down here as fast as you can." I heard an excited buzz of conversation in the background. Something big must be going on at WYME. Or as Vera Mae would say, "hellzapoppin."

"Ten minutes, maybe fifteen. Why?"

"Turn on the news, hon. Chantel is the big story this morning."

"Chantel? You mean she made another prediction? That's hardly news. That's her stock-in-trade."

"Not a prediction, sweetie. She's been taken into custody by the Cypress Grove PD."

"Whaaat?" I made a fast left onto Prince Street, tires squealing, and the guy in the car behind me blasted me with his horn before flipping me off.

"You heard me. She's down at headquarters right this minute. I know Rafe's been tryin' to get up with you. He called here for you a couple of times, and he told me he was going to try your cell. You've got to remember to leave that thing turned on, sugar."

"I know. I know," I muttered. I pulled over to the curb and checked my messages. I couldn't believe my rotten luck. Rafe had called four times while I was wasting time talking with Chris Hendricks.

But what had Rafe come up with? How could everything have hit the fan so fast?

"Don't keep me in suspense, Vera Mae. Why did they bring her in?"

"They're questioning her about the murders, hon." She paused. "Wait a sec. I've got to talk to Kevin." She must have slapped her hand over the phone, because her next words were muffled. Suddenly she was back on the line with me, excited and breathless.

"Okay, Kevin said that's the last he heard, but it seems to be changing minute by minute. At first they said she was a person of interest. But now it seems more serious than that. Kevin doesn't know if she's really been charged with murder or maybe she's just an accessory." She sounded like she'd just run up a flight of stairs, but I knew she was just jazzed over the latest developments.

"Rafe told you all this?" I was still scrambling to make sense of it.

"No, Rafe was pretty closemouthed. I'm just going by what I heard from Big Jim Wilcox. And you know what he's like. He might not have gotten his facts right. Maybe they just brought her in for questioning. Who knows? The point is, she's down at the police station right now."

So much for having her own show at WYME. A snarky thought, but I couldn't help it. That woman had been a thorn in my side since the first moment she'd come to town. And now she'd been hauled down to the police station. Career suicide, right? It didn't matter how it all turned out; she'd always be tainted by the charge. Her career in broadcasting was over, and maybe even her book deal.

Unless it was all a mistake? I shook my head in frustration. There were too many "if onlys" in the mix to really analyze the situation.

"Cyrus had planned big things for her at the station. I bet he's pulling his hair out by the handfuls right now."

"Damn straight, hon. He is." Vera Mae chortled. "Or what he has left of it."

Cyrus has one of the worst comb-overs I've ever seen. He keeps a can of industrial-strength hair spray hidden in the bottom drawer of his desk, just to keep the spaghetti-like strands glued in place.

"Big Jim's leaving in a few minutes to do a remote from down there. It's gonna be interesting to see how this all plays out. That's for sure. A break in the murder case is going to trump any news features on the time capsule ceremony. I'd bet money on it." I just realized I hadn't asked a very important question.

"But which murder is it?" My thoughts were racing. I still couldn't get my mind around the fact that the police had arrested Chantel. "What's that?"

"Which *murder*?" I repeated. I found myself shouting into the phone.

"What, hon? I can't hear you. You're breaking up."

"Who was it—Althea or Mildred? Who do they think Chantel killed?"

"We don't know that yet." Vera Mae came through loud and clear.

"How is that possible?" My thoughts were buzzing. I was still struggling to connect Chantel with either—or both—of the victims.

She'd held a séance at the historical society, but that was a dead end. I'd been suspicious of Chantel from the start, but facts were facts, and I never had any concrete evidence. Maybe Rafe was way ahead of me, though, because apparently he did. He never would have brought her in unless he thought he had a strong case. I told myself it was silly to speculate. I had to get down to WYME and see what was going on for myself.

There was another interruption while Vera Mae put the phone down for at least ten seconds. When she came back she said, "Gotta run, Maggie. See you in five."

Five? I sharked down Prince Street, slid through the next three intersections on yellow, and got to WYME in record time.

Big Jim was standing in the lobby, chatting up Irina. "I need to have an open line," he said, puffing his chest out with pride. "I'll be sending in breaking news alerts from the police department as they happen." You'd think he was Chris Hansen from *Dateline*, not a radio sports announcer from a little backwater town in south Florida.

Irina was busy filing her nails and barely looked up at him. She reached for a bottle of nail polish. Flamingo Pink. "Open line. I get it for you. You will haf it," she said in a bored tone. "You will haf everything you neet. I make it happen."

"What's going on, Jim?" I asked. I tried to breathe through

my mouth. Big Jim was drenched in stinky cologne again. The guy was the size of a jukebox, and he looked enormous in his pale blue blazer.

"The first break in the double murder case, that's what!" He took a step closer to me, peering at my face. "This could be the break I've been waiting for." I must have looked puzzled, because he added, "Career-wise."

I nodded. "Ah, I see. Yes, this could be the big one."

He gave me a hard look to see whether I was mocking him, but I kept my expression neutral.

Vera Mae flew into the lobby and grabbed me by the arm. "C'mon back to my office, Maggie. We've got to plan today's show."

"What's on the schedule?" I usually check to see who my guest is, but I'd been so rattled by the meeting with Chris Hendricks down at the frame shop that I hadn't gotten around to it. I wondered whether this news about Chantel knocked out my suspicions about the picture framer.

If Chantel was in as a murder suspect, did that mean Chris Hendricks was out? I didn't know how to fit Chantel into the puzzle, and I needed more information.

Vera Mae was talking nonstop as she pulled me down the hallway to her office. I tried to duck into the break room for a quick cup of joe, but she plucked at my elbow, propelling me forward. "I got your coffee all ready for you, just the way you like it." I must have hesitated, because she added, "Hazelnut double roast. And a bear claw. Plus a lemon cream."

I smiled. "You had me at the bear claw."

We zipped into her cluttered office and she shut the door. She whisked a pile of legal pads off the visitor's chair so I'd have a place to sit, and then she threw herself into her swivel desk chair. The coffee and doughnuts were laid out neatly on her desktop. She whipped a pencil out from behind her ear and tapped it on her mouse pad.

"Okay, Maggie, we've got to figure out how we're gonna play this. Cyrus wants a meeting with me thirty minutes before showtime. He wants to know our game plan."

I raised my eyebrows. "Our game plan?"

"He wants to know how much information we should release about Chantel."

"Why can't we just go with the truth? The cops brought her in for questioning, and that's all we know."

"Cyrus is worried about the sponsors. The last thing he wants is any hint of a scandal."

"If that's the case, I think we should say as little as possible. You could even mention that she's helping with the investigation." I couldn't believe that I was actually sticking up for Chantel. Maggie Walsh, team player.

"Helping with the investigation. That sounds good, hon. What does Rafe have to say?"

"I haven't gotten back with him yet." I sipped the coffee; it was very strong, just the way I like it. I felt a little jolt go through my system, and then I suddenly felt more alert. "So Big Jim is covering everything down at the police station."

"Only because you weren't available. If you can get some information out of Rafe, something that we can go public with, we can run it as a news item right now." Vera Mae pushed her desk phone toward me. "Do it, hon."

I nodded. Time to call Rafe.

He answered on the first ring. "Martino," he barked. Then he must have looked at the readout, because his voice softened. "Maggie, where have you been?"

"A long story. What's going on with Chantel?"

"This is off the record, right?"

"If it has to be."

"She showed up on Clemson's security tape. She was trying to get in Vera Mae's back door last night."

"So those cameras were real?" *Funny, I never thought we'd get a break like this.*

"Very real. The wacky neighbor has a pretty expensive system. First I thought it might be hot, and then he told us that he used to work for a security firm. When they upgraded their equipment, they let him buy the old stuff for a few bucks. He's paranoid, just like Vera Mae said. He let us search the place, and he's clean. I'm convinced he had nothing to do with the break-in. He's just a nut job, a loner, someone who thinks the world is out to get him."

"Wow," I said softly. "This puts a different light on things."

"Gina Raeburn showed up on the tape as well."

"She was dropping off some papers. I suppose her story checked out, right?"

"Absolutely. She entered the house with a cardboard box and exited thirty seconds later, without the box. She's in the clear."

I scribbled a few notes, knowing I couldn't use them. Vera Mae was watching me, and I made a no-go motion with my hands. She nodded. There was info on the case, but no way we could use it. It still made no sense to me. What was Chantel doing over at Vera Mae's last night? And why was she lurking around the back door?

"What does Chantel have to say? How does she explain herself?"

"She said she thought the front doorbell wasn't working. So she went around back and tried the back door."

"Pretty slick. Do you believe her?"

"I think she's lying through her teeth." He drew in a breath. "She said she wanted to go over some show ideas with Vera

Mae and she figured it would be better to do it away from the station. That it would be more private."

"Private? That's a crock. She could have called Vera Mae and invited her out to dinner. Or come in early to the station to see her. It makes no sense that she'd just pop up at her house like that."

"I know. She talks a good game."

"But if you have her caught on tape, for breaking and entering—"

"That's the problem," Rafe cut in. "We don't have a case against her for breaking and entering."

"Why not?"

"Some very bad luck. There's a glitch on the tape. The tape shows her walking up to the back door, trying the door, and then—nothing. There's some kind of interference. The tech guys are gonna try and clean up the tape, but that may be all there is."

"So she's not being charged with murder? Or as an accomplice or a person of interest?"

Vera Mae was sitting on the edge of her chair, taking in every word. I caught her trying to read my notes upside down.

"Charged with murder? No, of course not. Where did you hear that?"

"Big Jim Wilcox."

Rafe snorted. "He's an idiot. He's called me about twenty times. He's trying to get an exclusive for himself."

"You're right. He'll be on his way down there any minute. He thinks he's covering a breaking story."

"Well, he's wasting his time. We just released Chantel. She's probably heading back to WYME right this minute."

Chapter 25

I was more confused than ever. Chantel had been lurking around Vera Mae's backyard and had tried to open the back door. Why? Rafe thought she'd been up to something, and I *knew* she'd been up to something. I'd been suspicious of her from the start. I needed to settle a few things quickly, before she turned up here at the station.

I filled Vera Mae in on what Rafe had just told me. She looked dumbfounded.

"So you had no idea she was going to turn up at your place last night?"

"No, of course not." Vera Mae gnawed at her pencil. "And that story about wanting to talk to me privately is phony-baloney. We have nothing to talk about." She frowned. "So does this mean she wasn't the intruder? And she's not involved with either of the murders?"

I put my elbows on the desk and my head in my hands. "I don't know what it means. I'm in the dark as much as you are, Vera Mae."

I thought about Chantel's size. She was certainly an imposing figure; there was nothing petite about her. Could she have looked like a man in the darkened living room? "Vera

Mae, try to think back to that first moment when you walked in your living room and saw someone in a hoodie. Could it have been Chantel?"

"I told you, hon. I don't know who it was. It was pitch dark in there. I couldn't see a thing." She gave a little shudder. "Just this person who pushed past me and ran out the front door."

"But you said the person was wearing a hoodie. And you said it was a man. So you did notice something." I wondered whether Vera Mae had noticed more than she realized. Sometimes in a traumatic, high-stress situation, your mind takes a freeze-frame picture of the event. You do it unconsciously. Maybe if Vera could think about the situation, she'd be able to recollect some more details about the intruder.

"I thought it was a man. But maybe I just expected it to be a man. I don't know." She locked eyes with me. "When Chantel showed up outside my back door on that surveillance tape, was she wearing a hoodie?"

"I don't know. Rafe didn't say. Probably not, because he said her face was visible. Of course, she could have pulled the hood up around her face after she got inside."

"Exactly. That's what I'm thinking."

I looked at my watch. Rafe said she might be headed toward the station. We had to talk fast. "Can you remember anything else about the intruder? When you said you thought it was a man, did you mean because of the person's size? The build?"

"Yeah, I guess so." She hesitated. "But Chantel is a big woman. It could have been her."

"How are we going to play this when she gets here?"

"Very carefully, sugar, very carefully. From what you told me, they don't have any evidence against her. It's no crime if she was standing outside my back door."

I nodded. If the police had released Chantel, then all bets were off. It's possible that she was telling the truth. That she'd had an urge for a private chat with Vera Mae and had dropped by unannounced. A little far-fetched, but possible.

Cyrus would be pleased to learn that his new star wasn't a murder suspect. I could think of one person who'd take the news very hard.

Big Jim Wilcox.

I heard shouting in the corridor, and Vera Mae stood up and opened her office door. Right on cue, Big Jim stormed down the corridor, past Vera Mae's office, his face twisted in a scowl. "So they're letting her go? How is that possible?" He was moving at a good clip, trying to keep up with Cyrus, who was rushing toward the newsroom.

"They questioned her and decided there was no reason to hold her. She admitted she was at the scene, but she didn't break into the house. They've got nothing on her. It was all a mistake." Cyrus looked relieved, which seemed to aggravate Big Jim even more.

"A mistake? Well, I'm not satisfied with that explanation. The police have been wrong before," he said peevishly.

"They're not wrong," Cyrus said. "Give it up, Jim. It's not a story. It's a nonevent."

"It was a story, my story." Big Jim threw up his hands in defeat and then let them sink slowly to his sides. He watched as Cyrus disappeared down the hall into the newsroom, and then he saw us staring at him through the open doorway.

Vera Mae motioned for him to come inside. "Guess you heard the news," he said, his face a mask of despair. "The police are letting Chantel go. They didn't manage to pin anything on her. This time," he said darkly.

"And that means they're canceling your exclusive." Vera Mae winked at me. "Must be quite a blow, Jim. Of course, if

Maggie here solves the double murder, you'll have a big ole story that will probably go national."

He looked at me with a sudden interest in his eyes. "Are you hot on any leads, Maggie? Anything I should know about?"

I shook my head. "Nothing yet. When I come up with something, you'll be the first to know."

I glanced at my watch. I had plenty of time to follow up on a couple of leads right now. "Vera Mae," I said suddenly, "you don't need me for a while, do you?"

She shook her head. "No, everything's under control here. What's up?"

I smiled. "I've got to see someone about a painting. And then I've got to visit the library."

Vera Mae raised her eyebrows, and Big Jim looked puzzled. It didn't matter. I suddenly realized that a few loose ends were falling into place.

"Of course you can take the picture," Candace Somerset said to me a few minutes later. I'd rushed over to the historical society from the station, hoping that she hadn't already left town.

"Is it this one?" She stood on her tiptoes and lifted the Joshua Riggs off the wall. "It's not very attractive, is it?"

"No, but it might give us some information about what happened to your sister. I'll need to keep it for a few day. Is that okay?"

"Yes, of course." She hesitated. "You'll have it back by the end of the week, won't you? Because I really want to lock everything up and get back home. And the painting is part of the collection." She ran her finger over the Parsons bench in the hall and frowned. "I'm going to have this place cleaned professionally before the estate sale starts. There's a layer of dust on everything. I think it was too much for poor Althea to keep up. She did the best she could, poor thing."

I nodded. "I understand." I took the Joshua Riggs painting and carefully wrapped it in two plastic grocery bags before tucking it under my arm.

"Candace, this sounds like a silly question, but did you move this painting? I'm pretty sure it used to be hanging over here, on the other side of the watercolor."

She gave me a blank stare. "No, of course I haven't moved it. Why do you ask?"

I thought about what Shalimar had said about sunlight making colors fade. "Well, for one thing, see the empty spot where it was hanging?" I pointed to the burgundy-colored wall. "See how there's a large square that's a deeper color than the rest of the wall and larger than the Joshua Riggs painting? That tells me there used to be a bigger painting hanging here. It protected the wall from the sunlight, and that's why the paint is a darker color in that place." I gestured to the pond scene. "I'm pretty sure the Joshua Riggs was moved very recently. Someone switched it with the pond scene."

Candace took a closer look. "You're quite right. The color is deeper—and larger than the Joshua Riggs painting. Very strange." She shook her head. "Someone must have moved the painting. But why?"

"I don't know yet." I hesitated for a moment and glanced down at the floor. The hallway was dimly lit, but saw a faint dusting of blue powder near the baseboard. Again. Blue dust? Alarm bells were ringing in my brain. "Candace, can I ask you a favor? You mentioned you were going to get the place cleaned. Could I ask you to please hold off on the cleaning crew? Don't let anyone touch anything until I get back to you. Okay?"

Her blue eyes clouded with surprise. "Yes, I suppose so, but—"

"Please, just do it. It's important." If my guess was right, it was *vitally* important.

"All right, then." She gave a little shrug. "I'll wait to hear from you before I hire a cleaning crew." She shook her head. "I'd love to know what your plan is."

I grinned. "As soon as I know, you'll know." I put the painting in the trunk of my car and headed down to the Cypress Grove PD.

It was time to get Rafe in on the case. Vera Mae was right. There was only so much I could do on my own.

"Tell me again your theory about the painting," Rafe said half an hour later. "You borrowed it from the historical society because you think it's involved with Althea's death." Rafe looked a little haggard, as if he'd been up all night. He had dark circles under his eyes and a sexy stubble on his chin. Tired or not, he was still drop-dead gorgeous, and I felt a familiar little buzz go through me.

"It's not the painting," I said patiently. "Well, maybe it is the painting, but—"

"One sec," Rafe told me as his desk phone rang. He held up a finger. "Yo," he said softly into the receiver. He listened, nodding a few times, and then said, "Got it," and hung up. "Okay, Maggie, start over again. It is the painting, but it's not the painting? Is this a riddle or some sort of psychological quiz? Because I'm all tapped out. I'm not going to play games."

"This isn't a game!" I leaned forward out of my chair and slapped my hands palm down on the desk. The painting was leaning against a file cabinet. "Rafe, somehow that painting is involved in Althea's murder."

He stared at me for a long moment. He steepled his fingers. "And you know this how?"

"I just know it." I held up a hand to silence him. I knew he was revving up for a quick comeback. "But it's not the painting itself. I think there's something funny about the painting."

"You do?"

"Yes. Maybe there's something underneath the painting. I'm not sure." I told him what Althea had told me about painters sometimes hiding one painting behind another, and then I mentioned the blue chips that I'd seen in Althea's front hall. The same chips I'd seen over at the frame shop when I'd met with Chris Hendricks.

Rafe nodded, but I could see he wasn't wildly impressed with my theory. He leaned back in his desk chair, clasped his hands behind his head, and contemplated the ceiling. Meanwhile, I contemplated him. Always a pleasant diversion. Unfortunately, I couldn't give it my full attention, because I had to plead my case.

"And it's not just the blue chips I saw in both places," I said firmly. "There's more evidence I haven't told you about."

Rafe made a let's-speed-this-up motion with his hands and glanced at his watch. He'd already told me he was meeting with the chief of police in ten minutes to give a progress report, so I knew I had to cut to the chase.

I took a deep breath. "Chris Hendricks was acting very suspicious when I visited his shop."

"Really. Suspicious, huh?" He gave me a lazy smile, and the words hung in the air between us. I realized as soon as I'd said them that I hadn't been forceful enough. "I suppose you happened to psychoanalyze him in your brief meeting with him?"

"I didn't have to psychoanalyze him," I said forcefully. "The guy was a nervous wreck. He was sweating bullets and he had a facial tic. It wouldn't take Sigmund Freud to know something was really wrong."

"Ah. A facial tic."

"And his foot wouldn't stop tapping. It's like it had a life of its own." Oh, no. Rafe in condescending mode was more than I could take. Why wasn't I getting my point across? "He was definitely acting suspicious," I said. "I knew right away he was trying to hide something." I pulled out my ace in the hole. "In fact, here's something that will surprise you. Did you know that Althea had visited his shop? Right before she died?"

Hah. That got his attention. Rafe snapped his chair to the upright position and grabbed a legal pad. Suddenly he was all business. "He told you that?" He locked eyes with me, pen poised.

"Yes. He didn't want to, but he finally admitted it. At first he denied any knowledge of the painting, and then when I questioned him, he said she'd come into the shop. She was thinking about having this painting reframed, and they couldn't agree on a price. Althea wanted a discount, and he wasn't prepared to give her one. He said she walked right back out with the painting."

"Hardly a motive to kill someone."

I waited for a beat. "No, but there's more going on. Don't you think it's funny he never thought to come forward with that information? He kept his mouth shut even though he knew the police were looking for leads. I'd say that was suspicious, wouldn't you?"

Rafe nodded. "Maybe, or maybe he just thought it wasn't significant. I'm sure Althea visited a lot of shops in the week before she died. Who is this guy again?" I handed him the card Chris Hendricks had given me, and he copied down the information.

"What are you going to do?" I saw him eyeing the painting.

"We can have our CSIs analyze it." He walked over and touched the plastic wrapping. "You probably should have left it where it was," he said. "It makes more sense from an evidence-collecting point of view. It's better to examine it at the site where it was discovered."

"Maybe in theory that's true," I acknowledged. "But would you have bothered sending an officer over to the historical society to look at it?" I bit back a sigh. "Would we even be having this conversation right now?"

One eyebrow quirked. Rafe ran his hand through his thick, dark hair and gave me a knowing look. "Okay, Maggie, you win. I get your point. You took the bull by the horns, and maybe that's not a bad thing. If you hadn't brought the picture over here"—he shrugged—"who knows what would have happened? But since it's here, let's consider it as evidence. I'll get someone to look at it today. And I'll even get Officer Brown to have a chat with Chris Hendricks." He glanced down at the grayish linoleum. "I see what you mean. It looks like little blue particles are falling out of the picture. There must be a hole in the plastic."

"That's what I was trying to tell you. It's like blue confetti."

Rafe picked up a piece with the tip of a pen and dropped it into a clear plastic evidence bag. He held it up to the light, squinting at it. "Except it's not confetti. It's not even paper. It's hard, like plastic."

"Then what is it?"

He held the bag up to the light. "I'm not sure, but I think it's paint."

"Paint? Blue paint? That's odd, right? Because there's no blue in the picture. Look for yourself." The painting was a study in earth colors: muddy brown, with a few spots of tan and rust.

Rafe stared at the painting for a long moment, and then our eyes met. "There's something strange going on here. You're right. It may take the tech guys a little while to figure it out, but they will. They'll keep going until they've got the answer. They're the best in south Florida." His cell phone chirped then, and he flipped it open, glanced at the readout, and frowned. "Time for the meeting with the chief." He scooped up some papers off his desk and touched my cheek with one finger before he headed for the door. "Later, Maggie."

Chapter 26

"Terrible what happened to Miss Mildred," an elderly librarian told me a few minutes later. Her snow-white hair was tightly secured in a French twist, and her name tag said AGNES MILTON. I'd stopped by the Cypress Grove Public Library to pay a call on Miss Gina Raeburn, the library's director, and was waiting at the circulation desk while they paged her.

"Yes, it must be a great loss for all of you. And for the patrons, as well. I understand Miss Mildred had been here for a number of years."

"All her life." Her eyes brimmed with tears. "I still can't believe she's gone. It happened over there, you know," she added, lowering her voice. She glanced over her shoulder. "We've kept her office closed off since"—she paused delicately—"the incident."

"Oh, yes, I understand." Funny the way she referred to the murder as an "incident," but everyone has a different way of processing grief. I glanced over at the tiny cubicle that had been Mildred Smoot's office for nearly half a century. It was tucked behind the circulation desk and wouldn't be immediately visible to anyone walking past the main desk. I tried to imagine the awful scene when someone crept into the library and attacked her. She was frail and couldn't have put up much of a fight. Rafe had told me that there weren't any defensive wounds on her body. One swift stab with the letter opener and it was all over. Could she have known her attacker? Maybe she had even let the killer into the library after hours?

"Did she often work here late at night?"

"Yes, I'm afraid she did. She took on way too many responsibilities, you see." She gave a sad smile. "This library was her whole life. She was the first one here in the morning and the last one to lock up at night."

"So she was alone in the building twice a day. Did many people know that?" If the killer had time to plan the attack, then it couldn't have been a random crime. Someone wanted Mildred dead.

"Well, just about everyone who used the library knew it, I guess." She peered at me. "The police asked me the same thing." She hesitated and then added, "I suppose I shouldn't say this, but are you sure they're doing everything they can to find the killer? I can't believe they don't have any leads in the case. And coming so soon after the murder of Althea Somerset. What's our little town coming to?" She shook her head, her eyes misting with tears.

I was making sympathetic noises when a tall woman with silver-blond hair appeared next to us.

"Maggie Walsh?" she said briskly. "I'm Gina Raeburn. Please come into my office. We can talk privately. I hope you like chamomile tea." She smiled as she led the way.

"I love it. My roommate makes it every day. She finds it soothing."

"She's quite right. That it is."

Her office was a stark contrast to the rest of the library. It had sleek Danish furniture in polished teak, bold abstract paintings on the walls, and a colorful Mexican rug on the floor. She waved me to a love seat next to a bay window that looked out onto a garden in the back of the library. She'd set out tea and sugar cookies on a low coffee table.

"Thanks so much for seeing me."

"I want to do anything I can to make sure Mildred's killer is brought to justice," she said, her tone direct. "I'd like to think the police are on top of things, but I'm beginning to doubt it. They came by and did a cursory examination of her office, took the murder weapon, and that's the last I've heard from them." An angry flush crossed her porcelain-like skin.

"I'm sure they're doing what they can," I said diplomatically. "They probably can't show their hand too quickly because they're building a case. I'm sure the uncertainty is very hard to deal with." I waited until she nodded before I went on. "It sounds like Mildred didn't have any enemies, and I suppose nothing was missing from the library?"

"Nothing was missing. Not even the few dollars we had in petty cash." She paused to pour us both a cup of tea. "Do you think they have any leads yet?"

"I'm afraid I'm not really in the loop," I began, but she cut me off.

"But you do the news at WYME, don't you? You have every right to be involved."

I smiled. She must not have realized that I was low on the totem pole at the station. "I do a talk show, not really hard news. What I do is entertainment." I didn't want to admit that Big Jim Wilcox was unofficially covering the case for the station. I'd lose what little credibility I had.

"I thought you had some theories about the case and that's

why you wanted to see me." She gave me a speculative look. "You know that I gave Vera Mae a box of Mildred's personal papers, right? I dropped them off at her house the other night."

I nodded. "Yes, I know that. I wondered if they could have had anything to do with Mildred's murder, but I haven't had a chance to look at them yet. Vera Mae said they were connected to some research Mildred was doing on the time capsule celebration. A series of e-mails, that sort of thing."

"Yes. Mildred was fascinated by the time capsule, and she was communicating with historians all over the country. She was so excited when she was a guest on your radio show. It was quite a thrill for a small-town librarian. You know, she got letters from listeners in Boca and Miami after she was on the air."

"Really? I'm glad to hear it."

I had the feeling there was something Gina Raeburn wanted to say to me, and I wondered why she was holding back. Was there something I didn't know about Mildred, some dark secret in her past? It seemed unlikely. And it also seemed improbable that in a gossipy little town like Cypress Grove, I wouldn't have heard it by now.

I glanced at my watch. I needed to get back to the station to prepare for my afternoon show, so I took a chance. "Miss Raeburn—," I began.

"Call me Gina, please." She smiled.

"Gina." I took a deep breath. "Are you sure there isn't anyone who had a grudge against Mildred? For any reason at all? I'm sure the police have asked you this, but I thought that maybe you've had more time to think about it—"

"Everyone loved her," she said firmly. "There was no reason not to love her. She was a wonderful person." The words shot out of her mouth like bullets, and she tilted her chin defiantly. Vera Mae did the same thing when she was annoyed, so I knew that look very well.

"I'm sure she was wonderful," I said, hoping to placate her, "but sometimes people harbor a grudge for no good reason."

She gave me an intent look, reached for her tea, and stopped. She started to say something, bit her lip, and then said, "That can happen, I suppose."

"There can be misunderstandings, arguments going back decades." I waited a moment. "I've seen it happen again and again back in my psychology practice back in Manhattan. The presenting problem was just the tip of the iceberg. People would start to tell me all about their current problems, and suddenly they'd start talking about some long-buried grudge, something that should have been settled years earlier. And the anger was so fresh, you'd think it had just happened. Mildred could have been a wonderful person, and still have an enemy out there."

Gina nodded. "I know you're a psychologist. That's why I thought you might have some special insight into Mildred's murder. I figured you could be the one person who could connect the dots. No one in town seems to be able to do that."

"Well, I'm glad you have faith in me." I smiled at her. "I'd like to connect the dots, but first I need to find out more about Mildred." I glanced at my watch. I really needed to be going if I was going to have time to go over the guest material for today's show. I took a last swallow of tea and stood up. "Are you sure there's nothing else you can think of?"

"Nothing other than what I've already told you. You could start by reading her papers," Gina said crisply. "That would be the best place to begin. You might find the answer in her own words." I stared at her for a moment. Was she directing me to something specific in the papers? I had the feeling she'd read them. Gina leaned back and stared at the bright pink hibiscus bushes lining the garden. I knew with absolute certainty that she'd said all she was going to say on the issue.

Rafe had ruled out Gina as a suspect in the break-in at Vera Mae's place. According to the security tape, she'd been in the house for less than thirty seconds. She was seen on the security tape opening the back door holding a cardboard box, and then emerging without the box, seconds later. But was there something she wasn't telling me? I had the nagging feeling there was more to the story.

I left my card on the coffee table. "I'll go through the papers tonight, Gina. Maybe something will jump out at me. I certainly hope so."

"So do I, my dear, so do I."

I was passing the circulation desk on my way out when a display caught my eye. CYPRESS GROVE, THE LAST HUNDRED YEARS. Hmm. The librarian at the desk noticed my interest and smiled. "We just put that up last week, in honor of the upcoming time capsule ceremony. It's gotten quite a lot of interest."

"It's a lovely display," I said, wandering over for a closer inspection. Someone had made a montage of old letters, menus, and photographs that looked vaguely Victorian. A few yellowed textbooks were arranged on a table along with a genuinely old-looking Bible and a watermarked dictionary. "No newspaper clippings from those days," I said softly.

"No, it's a shame. I suppose you know the newspaper building burned down?"

I nodded. "I heard about that. And the courthouse records were destroyed as well. It seems sad that so much history could have been wiped out, just like that."

"Yes, it certainly is. Of course, people have their family Bibles for records of births and deaths, and some of the more prominent families were featured in the bigger newspapers. Regional newspapers, I mean."

"Really?" I hadn't even thought of that angle. Regional newspapers, of course. I should have been doing some research up in Palm Beach or maybe Miami.

"Of course, they didn't cover stories about ordinary folks, just the ones who were wealthy, or who owned lots of land and property. We do have some resources, though. We have some interesting pieces on microfiche. We haven't gotten around to putting any of it on computer. There's always so much to do, and we're understaffed at the moment."

"Microfiche?"

"Would you like to look at it?"

I glanced at my watch, wishing I weren't so pressed for time. I would have loved to take a look, but I couldn't spend the next few hours churning through spools of material. Probably ninety percent of it wouldn't be relevant, and just to make it more complicated, I really didn't know what I was looking for. "Maybe another time," I said.

"You should probably reserve it," she said. "We can leave them behind the desk for you, if you know when you'll be back." She pointed to a man in his forties seated at the far wall of the library. His eyes were glued to the screen, and he was making notes. "That gentleman's been sitting there for hours. Maybe all the excitement about the time capsule sparked his interest in local history."

"That must be it," I agreed. I felt a little shot of adrenaline go through me when I caught a better glimpse of the man viewing the microfiche machine. My thoughts scurried like a manic squirrel as I tried to remember where I'd met him.

Suddenly it came to me. Ted's wine party at the Seabreeze Inn. He'd introduced me to Trevor McNamara, who was supposedly in town looking for vacation properties. So why was a real estate broker looking at material from a hundred years ago?

"Was there something else you needed?" The librarian was staring at me, probably puzzled by my sudden fascination with the microfiche machine.

"Just one more question. There's nothing current on microfiche, right? Everything is old and out of date. It's all historical material, I mean," I amended quickly.

She looked surprised. "Yes, you're right. Everything current is on computer. The microfiche spools contain material with some historical interest. They date back several decades. Would you like to reserve something?"

"Not now, but I'll keep it in mind. Thanks." When would I ever have time to look at it? And more important, what was Trevor McNamara doing researching the past?

I was more convinced than ever that his story about looking for vacation properties was bogus.

"If you change your mind, you can sign up for it right here." She pushed a ledger across the counter to me. "We don't permit the microfiche spools to leave the library, but you're certainly welcome to look at them here, for as long as you like. Mildred used to be in charge of all this, but I'm handling the reference materials at the moment."

"Thanks." She turned to answer a phone call and I glanced through the ledger. There were very few entries. Apparently not too many people were interested in tripping down memory lane. The only name on today's page was Trevor McNamara. I glanced at my watch. He'd been looking at the material for more than two hours. What did he find so intriguing?

I idly turned the pages, and then one name jumped out at me.

Shalimar Hennessey.

She'd checked out some microfiche spools to look at a few days ago. Interesting. What was even more interesting was that she'd checked them out the day of Mildred's murder.

And they had never been checked back in.

Chapter 27

I drove over to WYME, my thoughts in a whirl. Shalimar didn't seem like the type of person who read books, much less historical material, and I couldn't imagine her spending hours hunched over a microfiche machine. I hadn't seen a single book in her house, just a copy of *InStyle* on a table in the foyer. And that wall of books-as-decor in the library. She'd told me she was fascinated by the upcoming time capsule celebration, but I was sure her interest was bogus.

I called Nick on my cell as soon as I pulled into the WYME parking lot and caught him at his desk. I filled him in on my visit to the Cypress Grove Public Library. I think it would be fair to say he was underwhelmed by the news.

"But don't you see?" I wailed. "This could be a big break in the case. First I spot Trevor McNamara zipping through a pile of microfiche spools, and then I see Shalimar's name on the same ledger. They both were looking for something. This has got to be significant. I'm positive of it!"

"I think you're reading too much into it," Nick said. I could tell he was multitasking, probably churning out a story while he kept the phone tucked against his shoulder. I could hear him tapping away on the keyboard, and every couple of minutes, I could hear him taking a big slurp of something. Probably his ever-present coffee.

"You don't think it means anything?" My spirits sank like a deflated balloon.

"Nope." More furious tapping and then, "Wait a sec. I just thought of something. Did Shalimar check out the microfiche materials herself? You said her name was on the ledger, but do you know if that was her handwriting?"

"Gosh, I don't know." I thought for a moment. I flashed on the page. All the patron names had been entered in the same delicate, precise handwriting. "Actually, I'm pretty sure it wasn't Shalimar who wrote her name in the ledger. Someone on the library staff must have made all those entries. Because the handwriting is the same in every one of them."

"Mildred Smoot?"

"Probably. Someone was very neat, very methodical. There was the patron's name listed, the time the material left the circulation desk, and the time it came back."

"And you're sure no one is allowed to remove the microfiche spools from the library?"

"I'm positive. They're valuable. That information isn't contained anywhere else. Or if it is, it would be hard to track down. You have to look them over while you're in the library."

A long pause.

"I think this could be important," he said finally. "I'm just not sure how."

I sighed. "Me, either." I thought for a minute. "Nick, you don't think Shalimar could be involved in Mildred's murder, do you?"

"I don't think so. I can't imagine what her motive would be."

I sighed. "Neither can I."

Vera Mae was waiting for me in the lobby. She waved a sheaf of papers at me as soon I walked in the double glass doors and waved to Irina at the reception desk. "Time capsule promos," she said by way of explanation. "Cyrus wants you to tape these today so we can run them every half hour during drive time."

"Every half hour?" I said, following her into her office. "He's really pushing the time capsule celebration, isn't he?"

"Big-time. It seems like people are excited over it. And don't forget the ceremony will be here in a couple of days, hon." She lowered her voice. "I'll give you a little heads-up. Chantel showed up. She came strolling down the corridor like nothing was wrong, about an hour ago."

I glanced around as if I expected the medium to suddenly materialize next to me. "She's got plenty of moxie. Did she say what happened down at the police station?"

"Not much. They released her. Apparently they can't hold her on anything. Big Jim tried to get a statement out of her, but she blew him off. She went right in to see Cyrus, and the two of them have been huddled in his office for the past half hour." Vera Mae gave a grim smile. "Thick as thieves. That's what they are."

"Interesting."

"Maybe he's gonna pull the plug on her. No more guesting on your show." Vera Mae said. Her voice went up at the end in a hopeful little lilt.

"Or maybe it's something else!" *Like maybe she's angling to take over my show, and maybe Cyrus is going along with the idea.*

"Here she comes," Vera Mae whispered. "Play nice."

"Hello, Maggie," Chantel said. Her eyes darted to Vera Mae and back to me, as if she knew we'd been talking about her. I tried to keep my expression neutral. She spotted the sheaf of promos I was holding. "I bet those are for the time capsule. Looks like a busy day for both of us in the production room."

"Really?"

"Yes, really." Her mouth twisted in a sneer. "I've been assigned a ton of promos." She lowered her voice to a silky purr. "It's going to take hours, but I have to do it. Cyrus says I've got the perfect voice for radio."

"So we're *both* doing the time capsule promos?" I asked. It came out shriller than I intended, but I was feeling pretty territorial at the moment. It was more than the promos; I hated the idea that she was intruding on my turf. Not that there was much turf to protect anymore.

As Irina would say in one of her favorite mixed metaphors, "The barn door is open and that ship has already sailed."

"Cyrus asked me to do them as a personal favor," she added snidely. "I told him I don't usually do promos, but it's for a good cause, so I'm willing to play along. After all, the time capsule celebration is important in the town's history. If it brings some attention to Cypress Grove, I suppose that's a good thing. Who knows? It might even put this place on the map."

"But I thought you chose Cypress Grove because it's *not* on the map," I couldn't resist saying. "You said you liked the rustic charm, the small-town feel of the place." The words hung in the air, and she narrowed her eyes, shooting me a hard look. Then she gave a forced little laugh.

"Yes, I did say that, didn't I? Well, a girl's allowed to change her mind, you know." She drummed her fingers on the desktop for a moment. "Now that I've learned about the radio business, I think I've found my true calling." She turned to Vera Mae. "I'll be in the production room if you need me. I want to choose some music to go under the spots. Something classical with strings, but not elevator music."

"Sure, hon, that's fine. I'll be there in a few."

Chantel turned to leave and was about to step into the hall, when Vera Mae's voice stopped her.

"Chantel, I've been meaning to ask you something. Something personal." Chantel turned, her expression guarded. "Is this your first time in Cypress Grove? Because you sure look familiar to me." She stepped closer and peered at Chantel under the harsh fluorescent lights. "I just can't place you, but I'm sure we've met before. You feel it too, don't you?"

Chantel pinned Vera Mae with an icy glare, clutching her Gucci knockoff handbag to her chest, a defensive gesture. "I don't think so." She tried a light little laugh but couldn't quite pull it off. "People tell me that all the time. Maybe I have a double."

For a split second, I saw one of those microexpressions that psychologist Paul Ekman had discovered. I looked into her eyes, and my own eyes widened in surprise. What was I seeing? Fear? Apprehension? Maybe even panic?

"See you later," Chantel said abruptly and sailed out the door.

"Well, she didn't take the bait, did she?" Vera Mae said, fiddling with some tapes.

"Not at all. I think you caught her off guard, though. She's got to be hiding something."

Vera Mae nodded and closed her cubicle door. "Speaking of hiding something"—she bent down and retrieved a cardboard box from under her desk—"here are some of Mildred's papers. I think you and I should have a look at them together. I put the interesting ones on top."

"I didn't know you had a chance to go through them. I was going to do that tonight." I thought of my meeting with Gina Raeburn over at the library. She was hinting that I'd find something significant in Mildred's papers; I was sure of it.

"I didn't go through all of them, but I found some unusual things in there." She shot me a meaningful glance. "Do you want to take a quick look now? We have about thirty minutes before we have to get things rolling for the show."

"Sure. Let's do it. Two heads are better than one."

"But not three heads." Vera Mae put her finger to her lips and pointed to the bottom of her office door. Was someone standing there? Or maybe it was just a shadow. She raced to the door, pulled it open, and stared up and down the corridor. "That woman's making me paranoid," she said, returning to her desk. "But you know what they say, Maggie: just because you're paranoid doesn't mean they're not out to get you."

I grinned at her. "Let's get started. Show me what you found."

We spent the next half hour going over a strange collection of Mildred's personal papers. Some were printouts of e-mails she'd sent to other librarians in south Florida, and I copied down their names and addresses. I knew that Mildred was doing her own research on the time capsule and especially on Mr. Paley, the patriarch of the prominent south Florida family. All I found were Mildred's requests for information; there was no hint of what the responses had been. Had she been successful in her quest? Is that what ultimately led to her death?

"This here looks like a journal entry." Vera Mae passed me a handwritten sheet from a file. The heading on the page was October 18, but that didn't mean anything. There was no year listed. "I never expected Miss Mildred to keep a diary, but that's what this looks like."

"It sure does. A page from a journal." I scanned the lines. The text was a bit overwrought, and Miss Mildred seemed to be in emotional distress. "She's talking about regret, about making mistakes"—I skipped down to the bottom of the page— "and here she says that some things can't be undone." I looked at Vera Mae. "Do you suppose she's talking about herself? What could she have done that she regrets?"

"I can't imagine. I've known her for thirty years." She passed me another sheet. It had the header November 12. "Read this one."

No matter how much time goes by, and how many ways I say I'm sorry, it seems some actions can never be undone. My choices have had consequences that I couldn't have foreseen. I never planned on ruining anyone's life. I've always had a strict idea of what is right and what is wrong, but maybe I've been too rigid in my thinking. Maybe justice should be tempered with mercy. I fear that C.K. will never forgive me. I've begged her, but she refuses. Her heart is hard, but then, who am I to judge? I think I have ruined her life.

"Wow," I said softly. "This is heavy stuff. It does sound like Miss Mildred did something she was ashamed of, maybe something innocent that backfired. I really don't know what to make of it."

"Neither do I. And I wonder who C.K. is," Vera Mae said, chewing on the end of her pencil. "It can't be Chantel. Her last name is Carrington."

"It wasn't always Carrington." I put the paper back in the box, on top of the others.

"What do you mean?"

"Chantel Carrington is a made-up name, a stage name. A pen name. Her real name is Carla Krasinski. At least it used to be." I paused, thinking. "Of course, that was a long time ago. She might have had several different names since then."

"C.K. Carla Krasinski. That would be quite a coincidence, wouldn't it?"

"I'll say. I've got to talk to Rafe about this. And a few other things," I added, remembering the blue paint chips. I wondered how long it would take to get them analyzed and whether they would tie Chris Hendricks to Althea's murder. If anyone was taking bets on Althea's killer, my money would be on him.

"Do you think Chantel was involved somehow in Miss Mildred's murder? And maybe even Miss Althea's?"

"I think Chantel isn't telling us the whole story. I think she had a relationship with Miss Mildred, maybe one that went back a long time. And for some reason, she doesn't want to come clean about it. But I don't think she killed her."

"Why not?"

"I don't know. I just can't picture her as a killer. She's not my favorite person in the world, but no, I don't think she's a murderer."

"Then who killed Althea and Mildred?"

"I'm still working on that." I chewed on my bottom lip.

"There could be two separate killers," Vera Mae said slowly. "I know we've been thinking the crimes were linked, but is there anything that concretely ties the two crimes together?"

I shook my head. "Not really. They could be completely separate. Maybe we were putting too much stock in coincidence. Both were elderly women. Both had lived here all their lives." I bit back a sigh. "But you're right. The crimes might be completely unrelated."

My mind flew back to the microfiche ledger with Shali-mar Hennessey's name written on it. The idea of Shalimar doing historical research was as unlikely as Pugsley taking up quantum physics.

I had a gut instinct that Shalimar was involved in Mil-dred's murder, but I couldn't prove it. I also believed that Chris Hendricks was involved in Althea's death and couldn't prove it.

What was my game plan? I was planning my next move when Vera Mae's eyes bulged like Homer Simpson's and she let out a gasp.

"Holy buckets, girl! Look at the clock!" She jumped to her feet, clutching her trusty clipboard to her chest. "We can't worry about this anymore, sugar. We've got a show to do."

Chapter 28

The show went well. One of my guests, Jon Tidings, was a retired architect, an authority on south Florida homes, and a history buff. The other guest was Shirley Taub, a local historian and gardening expert who'd written a book about indigenous flowers and shrubs. They both painted an interesting picture of Cypress Grove at the turn of the century, and the switchboard stayed lit up throughout the show.

As Vera Mae would say, it was a "solid show." Not the type of show that would rock the ratings or lead to a local Emmy for WYME, but it was educational and entertaining. I figure it ranked a six on a scale of one to ten.

We were heavy on history and academic experts at the moment, in honor of the time capsule ceremony. Next week, we could go back to our usual mix of zany callers and light, off-the-wall topics, like people who eat Häagen-Dazs in their sleep and women who are shopaholics.

I checked the log book and saw that Vera Mae had already scheduled a Monday show on hoarders, which would surely pull in the ratings. Tuesday was devoted to why spouses cheat, which is always a hot-button topic. I looked for Chantel's name on the schedule and didn't see it. She wasn't listed as a guest host on my show, and she wasn't listed as a solo host.

Interesting. Maybe Cyrus was waiting to see which way the wind blew on the popular medium. My gut instinct told me there was something going on with Chantel, but not murder. I kept waiting for all the pieces to arrange themselves into a pattern in my mind, but it just wasn't happening.

"Not bad," Vera Mae said as we finished the last commercial and closed the show. Today she was wearing a T-shirt that said, I'M NOT SUFFERING FROM INSANITY. I'M ENJOYING EVERY MINUTE OF IT. She took off her headphones and wandered into the studio chewing on a Twizzler. "The lines stayed busy pretty much all the time."

"I need to record a few more spots." Chantel strolled into the studio and slapped some pages down on the console. She plunked herself in my chair and adjusted the mike so that it was close to her lips. "I've already chosen the music, so I think we can knock them out fast." She tapped the mike to see whether it was live. "The sooner we get started, the better." She gave a thin smile. "You know what they say: time is money."

"Sure thing," Vera Mae said. She waited until Chantel's back was turned, threw her a mock salute, and marched back into the control room. "See you later, sugar," she tossed over her shoulder to me.

I grinned and headed to my office, pondering my next move. My cell rang as I tossed my show notes on my desk, and I answered it without looking at the readout.

"Maggie? We've got something going on." *Rafe.* His voice was hurried, excited.

"What's up?" For a moment my mind stalled. "Is there a break in the case?"

"You bet there is. The forensic guys came up with an

analysis of those blue chips falling off that painting you brought in. They're azurite. There's no doubt about it."

"Azurite?"

The word sounded vaguely familiar, but maybe I was thinking of my high school French class. *Azur.* Blue. As in "Côte d'Azur." My pulse was thrumming. "And this is important?"

"Very important. Swing by the station, and I'll tell you all about it."

I didn't waste another second pondering. I waved a quick good-bye to a stunned-looking Irina as I headed through the reception area. "I'm going down to the police station," I yelled. "You can reach me on my cell."

Big Jim had been lounging on the sofa reading a newspaper, and he jumped to his feet. "Are you finally going to confess, Maggie? Which old lady did you murder?" He whipped out a notebook from his back pocket. "Was it Althea or Mildred?" His round face had turned a bright red from excitement, giving him an unfortunate resemblance to an heirloom tomato. "Or did you kill both of them?"

"Calm down, Jimbo. I didn't kill anyone."

"I can see it now," he said, his eyes glazed, seeing a bright future for himself at one of the big Miami stations. " 'When Shrinks Go Mad: A Big Jim Wilcox Exclusive.' This one will take me to the networks. I know it will."

"I'm telling you, I didn't kill anyone," I said, scrabbling for my car keys in my oversized tote bag. I looked at Irina. "Tell Vera Mae to call me down at the station, okay?"

"You won't be able to make any calls in lockup," Jim said gleefully. "Just one call to your lawyer. And they'll give you a public defender if you can't afford one. I want an exclusive, Maggie. Don't talk to anyone else. I better give Cyrus a heads-up on this," he called over his shoulder as he headed down the hall. "You're smart to turn yourself in," he added as a parting shot. "Maybe they'll go easy on you. Especially if they think you're nuts."

Irina and I exchanged a glance, and she lifted her shoulders in a delicate shrug. There are times when I'm convinced Jim Wilcox is certifiably insane. Ever since the day Rafe handcuffed and perp-walked me out of WYME after an explosion, Big Jim has been waiting for me to snap. He's convinced that I'm teetering on the edge of madness and all I need is a little push over the edge.

"Big Jim is . . . How you say?" Irina began. She tapped her ballpoint pen against her temple.

"Insane? Crazy? Loco?"

She smiled and nodded. "Yes, he is all those things. He is the very big idiot. That is what we would be calling it."

The very big idiot. It was perfect. I loved it. For someone who speaks English as a second language, Irina certainly has a way with words.

"The very big idiot. You'll have to tell that to your instructor, Simon Brent."

Irina's face clouded. "I haven't been telling you the sad news. He is no more here in Cypress Grove."

"He left town? What happened?"

Irina shrugged. "He is not good man, I don't think." She raised her eyebrows. "Not what he seems, if you know my meaning."

I hesitated. Had Simon Brent dumped her? "Was he married?" I asked.

Irina shook her head. "Oh, no, he is not married man. Much worse. He is pretending to be English instructor, but is all a spam."

Spam? "You mean a scam?"

"Yes, that's it. He's here only to meet Chantel and write the biography of her. The kind no one gives permission to do." Irina gave a little sniff. "He called to tell me truth last night. He left town this morning. I can't believe I was taking in by him."

So Simon Brent was here to gather material for an unauthorized bio of Chantel. Interesting. "I'm sorry, Irina. I know you liked him."

"Is okay," she said, her face brightening. "As Vera Mae says, there are many more fishes in the sea."

I smiled. "You're right on that one, Irina."

"So tell me about azurite," I asked Rafe twenty minutes later.

"You really don't know what it is?" We were sitting in his office, and he was shooting me a sideways glance, part thoughtful, part amused. "I thought you were an art-history buff. You told me that was your minor in college."

"I know a little about painters and styles but nothing technical. What's so important about azurite?"

He rubbed his hand over his chin, his dark eyes rolling over me. "Azurite is a pigment that they used to add to paint. In the old days."

I waited a beat. I dredged through my memory banks and came up empty. "In the old days. As in past tense?"

"Very past tense. They haven't used it since the turn of the century. Newer paints don't contain azurite."

"Aha. And that's important because . . ."

"Because our forensic guys found another painting hidden under that monstrosity that Althea had hanging in her hall. Someone had slapped a very amateurish painting over the real one. It's the real one that has azurite in the pigment. Someone painted right over it."

"And this original painting, the one underneath, is valuable?"

Rafe leaned back in his chair and locked his hands behind his head. "It's worth a small fortune. And I think it's stolen. The presence of azurite helps to date it. We've reported it to the FBI, and they're scanning their National Stolen Art File databases right now. I wouldn't be surprised if they find the owner by morning."

I knew art theft is big business worldwide. And hiding a painting under another one is the latest trend. You can remove the fake layer with a solvent, and there's no damage to the original.

I thought of Chris Hendricks and the blue chips scattered on the floor of his shop. "Where is Hendricks in all this? He must have been involved somehow."

"We're going to bring him in for questioning." Rafe sat forward, put his hands on the desk, and cracked his knuckles. "He's trying to give us the runaround, but so far he hasn't lawyered up. If he does, he'll clam up and we won't get anywhere."

"What do you need to do to tie him to Althea's murder?"

"We have to tie him to the crime scene. We have to place him at the historical society. The azurite chips aren't enough. Even if he discovered the painting underneath and planned on keeping it, that doesn't link him to the murder. He could be a thief but not a killer."

I thought for a minute. Chris Hendricks *was* a killer. I knew it.

I suddenly remembered the dust in the foyer of the historical society. A few azurite chips had slid under a doily on a Parsons table next to the umbrella rack. How had they gotten there? I remembered that Candace Somerset was a tall woman, and she had to stand on her tiptoes to reach the painting. And Chris Hendricks was short, maybe five-six. There was only one way he could reach the painting without using a stepladder.

"Rafe," I said suddenly, "I think you need to look at the crime scene again. And this time look in the front hallway. There's a Parsons table—"

"A what?"

"A table, a big piece of dark furniture, in the foyer. I think Chris Hendricks probably stood on it and hung the picture back up on the wall. A few blue chips fell off the painting while he was doing it." Rafe nodded, listening.

"What makes you think he stood on it?"

"He's a little guy, really short. So I figure Hendricks had to hang it back up there fast and get out of there."

Rafe looked interested, his eyes flashing. "Go on," he urged me.

"He had to stand on something handy, and the table was the closest thing. I bet he jostled one of the other paintings and it fell on the floor. He was in such a rush, he grabbed both the paintings and hung them back in the wrong place. And I bet he never noticed those little blue flakes falling off the painting."

"And he was in a hurry because—"

"Because he had just murdered Althea." My pulse was jumping. It was just a hunch, but I felt good about it. Everything was falling into place. All Rafe needed was the trace evidence to nail Chris Hendricks.

"Somehow Althea found out that Chris had uncovered the real painting underneath the fake one and was planning on stealing it."

"Althea could have confronted him—" Rafe's voice trailed off as he started writing furiously.

"That's what happened. I'm sure of it. He killed her and hung the painting right back up on the wall. That would have been the smart thing to do. He didn't dare take the painting right then and there, because he was afraid Althea may have told someone that she was having it reframed. And it would raise suspicions if it was missing. This way, there's no paper trail tying him to the painting. He figured he'd be in the clear."

"That's quite a theory. The question is, will it hold up? Can we prove it?" he said, his brows furrowed in concentration.

"As long as he got in and out of the historical society without being seen, he knew he was in the clear." The scene was playing itself out in my mind like a DVD from Netflix. "After all, he'd had time to examine the painting. He was the only one who knew it was valuable. The painting wasn't going to go anywhere. All he had to do was hang it back up on the wall and bide his time." I sat back in my chair, my mind buzzing.

"So you're saying this is the perfect crime?"

"Chris Hendricks thought it was. He figured he could come by the historical society and steal the painting at another time, maybe when her sister closed up the place. Or maybe he'd offer to buy it from her for a few bucks. Anything is possible. I know the society is auctioning off some items to raise money."

"Candace Somerset is in the dark about all this. I've already talked to her."

"Exactly. Candace Somerset doesn't know the true value of the painting. She hates it. She told me so. She probably would have given it to him if he'd asked nicely."

"I'll get someone over to the historical society right away." Rafe reached for the phone, and I zipped out the door. It was tempting to stay and talk with Rafe, but Vera Mae had just texted me with a 911 in the subject line. What was this all about? I had my phone to my ear before I was out the door to the parking lot.

Chapter 29

"Something interesting happened right after you left, girl," Vera Mae said. Her voice was low, excited. "Chantel let something slip. Something big."

"Big as in she murdered someone?" I was only partly teasing. I didn't think Chantel was a killer, but I also didn't think she was as pure as the driven snow.

"Not quite. Big as in she's not telling the whole truth about coming inside my house the other night." Vera Mae paused for effect. "I'm positive that she's the person I walked in on. She's the one who went running out the door."

"Is that so?" I murmured. There's no way to hurry Vera Mae when she's telling a story, and even though I was seething with impatience, I got in my car, willing myself to be patient.

"In fact, I think she lied to the police and she left out a *major* part of the story."

Okay, now my nerves were stretched taut like a rubber band. "Vera Mae!" I wailed. "I can't stand the suspense. What happened? Why do you suspect her?"

"Well, we were doing those time capsule promos, and she was having a fit because Tweetie Bird was singing and ruined a couple of takes. It was no big deal. They were only thirty-second spots, so it was easy to redo them, but she raised a fuss about it."

"I don't think she's ever liked Tweetie Bird."

To be fair, a lot of people at WYME don't like Tweetie Bird, a perpetually molting parakeet who is the love of Vera Mae's life. She brings him to work every day in his cage, and he regales us with his limited repertoire of sound effects and warbly renditions of show tunes.

Cyrus once tried to ban him from the building because of health reasons, but Vera Mae held firm and threatened to quit. Cyrus knows when he's beat. Tweetie Bird stayed.

"You're right. She doesn't like him, hon. And that says a lot about her character. Never trust a person who doesn't like animals, because they have a soul as black as tar. That's what my momma always taught me."

"But what happened?" I turned on the ignition but waited to pull out of the parking lot.

"Tweetie Bird was making his fire engine sound. You know the one?"

"Yes, I do." It was particularly annoying, high-pitched wail that set my teeth on edge. Vera Mae told me he'd mastered it after watching an entire *Rescue Me* marathon with her one weekend.

"Well, he did it right in the middle of the spot we were recording, and Chantel practically hit the ceiling. She snapped, 'That's as bad as his police siren imitation!'"

There was a long beat while I absorbed this. To my knowledge, Tweetie Bird has never made a noise like a police siren. "A police siren? Is this something new he's learned?"

"It sure is, hon. And the first time he tried it out was the other night when that intruder was in my house. My little Tweetie Bird was screaming his heart out, trying to protect me. And I have to tell you, it was pretty doggone realistic. The intruder took off running."

"But Vera Mae, you didn't mention any of this to the police."

"No, of course I didn't. I'd forgotten all about it. The whole thing came back to me when Chantel was talking about Tweetie Bird just now in the studio. I was so upset that night of the break-in, I guess I blocked it out of my memory. You said that can happen when people are traumatized."

She had me on that one. Amnesia is often a by-product of PTSD. It was interesting that the whole scene had come back to Vera Mae as soon as Chantel had mentioned it.

"You're certain Chantel has never heard Tweetie Bird do his police siren imitation somewhere else? Here at work, maybe?"

"I'm positive. He just learned it. He hasn't had a chance to do it at work. And I know Chantel doesn't like him, so I usually toss a cover over his cage when she's around. It would break his heart if he could see the evil looks she gives him."

I had to smile. Chantel had thrown a few evil looks my way, as well.

"We have to tell Rafe about this," I said firmly. "Did Chantel realize the significance of what she'd said?"

"I don't think so. I suppose she might, if she thinks on it a bit. But she was so mad over having her spot interrupted, I don't think she was thinking clearly. It just slipped out." She let out a breath. "You think this is important, right? The only person who could have known about Tweetie Bird's police siren imitation is the intruder."

"And if Chantel really was breaking into your house, then we have to assume she was looking for something. Did you tell anyone about the papers?"

"I told Irina," she finally admitted.

"Was Chantel around at the time?"

"She was standing at the front desk, asking about her fan mail. She could have heard me."

"That box of Mildred's papers could be the key, Vera Mae. Be very careful with them. Don't leave them around the station. In fact, don't let them out of your sight."

"I won't. I plan on dropping them off at my cousin's and asking her to put them in her safe. That's better than Fort Knox. Tomorrow we can turn them over to the police, if you think that's the right thing to do."

"Good thinking."

I drove out of the parking lot then, my mind in a tizzy. Knowing Chantel was the intruder put things in a different light, didn't it? She was after Vera Mae, not to harm her, but to get ahold of those papers. The question was why?

I thought about the heartfelt journal entries in which Mildred had confessed to doing something that could never be undone. It was hard to imagine Mildred ever harming anyone, but it seems that she had, even if was accidental. So maybe Mildred and Chantel had a history, just like I suspected. But how could I get to the facts behind the relationship? Mildred was dead and Chantel wasn't talking.

I thought of the one person who'd lived in Cypress Grove her whole life and had asked me to contact her if I needed help with anything. I needed help right now.

And Lucille Whittier might be the one person to give it to me.

"Maggie, this is a nice surprise." Lucille welcomed me into her well-kept home on the end of Water Street, in the older section of town. She lived in a charming Victorian, with a wide front porch shaded by banyan trees. "Would you like to sit out here? I always have a glass of iced tea at this time of day." I spotted a pitcher of iced tea with lemon slices floating on top, on a white rattan table.

"I'd love to." She disappeared inside to get another glass, and I checked out the wide-planked porch with its wicker chairs and swing. Very Old South. A place to relax and watch the world go by.

After she'd reappeared with the glass and a tray of cookies, she sat across from me. "I know you didn't drop by just to pass the time of day." She shot me a shrewd glance.

"You're very perceptive."

"That comes from living a long time," she said with a light laugh. "And living in a small town for a long time." She paused. "People think it's boring to live in Cypress Grove, but believe me, it isn't. You learn a lot about human nature living in a place like this. Secrets and jealousies and regrets. Everything bubbling under the surface, just waiting to make it to the top. I always think that's why so many great writers come from the South. There's so much good material here."

I smiled at her. "I hadn't thought of it that way, but yes, I see what you mean."

"Some secrets are meant to be kept, don't you think, Maggie?" I felt a little buzz of excitement. She knew something about Chantel; I was positive. But was she ready to say it?

"That depends," I said carefully. "Sometimes the cost of keeping a secret is too great. There could be a lot at stake, you know. Keeping the secret just prolongs things. It might be better to shine a light on some of these things that are hidden."

She was silent for a long moment. The only sound was the chirping of cicadas in the lush trees in her front yard.

"I think you want to tell me about Mildred," I said softly.

"You wouldn't be breaking a confidence. I already found a few pages from a journal she wrote. She talked about how much she regretted something she'd done. She thought she'd ruined someone's life."

"The truth always comes out, doesn't it?"

I nodded. "Yes, one way or another. It certainly seems that way." I hesitated. "I think Chantel Carrington is involved somehow. That's where I hope you can help me."

"Oh, yes, Chantel is part of the story. Because you have to know what happened with both women to understand what really went on." I leaned back in my wicker chair, afraid to say a word and break the spell. "I'll tell you what I know, Maggie, and you can decide what you should do with the information. I always thought I'd take this story to my grave, but as you said, there's a lot at stake. I've heard that the police were talking to Chantel Carrington about Mildred's murder. She didn't do it, of course." She said this with absolute certainty.

"But there was something between them that goes back a long way, right?" I was careful to keep my voice neutral.

"Oh my, yes, it goes back a very long time. And it was all so sad. Things didn't turn out the way they should. Chantel was a young girl here in Cypress Grove—"

"She lived in Cypress Grove!" I blurted out. "Vera Mae swore she recognized her, but she couldn't place her."

"That's because she looks quite different now. In those days, she was Carla Krasinski. I knew who she was immediately when she came back as Chantel, but I decided to hold my tongue."

"Why did she leave town?"

"She had to. It was really a shame, but she did a very silly thing when she was a teenager. She was working over at the town library one summer, and she embezzled some money. It was only a small amount of money, but you know how Mildred felt about the library. It was her life."

"Yes, I got that impression."

"She was shocked that Carla would do something like that, and she reported her to the authorities. Carla begged her not to, but Mildred felt that she had to do the right thing. It would have been nice if Mildred could have seen that justice needs to be tempered with mercy, but she didn't look at it that way."

"What happened?"

"Of course Carla was fired immediately. But the consequences were worse than Mildred ever intended."

"In what way?"

Lucille took a sip of tea before replying. "Besides losing her job, Carla lost her college scholarship. She came from a very poor family, and they couldn't afford to pay her tuition. She was a smart girl, so it was really a shame. She left town in disgrace and vowed revenge on Mildred."

"And she never came back, until now?"

"That's right. She was down on her luck for many years and took a series of waitressing jobs here and there. I have relatives down in Pigeon Forge, Tennessee, who kept me up to date on her. She never really got her life straightened out, and then something really awful happened. She was badly burned in a grease fire at a diner. It took years of reconstructive surgery for her to look the way she does now."

"But you recognized her? When she first came back to town?"

She gave a light little laugh. "Oh, yes, because of the eyes. I knew that was Carla right away. They say the eyes are the windows of the soul, you know. There was no doubt in my mind."

"This is amazing." I sat back, stunned. This was the last thing I'd expected to hear. "But you do believe she didn't kill Mildred, right? Because I don't think she did it, either."

"I'm positive of it. I think Carla came back here for one reason. She decided that living well is the best revenge, and at an appropriate time, she was going to reveal herself to the townspeople. Not as a poor girl who'd made a mistake but as a wealthy, famous celebrity. She wanted to show everyone that she'd made something of her life. But she never had murder on her mind. Never."

"Did you ever tell her you recognized her?"

"No, I decided to play along. I figured she'd tell the truth when she was ready."

I nodded somberly, my thoughts skittering around in my head like dry leaves tossed by the wind. Chantel hadn't killed Mildred. So now that left . . . Shalimar?

"Thank you, Lucille," I said, standing up to leave. "This has been very helpful."

"Not as helpful as the time capsule unveiling will be."

My heart stuttered. Another revelation? "You're telling me the time capsule holds the key to Mildred's murder?"

"Very possibly. I think it holds the key to a lot of things," Lucille said. "And I think you're probably the one person in town who can put all the pieces together."

I blinked. Lucille was right. This was a giant puzzle. And I knew that I had less than forty-eight hours to solve it.

Chapter 30

"Want to grab a quick bite to eat at Gino's?"

Rafe called me just as I was leaving Lucille's. I knew he was deep into the double murder case, and I hadn't expected to hear from him. When Rafe's in the middle of an investigation, I see him only on the fly and sometimes not even then. I glanced at my watch. It was five thirty.

"Of course," I said, a pleasant little thrill of anticipation going through me. "Do you have time?"

"Not really, but I'll make time. See you in a few." He clicked off abruptly in typical Rafe fashion, and I felt myself smiling. I left a message for Lark, saying I wouldn't be home for dinner, and headed down South Street to my favorite restaurant.

"I thought you'd like to sit outside," Rafe said a few minutes later. He was sitting at one of the patio umbrella tables and half stood up when he saw me. He touched my arm very lightly, and we locked eyes for an instant. It was a golden time of day, with the sun setting low in a sky filled with paint-box colors. A light tropical breeze was blowing, and I really felt like I was in paradise. Of course, sitting across from Rafe added to the magic of the moment.

"You guessed right," I said, sitting down across from him. I noticed he was toying with a glass of iced tea, but a goblet of chilled white wine was waiting for me. I lifted it and took a sip and smiled at him. "Another good guess."

"I'd join you but—"

"You're on duty." I played with the rim of my glass. "Where do things stand with Chris Hendricks?"

"He's stonewalling us, but I think he'll talk eventually." He looked at me, his dark eyes flashing. "What have you been up to? I know you've been asking questions around town." It always amazes me that Rafe knows where I've been and whom I've been talking to. When he asks me for details, I figure it's just a formality. He's already been tracking me like a bloodhound.

"I'm asking questions and getting some interesting answers. But I'm still not sure what it all means." I told him about Lucille's revelation about Chantel and the part Mildred played in her life.

"So that would give her a motive to break into Vera Mae's the other night. She might have known Vera Mae had some personal papers belonging to Mildred, and that the whole story might come out." He waited a beat. "But Vera Mae said the intruder was a man."

I shook my head. "But now she thinks it was Chantel." I quickly filled him in on Chantel's comment on Tweetie Bird.

"He makes a noise like a police siren? That's pretty circumstantial," he said. I could tell he wasn't impressed.

"Well, maybe it's not hard evidence, but I think it's significant."

Rafe snorted. "Our best bet would be if the tech guys can clean up that tape and give us a clear shot of Chantel breaking in."

A pretty blond waitress came to our table, and Rafe ordered a roasted veggie pizza for both of us. Since Rafe isn't a vegetarian, I thought that was a nice touch. The server took the order, flashed Rafe a dazzling smile, and left. He didn't even glance at her, and I felt ridiculously pleased at this. "But the break-in is only a side issue."

"I think so, too." I wondered whether this was the right time to bring up Shalimar Hennessey and decided to go for it. I had the sneaking feeling Rafe would think that seeing her name on the microfiche list was more circumstantial evidence, but I believed it was important. I told him what I'd learned at the Cypress Grove Library, and he listened carefully, scribbling a few notes on a napkin.

"It was the day of Mildred's murder?" He frowned. "I wonder why that log wasn't taken into evidence."

"Because they keep it at the circulation desk. If you only searched Mildred's office, it wouldn't turn up. It would be easy to overlook it."

"And the check-out time was—"

"Just a few minutes before closing time." I raised my eyebrows. "Why would she check out a microfiche when she knew the library was going to close in a few minutes?"

"Maybe she knew the kindly librarian would stay late and let her look at it?"

"Exactly. And that's the sort of person Mildred was. She'd do anything for the patrons."

"I need to get someone on that first thing tomorrow morning." He smiled. "Good work, Maggie."

"Rafe, another place to check is the microfiche area. There could be trace evidence linking Shalimar to the murder."

"I've already got that covered. The only thing we're missing here is motive. Just proving she was in the library isn't enough."

He was right. I was convinced that Shalimar was involved

in Mildred's murder. I knew it in my gut. I thought about something Lucille Whittier had said. "The eyes are the windows of the soul." There was something odd and unsettling about Shalimar Hennessey's hazel eyes. But what were they trying to tell me?

It was dusk when I pulled up in front of my town house. I saw Mom's car parked outside and smiled. That could mean one of two things. If she had decided to drive back to Cypress Grove from Miami, that meant her movie audition had gone very well, or it had gone very badly. Mom has a dramatic flair and she tends to show up unexpectedly, especially in times of joy and times of crisis. And with Mom, you can be sure it's either one or the other. She's constantly jazzed or in despair about her career prospects, and Lark and I try to be supportive.

I'd just stepped out of my car when I spotted Trevor McNamara bounding down the steps of the Seabreeze Inn next door. He saw me at the same moment and gave me an uncertain smile. He was obviously heading for his car, but I decided to intercept him. I'd been dying for a chance to ask him what he'd been doing in the Cypress Grove Library. The timing couldn't have been better.

"Nice evening," he said politely when we both reached the sidewalk.

"It's gorgeous. Are you headed back to the library to do some more research?"

The question nearly knocked him off his feet. He looked stunned, and I continued to smile at him, pretending I didn't notice his discomfort.

"Well, I—" He blushed a few shades of red, and I could see the wheels turning as he tried to come up with a response.

"I saw you over at the library earlier today," I said quickly. "You looked pretty absorbed in those old microfiche records."

He managed an embarrassed smile. "I suppose you could say I'm something of a history buff."

And I suppose you could say I'm Angelina Jolie.

"Besides being a real estate developer," I said lightly.

"Er, yes." He immediately looked down and away. He certainly wasn't what the shrinks call a practiced liar, because he was obviously uncomfortable with the conversation. And with lying.

"So I guess you'll be at the time capsule celebration?"

"Oh, yes!" He spoke quickly, and his face lit up with genuine pleasure. Interesting. It was obvious he was really looking forward to the event; he could hardly contain his excitement. "I wouldn't miss it for the world." He paused. "I suppose you're covering it for the radio station?"

I was surprised he even remembered I worked for WYME. "Actually, one of our newsmen is covering it. I'm just going out of interest." I gave him a steady look. "Like you."

This time the flush was back and creeping up his neck. "Well, I hope to see you there," he said. He gave an awkward little wave, reached for his car keys, and made a fast exit to his car.

I filed another puzzle piece away. Trevor McNamara was hiding something. But what?

"So you don't think Chantel was involved with the murders? I always had my suspicions about her, you know." Lola pulled her dressing gown around her and filled our cups with fresh-brewed chamomile tea. It was almost ten in the evening, and Lark and Lola and I were sharing a walnut-cinnamon torte fresh out of the oven. Sometimes I can hardly believe my good fortune: I have a roommate who loves to cook—from scratch!

"Chantel is a lot of things, but I don't think she's a murderer."

"But she's not what she seems, is she?" Mom said astutely. "I knew that the moment I met her. There was something a little off about her, a little je ne sais quoi."

"Je ne sais quoi?" Lark repeated.

"It loses something in translation," I said. Mom studied at the Sorbonne, and she's fond of slipping into French on occasion. "Literally, it means 'I don't know.' It means it's hard to put your finger on something."

"Well, that certainly fits. I love to analyze personality types," Lark confided, "but I never felt like I had a handle on Chantel. There was always something a little off about her. I always felt she had adopted a whole different persona." She gave a little sigh. "When I first met her, I really wanted to believe in her. But I always felt she was keeping parts of herself hidden."

"Exactly!" Mom exclaimed. "I always felt like she was hiding her true self and playing a part. What do you call that in psychology, Maggie? When someone adopts a whole personality that really is not their true self. You call that a false self, don't you?"

"Something like that. It's often found in people who are narcissistic. They're chameleons. They can be whatever you want them to be. It's very easy to be fooled by them."

I quickly described what I'd learned from Lucille Whittier about Chantel's sad and tragic past. If anyone had a reason to feel bitter and betrayed by life, it was Chantel, but somehow it was hard to feel sympathetic toward her. Possibly because there was something twisted and deceitful at the core of her personality? Or was I just jealous that she'd managed to breeze into town and pull in good ratings at WYME?

"And you believe she might have broken into Vera Mae's the other night?"

"Well, that's a tough question. They can't really prove it. She was there in Vera Mae's backyard, but there's no evidence she really entered the house. And she had no reason to be there." The notion that she'd dropped in to discuss show ideas seemed pretty lame.

"She certainly came up with a pretty silly excuse," Mom said archly. "That would make me very suspicious, right there. If someone lies about one thing, I immediately suspect everything else they say."

Lark nodded. "I'm the same way. It does seem a little far-fetched that she just happened to be in the neighborhood and wanted to talk business with Vera Mae. She could see her at the station anytime."

"Exactly. The whole thing is ridiculous!" Lola's tone was adamant. "I hope no one believes her." She turned to me. "Please tell me no one does, Maggie."

"I don't think Rafe does. But without any evidence that she was inside the house, there's nothing to charge her with. It's just a shame that the video surveillance camera went on the blink. It shows her walking up to the back door, and then it goes blank. So we're at an impasse," I said, "at least as far as Chantel is concerned."

"But if you're patient, the truth becomes clear, as my granny used to say," Lark offered. She cut us each another huge wedge of coffee cake; it was too delicious to refuse. Lola held up her hand like a traffic cop and then caved and took another piece.

"Yes, there are plenty of suspects." I told her what I knew about Chris Hendricks, the picture framer, and how he could have been involved in Althea's murder. "I certainly think he was involved with that painting, but beyond that, I can't be definite." I explained about the azurite chips the crime scene techs had discovered. I was glad that I had noticed that strange blue powder and even happier that it was related to the case. All my instincts about Chris Hendricks had been on target. He was a thief, at the very least, and maybe a lot more.

"It seems like the past comes back to haunt us," Mom said slowly. "I was thinking of those boxes of papers." She waved her hand. "It's hard to believe that someone would kill over some musty old notes, but maybe they did."

"It does seem amazing. If Mildred hadn't kept a journal, we never would have known about her connection with Carla, or Chantel as she calls herself. And if Chantel knew that Vera Mae was going to have possession of those papers, she would have to do everything in her power to get them. Even if it meant breaking into Vera Mae's house."

"Or worse," Mom said tightly. "What if she had harmed Vera Mae?"

I felt a little shiver go up my spine. I had thought exactly the same thing. I honestly didn't know whether Chantel was capable of violence. She was loud, pushy, deceptive—but a killer? Who could say?

"Secrets always have a way of coming out, don't they?" Lark mused. "All you need is one person with a heavy heart, maybe someone who wants to unburden herself, and it's like opening the floodgates."

"Exactly. And there might be a few more floodgates opening this week," Mom said. "Who knows what will happen at the time capsule ceremony. We all might be in for a surprise."

"Did you ever pick a winner for the WYME time capsule contest?" Lark asked. "They've been running those promos night and day."

"I know. I think Cyrus overdid it a little." I swallowed the last of my tea and stood up. "As a matter of fact, we did. We asked listeners to describe what they would put in a time capsule, and the winning entry was a quilt."

"A quilt?" Lola looked up.

"Not just any quilt. But a quilt that had a family tree woven into it, with all the births and deaths and babies and major events in a family's history. Cyrus thought that was the best entry of all."

Lola smiled. "You know, for once I agree with him. Maybe I underestimated that man."

Chapter 31

"This is going to be big," Cyrus said, looking up at the podium in front of the courthouse. It was a bright, sunny morning, a picture-postcard day for the time capsule ceremony. All the town's leaders were there, and the mayor was standing on a small platform draped with a red, white, and blue bunting. Cyrus had finally decided to let Big Jim cover the time capsule ceremony, and I was fine with that. Cyrus always takes the line of least resistance, and he knew Chantel and I were angling for the spot, but Big Jim had seniority at the station.

"It's certainly a good turnout," I said. Mom had come with me to the ceremony. It was nine o'clock and she had to be in Miami later that day, but she said she didn't want to miss the big unveiling.

There were hundreds of people milling around the square, and the town merchants had set up tables, selling handcrafted items and souvenirs. "Do you suppose they'll find a buried treasure inside?" Mom asked.

"I think you've been watching too many pirate movies," I told her.

"I bet they'll find a bunch of moldy old papers in that thing," Vera Mae said. "Let's just hope there's no water damage. It's gonna be pretty darn disappointing for all the media folks if this is a dud."

Nick was standing on the edge of the crowd with his notebook, getting quotes from the dignitaries, and I recognized a few reporters from the *Palm Beach Post* and the *Miami Herald*. Like Vera Mae, I hoped their trip hadn't been in vain. Big Jim Wilcox was hovering at the edge of the platform, with a WYME microphone prominently displayed. I spotted Mark Sanderson, the real estate developer, a few yards away; he looked tense and preoccupied.

Mayor Riggs stepped to the podium, greeted the crowd, and gave the usual politico spiel. Nice weather, beautiful day, good to see you all here. Yada, yada, yada.

I glanced back at Nick. He wasn't recording the mayor's remarks for posterity, and he was shifting from one foot to the other. I smiled to myself. He probably hadn't had his morning coffee and doughnuts. That's why he seemed edgy and distracted. I walked over to him and handed him a flask from my tote bag. "You're in luck," I told him. "I brought an extra mug of coffee."

"You are my hero!" He grinned, took the flask, opened it, and took a sniff. "Hazelnut?"

"Is there any other kind?"

"I think they're starting," he said, craning his neck to get a better view. A low buzz of excitement went through the crowd. I noticed Trevor McNamara just a few feet away from me. He was staring at me with an intent look on his face. I smiled, and he gave an uncertain nod.

Trevor McNamara, the mystery man. Somehow he was a part of the puzzle, and I was frustrated that I couldn't quite figure out where he fit in. Not as a killer, as something else. A word drifted through my mind. *Catalyst.* Where had that come from? What did it mean?

I felt the back of my neck prickle. Chantel was standing right behind me, a smug smile on her face. She locked eyes with me and said very softly, "Catalyst."

I nearly jumped. Had she read my mind? The notion was ridiculous, but the timing was uncanny. How could it be a coincidence?

I tried to gather my thoughts. Maybe she'd whispered the word and it hadn't registered with me but my brain had picked it up anyway. So the word "catalyst" had just been floating around in my synapses, and I thought it was something original, something I'd dreamed up. That was the only rational explanation.

"This could change everything," Nick said, his voice excited. His head was bent in concentration, and he was writing furiously in his notebook.

I dragged my attention back to the podium. While I'd been daydreaming, Mayor Riggs had already opened a dingy aluminum capsule the size of a cocktail shaker and pulled out some documents.

He began listing them as the handful of television cameramen huddled around the platform zoomed in for close-ups. Big Jim was elbowing a reporter from WTVJ out of the way so he could take a better look.

"I have here the original copy of Ronald Paley's gift of land to the city." Mayor Riggs's voice crackled a little over the microphone. "That's right, folks. This is the deed to the land you're standing on. The land this courthouse was built on." He unfolded the paper and peered at it more closely. "You know, this is truly a historic document." He passed it to the head of the town council. "Put this somewhere safe, Ed," he joked. "I don't recall seeing this anywhere else. This must be the only copy that survived the fire."

"Would you like me to read it aloud?"

"Well, there's probably nothing there but a bunch of legal mumbo jumbo," Mayor Riggs said in a low voice. "No surprises, right?" He suddenly remembered that his mike was live and put on a somber expression. "But this is a good opportunity for us to thank the Paley family for their generosity over the years. Without this land, there would be no courthouse."

Ed Taylor glanced at the document, and a shrewd look flitted across his face. "And according to this document, there will *always* be a courthouse here," he said. "No Royal Palm Towers, just our very own courthouse. That's what Mr. Paley intended, and that's the way it's going to be."

There was dead silence. No one reacted except Mayor Riggs, who drummed his fingers impatiently on the podium. He probably had a flowery speech all set to go, and I could see the news hadn't sunk in yet.

There was a vague murmuring in the crowd, and one of the town council members, Norton Townsend, stepped forward and whispered something in the mayor's ear. Mayor Riggs leaned forward, grasping the podium with both hands like he was on a sinking ship.

"What are you talking about, Norton?" This was followed by a nervous chuckle. "It sounds like you know something the rest of us don't." He shot Norton an annoyed look and turned his attention back to Ed Taylor. "Ed, on second thought, maybe you better fill us in."

There was an edge of uncertainty to his voice. I had the feeling he was wishing he'd never opened the time capsule.

"This is a deed restriction to the original land gift from Ronald Paley. We should give this to the town's attorney, but it seems pretty cut-and-dry to me. It says that this property can only be used as public land, never for any commercial enterprise. So no high-rises, no condos. Mr. Paley was very clear about what he wanted."

I heard a muffled gasp and turned to see Mark Sanderson's face go white. He had his arms folded across his chest as if he was literally holding himself together. In the space of a few seconds, his entire condo plan had gone up in smoke. It was like a magic trick. Now you see it, now you don't. Goodbye Royal Palm Towers.

For a moment, Mayor Riggs was flummoxed. "Ed, we'll have to discuss this later," he said quickly. "In private. That document you're holding—that wasn't part of the original papers that were filed with the Paley estate." He was obviously trying for a quick save, but it wasn't going to work.

"Not much to discuss." Ed Taylor gave a wry smile. "Everything you need to know is right here in black-and-white. This is a deal breaker. There won't be any condo project on this land. Ever." His voice was strong and carried all the way to the back of the crowd. "It's like a voice from the grave."

I gave a little shudder. *A voice from the grave?* Well, it was certainly true that Ronald Paley was reaching out across the years. Vera Mae nudged me and smiled. "Didn't I tell you things have a way of working out, sugar? Our little town can stay just like it is."

I stared at her. "You didn't have any advance notice about this, did you?" Sometimes I think Vera Mae is the psychic one.

"No, but I had one of my feelings about it. We don't need a condo project here in our Cypress Grove. And now it's not gonna happen. It all worked out the way it was supposed to." I had the feeling she wanted to give me a triumphant fist bump, but she restrained herself.

"Mark Sanderson looks pretty unhappy," I said, gesturing to the developer, whose face had turned from ghostly white to ashen gray. "This is disastrous news for him." His eyes were glazed, and he looked as if someone had kicked him in the chest. Hard.

"Cyrus won't be doing the happy dance either," she said. "Think of all that ad revenue sliding down the drain. We're just gonna have to work harder with our local accounts."

"So this is it? The surprise is over?" Nick said.

I nodded. News of the deed restriction was a shocker, and I figured it was going to be the big news of the day. I figured it would eclipse anything else that would happen.

I was wrong. Something even bigger was lurking on the horizon.

"There's more," Mayor Riggs said uncertainly. He pulled out a yellowing sheet of paper and examined it. "This seems to be a personal letter here that Ronald Paley wrote to . . . uh . . . one of his relatives." He read a little further and his eyebrows lifted in surprise. "This is not . . . Let me just say, the contents are very . . . uh . . . private." He shook his head, his face reddening.

A little excited buzz went around the crowd, and Nick raised his eyebrows. "Private? Sounds like a juicy scandal to me. I bet Big Jim Wilcox is salivating at this."

"Read it!" one of the Miami reporters shouted.

The mayor looked distinctly uncomfortable. "It wouldn't be appropriate to read this letter in a public forum, but I'll make sure this gets to the recipient immediately after the ceremony." He looked around at the town council members, and I figured he was trying to find a way to wrap things up as quickly as possible.

"Bobby Hennessey is Ronald Paley's grandson, his only living relative." Nick frowned. "So what's the big mystery? Where's he going with all this?"

"I don't know. But look at the expression on his face. I

bet he never expected to be sandbagged like this. And I don't think he's talking about Bobby Hennessey."

"You may be right." Nick gave a wry smile. "Riggs probably figured today was a great photo op. All he had to do was unveil the capsule, pose for a few pictures, and call it a morning. Now he's opened Pandora's box."

"And we both know how that turned out," I quipped.

Mayor Riggs put his hand over the mike and had a whispered conversation with the town's attorney, a reedy, nervous man, who'd joined him on the platform. After a couple of minutes, the attorney took the letter and stepped off the platform. Suddenly a silence fell over the crowd. Everyone was waiting for the other shoe to drop.

"There's one final document in here." Mayor Riggs's voice trembled, and he took a deep breath. He looked like he was afraid to open it. I could hardly blame him. Somehow the time capsule ceremony had taken on all the drama of a reality show. "It's a codicil to Ronald Paley's will."

"Uh-oh, now the real fun begins," Vera Mae said.

We waited as the mayor read the document silently and shook his head slowly from side to side.

"He's not gonna read it out loud?" Nick muttered.

The mayor cleared his throat. "I believe this codicil is genuine." A long beat. "But again, the contents are private and affect the disposition of some very important property. There are legal implications to all this. I'll need to notify the parties involved and meet with them and their attorneys later today."

"Somebody's going to get stung. I just know it," Nick whispered.

"I hope you'll all stay and enjoy the music"—he gestured to a brass band that was making its way down Main Street blasting a Sousa march—"and the Florida sunshine. Have a good day, everyone." His voice was ragged, but he forced a smile for the cameras and made his way off the podium to some scattered applause.

"Let's see where he's headed," Vera Mae said.

I watched as Mayor Riggs conferred with the town's attorney, and then the two of them joined Trevor McNamara. I stared for a minute, trying to figure it all out. Trevor McNamara was involved—but how?

"Maggie, who is that guy talking to Riggs?" Nick's tone was urgent.

"That's Trevor McNamara. He's staying at the Seabreeze."

"Who in the world is Trevor McNamara?" Mom chimed in.

"He's new in town. He says he's looking for vacation properties in town." Trevor McNamara was attracting some curious stares. He had his hand in his pocket, looking surprisingly calm and focused, talking to the mayor.

I saw Shalimar Hennessey out of the corner of my eye. She reached into her bag for her cell phone and started moving swiftly to the edge of the crowd. Interesting. She had a stricken look on her face, as if the news had hit her hard. But what were the implications for her and her husband, Bobby? I couldn't even begin to guess.

The ceremony continued, but it was anticlimactic, like a party balloon that's fizzled and gone flat. The handful of other items in the time capsule were held up for display, but they were mundane, of passing interest. Some handwritten recipes on yellowed paper, a bottle of laudanum for women "suffering from the vapors," a geological map of the county. The only interesting item was a photo of the town's first firehouse, complete with a Dalmatian. Odd choices for a time capsule. Either Mr. Paley wasn't imaginative, or he really couldn't be bothered with trivia.

"I knew it," Chantel said softly. "I knew this was exactly what would happen." I'd forgotten she was still standing behind me.

"How did you know?" The words slipped out before I could stop them.

"Because I'm psychic, you silly girl."

"And I'm a Victoria's Secret model," Vera Mae hissed as Chantel flounced away.

"What happens now?" I asked Nick. I saw Trevor McNamara walking toward the courthouse with the mayor and a couple of town councilmen. Apparently they were all going to get together privately and discuss Ronald Paley and the contents of the codicil.

"I wish I could get in on that meeting," Nick muttered.

"Forget it. It's going to be closed to reporters."

"We can always use FOIA." I knew Nick had used the Freedom of Information Act to gain access to other public records. Newspapers do it all the time. "But I bet the cops can get the information for themselves right away. All they have to do is say that it's relevant to an ongoing murder investigation."

"That's an interesting angle." I wondered whether Rafe was already on it.

I spotted Shalimar again. She had stopped near a park bench, and she was talking on her cell phone. She started moving away from the square, heading south, with the phone still pressed to her ear.

I was baffled, still trying to figure out how Trevor McNamara was connected with Ronald Paley.

Mark Sanderson, the real estate developer, was walking quickly toward his car, looking somber, and he also had his cell phone glued to his ear. Maybe he was calling all his investors, telling them the deal was off. Or maybe he was calling his accountant to tell him he was broke.

"Well, this has been fun, gang, but we still have a show to do. See you at the station, Maggie. Lola, if you need a lift, I can drop you off at home first. It's right on the way."

"Thanks. That would be great. I need to be in Miami by three for my big audition." She gave a girlish giggle and a quick hug good-bye.

Vera Mae peered at me. "Maggie, are you sure you're okay? You're gonna get wrinkles if you keep frownin' like that."

"That's what I always tell her," Lola tossed over her shoulder.

"I'm not frowning. I'm thinking." I gave a little distracted wave. "I'll be there in a few." I felt like all the principal characters were fleeing the scene and I was going to be left in the dark.

"Well, that wasn't quite what I expected," someone said behind me. I turned to see Gina Raeburn from the Cypress Grove Library.

"It was a total surprise," I replied. I was still puzzling over the news about the deed restriction and the codicil. Two bombshells in one day. I suddenly remembered that Rafe was supposed to be collecting evidence at the library this morning. "Have the police been by this morning?"

"Oh, no. We're closed for the morning, so our staff could attend the celebration," Gina said lightly. "We don't open till after lunch today. A lot of businesses are closed, you know." She frowned. "Are the police planning on paying us another visit?"

"Possibly," I hedged.

I was distracted for a moment, watching Shalimar making tracks down a side street. There was something furtive about her movements, and I wondered where she was headed.

Gina put her sunglasses on. "I better get going. I need to catch up on some paperwork at the library before we open."

"Are you walking over there now? I'd love to go with you."

She looked surprised. "Of course. I'd be glad to have the company. I've been wanting to talk to you about something."

"About the murder investigation?"

"No, something pleasant. I'm hoping you'll be our keynote speaker at our annual fund-raiser. We'd love to have someone with your expertise."

My cell rang just as I was pondering my answer. I flashed an apologetic smile at Gina, and she gave an understanding nod.

I flipped open the lid. *Rafe*. "You heard what happened at the time capsule ceremony at the courthouse just now?"

"Yes, I'm down at the town square right this minute. I heard the whole thing. Where are you?"

"I'm back at the station." He sounded regretful. Rafe hates to be out of the loop. "I have some information, though. Our contact at city hall just called us. According to that codicil, it sounds like the Hennesseys' home, Magnolia Hall, is changing hands."

I was surprised that Rafe had gotten the information this quickly, but this is the kind of thing he always does. "Magnolia Hall? Really?" Gina gave me a curious look, and I tried to keep my expression blank.

"That's what my source tells me. The mayor and the town's attorney are going to bring Bobby and Shalimar Hennessey in there for an emergency meeting later today. But guess who they're meeting with right now?"

"Trevor McNamara."

"You knew?"

"Yes, I saw them all going into the courthouse together."

"What do you know about him?"

"Not much. I've only seen him at the Seabreeze and at the library."

"I think he's the key to all this. He's the one who's inheriting Magnolia Hall. McNamara is in, and the Hennesseys are out."

"How is that possible? Is he even part of the family?" I pictured him as the black sheep. Maybe he'd been estranged from the family and then returned to town after all these years.

"I'm not sure. The information is still coming in. Got to go. Later. And Maggie—"

"Yes?"

"Keep this to yourself."

"You're quite the mystery lady," Gina said as I dropped the phone back in my purse. She gave me a curious look as we fell into step together.

"Not really. That was just a call about—about a show I'm thinking of doing."

She smiled. "Whatever you say, dear." I knew she didn't believe a word of it. We walked quickly past a row of stores, and I spotted Officer Duane Brown on patrol. The crowd was dispersing fast now that the excitement was over. I wondered what the newspeople would make of the information from the time capsule and how they would spin the story.

It was bad news for Mark Sanderson and his development company. But a windfall for Trevor McNamara if what Rafe had said was true.

Chapter 32

We'd reached the Cypress Grove Library and Gina was fumbling for her key in her purse when she gave a little gasp. "Oh, that was silly of me." We were standing outside the staff entrance in the back, and the door was open slightly. "I was working late last night and I didn't pull the door shut tight. That's the second time this month I've done this. I've got to be more careful."

"Gina, are you sure—" I felt a chill go through me. I reached for my cell phone, my heart hammering in my chest. "I don't think we should go in there."

"It's nothing. Don't be silly." She gave me a reassuring smile. "The wooden frame is a little warped, that's all." She pointed to the lock. "See, it's still locked. It's just because I didn't give the door a good strong pull. I must have been distracted."

She walked inside before I could stop her, and I followed. Gina made her way through the storeroom, past the employee lunchroom, to the door leading into the main part of the library.

As I looked through a glass panel in the door, I thought I saw a shadow move across the room. My heart stuttered to a stop. In a panic, I grabbed her forearm. "Gina, stop! I think someone's in there!" I hissed.

"Well, of course there is. Agnes Milton said she was coming in to do some work this morning, too." She gave me a sympathetic look. "I think you've been working too hard, Maggie. You're a bundle of nerves."

She pushed through the door into the main part of the lobby. We were behind the circulation desk, and the thick carpeting masked the sound of our footsteps. I noticed that only a few lights were on and the back of the room was shrouded in shadows. It was very still except for a faint noise coming from the direction of the microfiche machine.

I put my finger to my lips and motioned for Gina to hang back. This time she took me seriously, because her face paled and she put her hand to her throat. I inched forward and saw Shalimar Hennessey down on her hands and knees, plucking at the thick carpet and cursing under her breath. What was she looking for? Surely not the microfiche ledger book. As far as I knew, that was tucked away behind the circulation desk.

At that moment, Gina took a step backward into the shelving cart. A dozen books clattered to the floor, and Shalimar's head jerked up in alarm. For a moment, she was perfectly still, glaring at me. She reminded me of a jungle cat, crouching there. Her hazel eyes were fiery as she scrambled to her feet, pinning me with her stare.

Then I knew what had happened. It was her eyes that had driven her back to the library. Shalimar's eyes had been an electric shade of green before Mildred's death. But recently, her eyes had been a rich hazel color. Her natural color. One or both of her colored contacts must have become dislodged in a scuffle with Mildred and the CSIs had overlooked it. She figured this was her one chance to find the contact lens before they did another sweep of the place.

I reached for my cell phone, but she was too quick. In an instant, she closed the space between us and pulled a gun from her purse. Even though my thoughts were racing, I noticed that it looked like one of the antique weapons from her husband's collection. It was like a ladies' gun, a derringer. Was it loaded? Silly question. How could it not be? And what was she going to do to us?

My heart thudded in my chest, and an icy chill ran down my spine.

"Shalimar, don't—," I began, and I heard a muffled sob from Gina.

"Shut up!" she shouted. She put her left hand to her forehead, her brow furrowed, her mouth twisted in despair. "I need to think. I've got to figure this out!" Her voice had a crazed, almost pleading note to it, and she waved the gun in the air, finally pointing it right at my chest. She took a few steps toward me, walking in a straight line, the way a cat does when it's going to attack a small rodent.

Gina stretched her arm out, as if to ward her off. "Why . . . why did you bring a gun, Shalimar?"

Shalimar gave a high-pitched laugh and waved the gun in the air. "Oh, this thing? Bobby left it at a gun dealer's to be appraised and he asked me to pick it up when I came into town." Another maniacal cackle. "Pretty funny, isn't it? I never thought it would come in handy. Good thing he was stupid enough to forget it was loaded."

"You're just making things worse for yourself, Shalimar," I said, forcing myself to be calm. My mouth felt dry, and I struggled to keep my voice steady. Moving very slowly, I pushed Gina into a chair at the circulation desk and positioned myself in front of her. "We know you're here because you're looking for your contact lens."

She stared at me, breathing hard. "You do?" She looked

wildly around the room. "How did you—" She paused, licking her lips. "Okay, you know about the contact lens. That makes it easier. I know I lost it somewhere around here, but where . . ." Her voice trailed off. "I'm not leaving here until I find it. And if I have to kill you two, so much the better."

"The cops have already found the contact lens, Shalimar." She took another step toward me, her expression faltering. I improvised quickly. "It was over there, in that potted palm. I'm afraid the game's over." I paused, watching her. Her face sagged, and she leaned against the counter. "They know you killed Mildred," I said in a low voice. "The best thing you can do right now is turn yourself in."

"Maggie's right," Gina said, her voice surprisingly level. "Please put the gun down before someone gets hurt. There's still time to do the right thing. You can turn yourself in."

"Shut up!" Shalimar shouted, her face contorted. "I told you I need to think." She raised her left hand to brush her hair out of her eyes. "I think the best thing is to get you two down in the basement," she said, her words clipped.

Off to the left, I saw a slight figure enter the front door of the library. He was in a semicrouched position, moving slowly, clasping a gun in two hands like someone on a SWAT team. I knew I had to keep Shalimar talking to distract her. I strained to make out who it was, and then it dawned on me.

Opie!! Officer Duane Brown was on the scene. I nearly cried with relief. But what in the world was he doing here?

"Shalimar, you really don't want to do this. Listen to me. I have no idea why you killed Mildred, but you need to turn yourself in and let the police sort this out." I managed to keep the quaver out of my voice.

Shalimar's face clouded, and when she spoke, her voice was hardly a whisper. "But I didn't kill Mildred," she said slowly. "I swear I didn't."

"Then who did?" I asked. The question hung in the air between us.

"It was Bobby," she said, a flash of fire returning to her voice. "I came inside to talk to Mildred and to look through those stupid old spools on the microfiche. Bobby was waiting in the car. He was positive Mildred had found a copy of Paley's will. She said she didn't. When I went outside and told Bobby that she couldn't help us, he went inside to talk to her." She was staring straight ahead, and her voice had a flat, robotic quality. "He thought she was lying. Maybe even holding out for money." She gave a little sigh. "He was only inside a few minutes when he came running out and told me to hit the gas. It wasn't until we were halfway home that I realized he'd killed her." This time her voice rose half an octave and ended in a sob. "He's the killer. Bobby, my own husband."

Shalimar still had the gun in her right hand, but then she let her arm drop slowly to her side.

In one smooth movement Officer Brown rushed forward and knocked the gun to the floor. As Shalimar whirled to face him, hands outstretched, her nails aiming for his face, he said coldly, "You really don't want to do that."

And just like that, it was over.

Everything happened very fast then. Gina clutched her hand to her throat, her face pale, looking as if she might faint. "Take deep breaths," I told her. "Deep, slow breaths. You'll be fine."

She gave me a watery smile. "Thank you, my dear. You're very brave."

Brave? I was shaking like a leaf, my heart hammering in my chest.

Rafe turned up then with three uniformed officers. Shalimar was taken into custody. Nick Harrison walked right into the library behind the cops, until they spotted him and shooed him out the front door. He grinned and put his hand to his ear, in a call-me gesture.

Gina Raeburn quickly regained her composure and was remarkably calm after what she called her near-death experience; she asked Rafe if that "fine young officer" could be commended by the city. Opie blushed bright pink and insisted he was just doing his job.

Rafe gave me one of his unreadable looks and said he'd get up with me later. I think he was relieved that I hadn't been shot with that doll-sized pistol, but Rafe plays his cards close to his chest and it's impossible to be sure.

My cell chirped just then, and I glanced at the readout. Vera Mae.

"Are you alive, sugar?"

"I'm here," I told her. "Did you hear what happened here at the library?"

"I surely did, hon. I heard you tell Ms. Raeburn you were going to head over there, and then I realized you might be following Shalimar. She was hightailing it away from the square, and I knew something was up. I had one of my 'feelings,' you know?"

"Yes, I do," I told her. Vera Mae has the "feeling" that something dire is going to happen at least once a week. Naturally, her worst fears are never realized—at least, not usually— and they're forgotten.

"So that's why I called him," she said, breaking into my thoughts.

"Who?" I glanced at Gina Raeburn. One of the officers had brought her a paper cup of water and she seemed relaxed, with color in her cheeks. I knew she was going to be okay.

"Why Rafe, of course," Vera Mae said. "I told that boy

something was up and that he needed to get over there quick."
She paused. "He takes my feelings real serious, you know."

I had to smile, in spite of the fact that I'd nearly been shot.
"I'm sure he does, Vera Mae."

"So he sent that nice young Officer Brown to investigate
and said he'd get over there himself as soon as he could."

"Ah, it all makes sense now."

"Maggie, can you get over to the station? Cyrus wants to
do a news feature on you, and we need a couple of sound
bites. This is going to be even bigger than the time capsule
ceremony. Cyrus wants to do some promos and run them all
day long. That is, if you feel up to it, sugar," she added as an
afterthought. Ironic. My terrifying ordeal in the library would
be a ratings bonanza.

Did I feel up to it? I felt a little shaky and weak at the
knees, plus my heart was still pounding. I longed to have
a cup of coffee and go home and curl up on the sofa with
Pugsley.

And then Vera Mae said the words that made me pull
myself together and rush right over to WYME.

"If you don't feel up to it, hon, Chantel said she'd be glad
to step in and host your show today. She said she had a vision that Shalimar was going to be arrested and she'd love to
have the chance to talk about it with your listeners." Vera
Mae chortled with laughter. "Not that Cyrus would let her,
but I'm just saying she offered, sugar."

Chantel had a vision and figured she was going to get
away with hijacking my show? Hah. Not in a million years!
"I'm on my way," I said through gritted teeth. "And tell that
chick to get her own show."

Chapter 33

It was nearly six o'clock when I finally went down to the Cypress Grove PD to give my statement, and to see Rafe. He was waiting for me in his office, leaning back in his desk chair, his hands behind his head.

"Maggie," he said, jumping to his feet. The way my name rolled off his lips, it sounded like a caress. He crossed the room and grabbed me by my upper arms and rested his cheek against mine, just for a second. It was so fast it was almost subliminal. I think he would have drawn me into a tight hug, but the door to his office was wide open and people were milling by. "How come you always end up in the thick of things?" he whispered into my ear before releasing me.

"Just lucky." I smiled at him.

He grinned and motioned me to his visitor's chair. "Want some coffee?" He gestured to a pot that I knew had been brewing brown sludge all day long.

"Please, I've already cheated death once today." A beat passed. "So what happens now?"

"Well, technically, you're supposed to give me a statement about what happened in the library, and I write it down.

Then one of the officers types it up and you sign it. But I figured you probably have some questions for me."

"I do." Rafe was right. I was bursting with questions. "I'm still trying to put the pieces together and figure out what happened today. With the time capsule and Magnolia Hall. And everything else, I guess."

"Where do you want me to start?"

"Trevor McNamara. What does he have to do with all this? And is it true? Did he really inherit Magnolia Hall?"

Rafe nodded. "Yes, he did. That codicil to the will was a bombshell. Trevor McNamara is Paley's illegitimate grandson. Ron Paley never acknowledged him in life, but he always felt guilty about it. He even kept a copy of his birth certificate. That was another item in the time capsule, but the mayor didn't make that one public. Trevor McNamara was illegitimate. Paley's daughter, Eleanor, gave birth to him, and she and the baby were whisked out of town to cover it up."

"Trevor is his grandson? So maybe that explains why I saw him in the Cypress Grove Library a couple of days ago," I said softly.

"Apparently so. He said was trying to dig up some information on his biological family. He had no way of knowing what was in the time capsule, but he guessed that some family secrets would come to light."

"So he knew he was part of the Paley family? And that's why he came to Cypress Grove?"

"He'd always suspected it. He knew that this might be his one chance to claim his inheritance. A family in Massachusetts had adopted him as a baby, but he was sure he was related to the Paleys. He even carries around a picture of his mother, Eleanor Paley. Eleanor died shortly after he was born, but a maid mailed a photo of her to his adoptive parents, and they saved it for him."

"So Trevor is Bobby's half brother, but no one ever acknowledged him."

"That's right. Ronald Paley thought he could make things right by leaving Trevor Magnolia Hall. After all, the Paley family had ignored Trevor and rejected him his whole life. They'd do anything to keep up appearances. But in the end, Ron Paley tried to do the right thing and added that codicil to his will."

"But the codicil never saw the light of day?"

Rafe nodded. "It disappeared in the fire at the courthouse, so the provisions of the original will were in place. Everything went to Bobby. If the time capsule hadn't been dug up, Trevor's claim to the estate never would have come to light. It was just sheer luck that Mr. Paley decided to put a copy in there."

"But why did Mildred have to die? Did Bobby kill her because she knew too much?"

"He thought she did. Mildred suspected there was a missing heir, and she did one of those ancestry searches online. She'd always suspected that Paley's daughter, Eleanor, was sent away because she was pregnant. In those days, an unwed mother was considered a disgrace to the family. Bobby had heard the rumors that he might have a half brother somewhere up north, but he ignored them. He killed Mildred because he was convinced she knew the secret and was going to go public with it."

"So Shalimar wasn't involved in the killing." I shook my head, remembering the scene in the library, and a little chill went through me.

"No. She's turned state's evidence. She's helping us nail Bobby."

I was silent for a moment, turning everything over in my mind. Layers upon layers of misunderstandings, greed, deceit, and murder. As Lucille Whittier had said, "a lot happens in a small town."

Suddenly I remembered the blue chips of paint. "Chris Hendricks!" I had almost forgotten about the jittery picture framer. "What happened? Did he kill Althea Somerset?"

Rafe nodded somberly. "Yes, I'm sure he did. He's in custody right now. We got a warrant to search the historical society again and found the blue paint chips on the hall table, just like you said. And there's more. We also found a footprint on the tabletop that's a match for his sneakers. There were traces of blue powder on the top of the Parsons table—they'd gotten pushed under a doily. I guess that's why the crime scene techs missed them the first time around. Plus they weren't really concentrating on the hall, because Althea was murdered upstairs in her apartment."

"So Chris Hendricks really did stand on the Parsons table to hang the picture back on the wall?"

"He must have. I think everything happened just like you said, Maggie. We've got him." He glanced down at a notepad on his desk. "It seems Althea suspected the painting was valuable. One of the old dears at the historical society told us today that Althea planned on getting it appraised. She'd forgotten to mention it before. So Althea never would have given it to Hendricks. He figured he'd have to kill her for it."

"It was all about money, about the painting," I said, turning it over in my mind. I thought of Althea, losing her life over some paint on canvas. What a waste.

Rafe gave a wry smile. "It was definitely all about money. The root of all evil."

"The painting is worth a lot?"

"A small fortune. The FBI tracked it down for us. It belongs to a wealthy Miami collector. No one seems to know how it ended up at the historical society. Hendricks thought he could get away with the perfect crime. He might have, if you hadn't noticed those tiny blue paint chips."

"Glad I could help." There was something else. *Chantel.* "Did the tech guys ever clean up that security tape?"

"Afraid not. We can't pin anything on Chantel. Maybe she broke in to Vera Mae's, maybe not. We can't prove it, and she's not going to admit it."

"I think she probably did," I said. "She was snooping around, probably hoping to get that box of papers."

"There's enough of a cloud hanging over her that I think she's lost her credibility. When the story gets out of who she really is, her career here is over."

"I think so, too." Vera Mae had told me after my show that Cyrus and Chantel were huddled in his office again. This time, when Chantel emerged, she told Vera Mae that Cypress Grove was too small for her, and she was ready to move on. "I wish I'd asked her how she did that trick with the pen."

"What's that?"

"She said she could do telekinesis. She made a ballpoint pen move across the console in the studio, just by using her mind. We were live on the air. It was pretty impressive."

Rafe laughed. "That's an old trick, Maggie. Was she alone in the studio at any time before she did the trick for you?"

"I thought for a moment. "I'm not sure. I might have zipped back to my office to get some notes," I said finally. "But what could she have done? How would she make the pen move?"

"Magnets, Maggie. That's the secret."

"Magnets?"

"Two magnets—that's all you need. She probably planted

one under the counter, out of sight, and another in the ball-point pen. All she had to do was slide her hand under the counter and move the magnet. Once she had her hand on the magnet, she could make the ballpoint pen move anywhere she wanted."

"Oh." I laughed. "She really had me fooled. Maybe I'm too gullible, too trusting."

"Or too easily impressed. You're full of surprises. I thought you didn't believe in magic. That's what you've always told me." He had a devilish glint in his eye, and my pulse jumped as he crossed the room in a few powerful strides.

"Have I?" I thought for a moment. "Well, maybe I spoke too soon. Because there are some types of magic I really do believe in. At least I think I do." I remembered the scene in the town square. I'd been thinking of the word "catalyst," and to my amazement, Chantel had said the word out loud.

I stopped mulling over the problem when Rafe shut the door to his office, a smile playing over his lips.

Then he locked eyes with me, his black eyes flashing, and it dawned on me. He swept me into his arms and pulled me close to him, so close I could hear his heart beating.

"Do you believe in this kind of magic?" he said, nuzzling my neck. "Or maybe this?" He planted a string of kisses below my ear, setting my pulse thrumming. "Or how about this?" He brushed his lips against mine; his lips were incredibly warm and soft. I felt myself melting. I gave a happy little sigh, tightened my arms around his neck, and snuggled against him.

"You're very persuasive, Rafe," I murmured. "I think you just made a believer out of me."

He gave a low, sexy chuckle, and I felt my heart start to tap-dance in my chest. "Maggie, my love, that's exactly what I was hoping for."

ABOUT THE AUTHOR

Mary Kennedy is a former radio copywriter and the award-winning author of forty novels. She is a clinical psychologist in private practice and lives on the East Coast with her husband and eight eccentric cats. Both husband and cats have resisted all her attempts to psychoanalyze them, but she remains optimistic. Visit her Web site at www.marykennedy.net.

<u>Also Available</u>

Mary Kennedy

Dead Air
A Talk Radio Mystery

Maggie left her clinical practice in Manhattan and moved
to sunny Cypress Grove, Florida, where she became host
of WYME's *On the Couch with Maggie Walsh*. From
co-dependent wives to fetish fiends, all the local crazies
love her show.

Then threats start pouring in against one of the station's
special guests: self-styled new age prophet Guru Sanjay
Gingii. When one of the threats becomes a deadly reality,
Maggie's new roommate, Lark, is surprisingly the prime
suspect. Now, Maggie has to prove Lark is innocent while
dealing with a killer who needs more than just therapy...

**Available wherever books are sold or
at penguin.com**

The Crime of Fashion Mysteries
by Ellen Byerrum

Killer Hair

An up-and-coming stylist, Angie Woods had a reputation for rescuing down-and-out looks—and careers—all with a pair of scissors. But when Angie is found with a deadly haircut and a razor in her hand, the police assume she committed suicide. Lacey knew the stylist and suspects something more sinister— that the story may lie with Angie's star client, a White House staffer with a salacious website. With the help of a hunky ex-cop, Lacey must root out the truth.

Hostile Makeover

As makeover madness sweeps the nation's capital, reporter Lacey Smithsonian interviews TV show makeover success story Amanda Manville. But with Amanda's beauty comes a beast in the form of a stalker with vicious intentions—and Lacey may be the only one who can stop him.

Also in the Crime of Fashion series:
Designer Knockoff
Raiders of the Lost Corset
Grave Apparel
Armed and Glamorous

**Available wherever books are sold or at
penguin.com**

OM0016